"An ur   ınd well-told story of love against the odds."
The Observer

"Here is a novel that needs a trumpet to be blown for it…
The pleasures lie less in plot surprises than in the plain, exact
and elegant language that takes you to the heart of each
character's feelings." Adèle Geras, *The Guardian*

"Historical details are deftly handled, building a rich picture
of momentous events set against personal, domestic lives,
particularly those of women. A pleasingly unexpected take
on the boy-meets-girl romance, set in a fascinating context."
Booktrusted News

"The unembellished but quietly passionate tone of the story
perfectly realizes the Quaker ideals of simplicity and truth,
and the privations which they endure with courage and
dignity serve to engage reader sympathy in a powerful,
understated way. Historical context is accurately and carefully used, but it is the measured tone of the narrative and
its humble, quiet characters with their rock of religion which
leave a lasting impression." *Books for Keeps*

"A novel of huge integrity told in a fittingly simple voice…
Turnbull has written a powerful and moving book that never
becomes shrill; she creates a past that is wholly credible and
sets out a thoughtful blueprint for tolerance."
Julia Eccleshare, *The Guardian*

"I was surprised to find how easily I was drawn inside this
gentle love story… This is a book for all teenagers and
adults who want to remind themselves how powerful
teenage passion can be." *Carousel*

Books by the same author

No Shame, No Fear

Forged in the Fire

Alice in Love and War

Greek Myths

Seeking Eden

ANN TURNBULL

WALKER
BOOKS

Heartfelt thanks to everyone who helped me with both research and structure for this book, and to all those who encouraged and supported me along the way.

First published 2012 by Walker Books Ltd
87 Vauxhall Walk, London SE11 5HJ

2 4 6 8 10 9 7 5 3 1

Text © 2012 Ann Turnbull
Cover photograph © Tyler Stalman/Getty Images

This book has been typeset in Cochin and Aqualine

Printed in Great Britain by Clays Ltd, St Ives plc

ISBN 978-1-4063-2542-3

www.walker.co.uk

To the memory of Viera, with love

APRIL, 1683

One

$\mathcal{I}$ could not see my face, but I guessed I had a black eye. And the knuckles of my right hand were bruised and bloody: that would tell its own story.

I hoped they had all gone to bed, but when I opened the back door I saw both parents there, sitting on the bench in the kitchen, my father with the Bible open in his hand.

"Jos!" My mother sprang up. Relief, then shock at my injuries, showed in her face.

My father rose in a more measured way. "Where hast thou been, Josiah?"

I'd had too much to drink. I felt queasy, and wanted nothing more than to crawl upstairs and fall on my bed. But he was waiting.

"Limehouse. The Blue Anchor." I tried not to slur the words.

I knew from the set of his lips that he was angry. But my father has never beaten me, never even raised a fist. Friends do not approve of such methods of chastising their children. Instead, my parents express sorrow and disappointment, which always makes me feel guilty, as if I could never be good enough for them. And who *could* live up to my parents, so brave and determined over years of persecution, so strong in their faith?

My father had noticed my hand. "Thou hast been fighting?"

"Some youths set upon us. I hit one of them." I remembered the satisfaction of that punch, my shock as the blood spurted, the approval of Ned and Sam.

"Jos, Friends don't strike back," my mother said.

"Perhaps I am not a Friend."

And yet I knew I was. I had been born a Friend. I dressed like one, looked like one, went to Meeting – usually. But there were Friends and friends. I had other friends at the Blue Anchor, drinking companions, friends who were outside the narrow world of the meeting house.

"I could not stand by and let others fight for me." I swayed, and steadied myself against the doorframe. I was having trouble forming my words and wished my father would leave me alone.

"It's those false friends who lead thee into this trouble," he said, and I could hear his mounting anger.

"Thou refused to come to Meeting on first-day—"

"Meeting!" I spoke contemptuously. "It's a fool's game to go to Meeting! To let the sheriff's men turn you out and lock the door, and then charge you with ri … righteous and…" The words "riotous and tumultuous behaviour" – the accusation frequently levelled at our people – proved too much for me in my drunken condition, and I finished lamely, "And arrest you because you hold the meeting in the street."

"But we do hold it."

"For what? To be beaten and fined – or dragged off to prison?"

"Art thou afraid of that?"

"Husband…" My mother touched his arm, her eyes pleading.

I had turned sixteen two months ago. I was old enough now to be arrested for being at a conventicle; my youth would not protect me, as my sisters were protected.

I glowered at my father. "I'm not afraid," I said. "But if I'm going to be charged with causing an affray I'll make sure I start one first."

Without warning, I retched. A sour burning was in my throat. I rushed outside, but did not reach the privy in time. My parents must have heard as I splashed my dinner and the evening's beer onto the cobbles of the yard.

I felt dizzy and foul. I wiped my face with the back of my hand and slunk back in.

"Sorry, Mam."

She was already moving instinctively towards the scullery, where the pails are kept. My father restrained her. "Let him do it."

He turned to me. "Jos, it's late. Draw a bucket of water and sluice the cobbles. Then wash thyself and go to bed. And in the morning, when thou'rt more sober, take time to wait on the inward light – it will guide thee if thou attend to it."

As I went into the scullery I heard him say to my mother, "It's as well we are leaving England."

And she sighed – a great, heartfelt sigh, it sounded, and said, "Oh, Will!"

I cleaned up, and went to bed. I felt ashamed of my behaviour and yet aggrieved at my father's response.

I had grown up resenting Friends. Not their beliefs – those I shared; they were part of my being – but their stubbornness, their refusal ever to defend themselves or even to worship in secret, the way they made my childhood a time of fear. I remembered a day – I know now it was in January 1671, at Ratcliff, for it is written up in our Society's records of Sufferings. I would have been a month short of my fourth birthday and was with a group of children being minded by a woman Friend at her house while our parents were at Meeting. We heard the soldiers – the trained bands – come marching up the street, heard their harsh voices, the tramp of boots. And the woman, who had been telling us a story, stopped speaking and looked towards the door. Fear flooded through me. I knew something bad was going to happen, and I wanted my mam, I wanted her now. *Now.* I began to cry, and Tabby Lacon (she'd have been about seven, then, one of the older ones in the group) took my hand and said, "Don't be scared, Jos." But she was trembling, too.

Almost at once we heard a great shout and commotion, and banging, and people crying out for help. The woman ran to the door, and we with her.

The priest of Stepney, the one I called "the bad man", the one like a crow in his black robes, was dragging someone from the meeting house. His two servants struck out with canes, hitting, hitting, right, left; and people were screaming. No one fought back. Men and women let themselves be hauled out, struck and pushed to the ground. Some knelt and prayed. And the soldiers didn't help them; instead they seized and beat them and put guards around them.

"Mammy!" I screamed.

I saw her, blood on her gown, on her arm, streaming between her fingers; and Dad, helpless, forced back by the soldiers. One of them struck him a blow with the butt of his musket.

I tried to run to them, but the woman pulled us in, close against her skirts that smelt of smoke from the hearth fire. I clung to Tabby's hand and wailed out my terror and desolation. I understood at that moment that the world was not a safe place, that my parents could not protect me. The bad men were hurting Mammy, and Dad couldn't help her. He would not fight back, and neither of them resisted as they were led away.

After my night at the Blue Anchor, the morning brought me a thumping headache. I rose unwillingly and went downstairs to join the rest of the family on the benches either side of the table.

As always we sat in silence: Mam, Dad, Betty, Sarah and me. I would not admit it, but I liked to start the day this way. It felt right. Even when we had eaten and begun to make ready for work, we moved quietly, without bustle or needless talk.

Our home was five rooms over the print shop. I had grown up to the smell of ink, the thump of the press when big Matthew Crale was operating it; the dusty quiet of the bookshop after hours. My father's business partner, Nat Lacon, had the adjoining house. The two of them had been running the printer's and bookshop in Stepney ever since 1667 – the year after the Great Fire; the year I was born.

The girls went off to school, and I put on an old shirt and breeches and set off for the shambles, where I worked for one of the butchers. Not jointing carcasses – that's skilled work – but cleaning up, emptying the tubs of entrails, scrubbing tables, sweeping blood and debris into the channel that runs down the centre of the road.

It was filthy work and I hated it, but I'd taken it because I was angry and wanted to strike back at my father, who had called me lazy and unwilling after my apprenticeship to Thomas Green the notary was broken off.

"I will not have thee idle about the house," my father had said – as if I had wished such a thing – so I had gone out and found myself this employment. And I took pleasure now in coming home stinking of the shambles and, on first-days, feeling the eyes of the meeting on me and knowing Friends felt sorry for my parents for having such a wayward son – though I suspected that some of them also felt a little complacent that their own children had turned out better.

When I arrived Ned was already starting work; he was my friend of the night before, and one of the butchers. He grinned at my black eye. "Bet that pleased your father. *Thy* father," he corrected himself, mockingly.

I endured much teasing from my workmates about

Quakers (as they call us) and their ways. "I threw up in the yard too," I said, eager to be seen as one of the group.

We laughed. It had been a good night. Ned appeared unscathed by it: his eyes blue and clear, his complexion pink. He wielded the cleaver with swift, well-placed strokes. Ned was twenty. He was in a well-paid trade, earned enough to buy drink, clothes, and women, when he wanted. He went to church on first-days, but religion did not seem to invade his weekday life as it did mine. He felt no guilt for the brawl we'd been involved in last night, nor for our drunkenness.

"They hope I'll reform when we go to America," I said. I began sharpening knives on the whetstone.

"When do they mean to go?"

"Fifth or" – I'd started to give the Quaker names of the months – "July or August. It's best to make landfall in spring or autumn, we're told."

Landfall. I liked that word. It spoke of voyage, of adventure.

"And will you go with them?"

"They expect it."

It had crossed my mind to refuse. They would not force me, at sixteen, I was sure. But not to go would be hurting myself, for the New World drew me with a sense of strangeness and wonder. People who sailed in the winter season said that even before land was sighted there came from it a scent of sweet herbs and flowering grasses blown on the wind across the ocean. The truth was, I wanted to go.

"I'd go," said Ned, grinning. "Have you seen those pictures of the savages? The women with their breasts bare and only a little apron in front – nothing behind! Hey, that'll liven up you Quakers!"

I had, of course, seen the prints he spoke of and had thought about encountering such a woman. The respectable girls I knew were chastely covered and I had to imagine what lay beneath. Tabitha Lacon, for instance. I had known her all my life, but two years ago I had begun to have quite different feelings about her. She was older than I and for many years had been taller; but I had grown fast – five inches last year – and now she barely reached my shoulder. She was small, blonde and slender, with a narrow waist that she would set her hands on, either side, when she was arguing with me or telling off Nick, the apprentice. I was afraid to touch her now, and yet I wanted to. But I loved Tabby in vain. To her I was simply little Jos next door; she was twenty now, and worked in the print shop downstairs; and she was promised in marriage to Francis Eldon, a bookbinder in the City. There were other girls in Stepney and Ratcliff meetings, but none I admired as much as Tabby. And the girls I met in Limehouse, at the Blue Anchor or the Mermaid, were too coarse for my liking.

When I arrived home that evening my father said no more about my behaviour of the night before. That was his way. But I saw him glance with distaste at my blood-spattered clothing and dirty hands. I went into the scullery and washed away the filth of the shambles and presented myself clean and sober, though still with the black eye.

It was then that I noticed the letter in my mother's hand, and the expectant faces of my sisters.

Two

When we were all seated around the table, my mother said, in a voice of simmering excitement, "This letter came today, from Pennsylvania; from our friends, Daniel and Judith Kite. Your father and I have both read it." She offered the letter to him. "Wilt thou read it aloud, husband?"

But my father said, "No, no! It's thy letter. Judith wrote to thee. Thou should read it."

I saw that she was pleased at this. She said, "It was sent nearly three months ago. They are all in good health, and have a plot of land, and – well, Judith says, '*Forgive me, Susanna, for not writing earlier. We arrived, as planned, before winter set in and have been hard at work ever since, clearing the ground for planting, building a house, buying animals (we have a fine horse now, and chickens, and a pig), and setting up the forge. All is new and promising here and exactly as described by the Proprietor in his writings. The necessities of life are to hand, prices are cheap, Daniel has plenty of customers, and I shall be kept busy growing food and caring for the animals. The young ones help us, and are well. Now in this winter season, we have great quantities of snow, and the rivers are locked in ice. We look forward to spring. Are your plans made? I long to see thee again, dear Su, and thee too, Will, after so many long years…"* Here my mother's voice wobbled.

"When did thou know Judith, Mam?" asked Betty. And Sarah, wriggling on her seat as she always does when interested, exclaimed, "They have animals? Will *we* have some?"

"We may have chickens, Sarah," my mother said. "We know Judith and Dan from our Shropshire days, twenty years ago. Judith had her first child there – Benjamin; he'll be about eighteen now. They emigrated to Boston before Jos was born, to take the Truth to the New World. Dan is an outspoken Friend, a preacher – a troublemaker, the authorities would say – and Boston was a challenge for him, since Friends have never been welcome there. He and Judith have suffered years of persecution."

"Like us?" said Sarah.

"Worse than us," said Betty, who read the books and pamphlets in our shop.

My mother agreed. "Often worse than us."

She read on: *"'This new colony of Pennsylvania will be*

a haven for many people. There were Dutch here already; and Swedes who have long been settled – we see their log cabins all around. English, Welsh, Germans and French come now, all fleeing persecution for their faith. There is constant activity, new houses finished every day, new streets, new settlers arriving, fair prices for plots of land, and fair rents, and plenty of work to be found. We have great hopes for this venture, dear friends. It is truly a holy experiment, as William Penn has called it. Without a militia, without arms, with freedom of religion, and seeking fellowship with all people, we shall be living the gospel every day. We have come seeking Eden, and believe we will find it here.'"

She laid the letter down, and we all fell silent for a few moments. I listened to the crackle of the fire and lost myself in imagining that far-off land where Eden could be found.

When the silence ended, my mother said, "This strengthens my belief that we have made the right choice." And then she got up and said, "Now let's eat."

The girls immediately broke into chatter. Betty helped my mother bring the food to the table and Sarah set out the cutlery. All three females were unusually talkative – but this was no ordinary day. After supper we all went down to the bookshop and my father brought out the pamphlet written by the Proprietor, William Penn, to encourage settlers to come to Pennsylvania. He found a map, and spread it out on the counter so that we could see where the new city of Philadelphia was being built: sixty miles up the Delaware River, near its convergence with the Schuylkill, so that the city stood on a promontory between the two rivers.

"We will land here," he said, pointing, "on the Delaware side, though there is no wharf yet, and we must be brought off the ship in small boats. The voyage will take two months at least."

My mother put a fist to her mouth and shook her head. I knew this sea crossing was the part she dreaded, especially for Sarah, who was often ill.

"Many others have made this voyage and survived," my father said gently.

"I know, husband. I know. And if Judith has endured it, so shall I. And put my trust in God."

"Life will be hard at first," he said. "The Proprietor says here, *'They must be willing to be two or three years without some of the conveniences they enjoy at home.'* But, *'There is better accommodation, and English provisions are to be had at easier rates…'* And see here" – he took up a second pamphlet, *The Present State of the Colony of West-Jersey* – "this is another settlement on the Delaware, more old-established than Pennsylvania, where many are Friends. They say, *'The air is temperate and healthy, winter not so long as it is in England'* – so it will be better for Sarah – *'few natives in the country; but those that are, are very peaceable, useful, and serviceable to the English inhabitants…'"*

I read on, to myself, and found descriptions of the many creeks and bays, and navigable rivers; of the woodland bought from the natives, full of familiar trees like oak, cedar, chestnut, walnut and mulberry, and others that were new to the English.

"What will our house be like?" Betty asked.

"We'll have no house at first," my father said. "We'll have to build one."

Betty gave him a sceptical look. None of us could imagine our father building a house, and he knew it.

He smiled. "We will employ builders," he said.

"Will there be a school? A meeting house? Shops?" The girls were full of questions.

"There will certainly be a place to meet," said my mother, "probably in someone's house."

And my father added, "We will be free to worship without fear of persecution. And in a few years we'll have a better life, a new country…"

I looked at the map, and saw how the land granted to William Penn stretched far, far to the north and west of Philadelphia, with almost nothing marked but rivers and a skein of mountains running north to south.

I ran my hand across it. "What is here?"

"Wilderness," my father said. "Forests, rivers, wild

animals. 'A red man's wilderness', George Fox called it."

And William Penn was the owner of this vast tract of land, having dreamed for years of setting up such a colony. He was given this territory, the size of southern England, by Charles Stuart, the king, in settlement of a debt the king had owed his father, Admiral Penn; and now he would use it for his holy experiment, and we would be part of that great cause.

My father turned to me. "Well, Jos? How dost thou feel about all this?"

I shrugged. Enthralled as I was by the maps and pictures and by William Penn's vision, I was unwilling to admit any of this to my father. "I'll come," I said.

My mother spoke sharply: "Of course thou'll come! I won't go without thee!"

"Judith says there is plenty of work there," my father said. "We must find thee something to thy liking."

I looked at my hands, at the bruised knuckles, the broken nails, the blood of the shambles still in the creases of my skin. "I suppose they'll have butchers there," I said, "and butchers'll need swabbers and sweepers."

"Thou'rt determined to provoke me, Josiah. Thou could do better than sweeping; thou know it. Thou should endeavour to learn a trade."

"I'll get work there," I said, "but I'll find my own master."

I imagined an explorer, or a trading voyage up one of those great rivers that flowed out from the wilderness; saw myself as ship's boy.

"Good." He laid a hand on my shoulder. "But think about thy natural talents. Thou can cast accounts, and read well, and write a fair hand."

"A clerk!" I said, and sighed.

"Why art thou so hurtful to Dad?" Betty said later. She had joined me, uninvited, on the bed in my attic room.

This room was one I had chosen for myself years ago, and kept – against all common sense, since these days I could stand upright only in the very centre. But I liked the feeling it gave me of being apart from the rest of the family. I had a few books there – Friends' writings, *The Pilgrim's Progress*, and also books with maps and drawings. My own drawings – for I loved to draw – were tucked away in a folder, not displayed. Friends do not approve of drawing and painting unless for some useful purpose, such as a herbal or a map. My parents knew of my interest, for I used scrap paper from the shop; they tolerated it, but my mother urged restraint: "Thou must not make likenesses of

people, Jos, or any other work that leads to vanity."
I did not make portraits, but I drew the view from
my attic window, the rooftops and spires, the gulls
that perched on the windowsill and glanced about
with fierce eyes, their feathers lifting in the breeze.
From that window I had a glimpse of the docks, the
network of masts and spars, a sense of ships coming
and going, all the life of the great river.

And up here I was away from my father's eye.

"He bullies me," I said in response to Betty.

"He tries to help! And he's right: thou should be a
clerk – keep tallies and ledgers – "

"Huh! Like I did for Thomas Green? *He* didn't
think much of my skills."

"Thou didn't try."

"I didn't like him."

But it was true I'd been unwilling – lazy, even. And
Thomas Green's business was up north, in a dull part
of London, far from the docks and the vigour of the
City. I hadn't wanted to stay. I'd been on a month's
trial, and had failed. I was glad to come home, but
it had angered my father, who had put effort into
arranging the bond.

Betty said, "I shall work with Dad in the print
shop when we go to America. He says I can. I'll be
fourteen by the time we sail – no need for any more
schooling."

I looked at her in surprise. I'd thought of her as a child, but it was true, she'd be old enough to work.

She was clever, my eldest sister, and eager to learn. She and Sarah went to Hester Lawrence's school for the daughters of Friends, at Mile End. There they learned to read, write and cast accounts; also to sew, and darn hosiery, and knit, and launder and prepare herbal remedies – all those womanly tasks that I was spared. And of course they were guided gently but firmly towards the light. Silence and Bible-reading took up much of their day at school, as it had at mine. Betty was proficient in everything. Sarah, who had always been a frail child, was often ill and absent from school; she was slower to learn; and our mother, who feared for her, kept her close at home. She was Mam's baby, the youngest since Henry had died.

So there we were: the protected Sarah; Betty, who spent all her spare time in the print shop or among the books – Betty, who was our father's pride, his "clever girl"; and me, his only surviving son, and a disappointment to him.

"I'll miss my friends at school," said Betty. "Ruth, and Damaris. And I'll miss Tabby." She gave me a teasing look. "Thou will, too. Thou'rt blushing, Jos!"

"Tab's spoken for," I growled. "Anyway, she's too old for me."

"Too old! Thou make her sound ancient!"

I changed the subject. "Dost thou think Mam wants to go? I know what she *said*, but…"

I knew Mam had been less certain than our father, who was such an admirer of William Penn, and had been inspired by his writings from the start. My mother thought more of those people we would leave behind and probably never see again: her Shropshire family – our grandmother Elizabeth Thorn, for whom Betty was named, Uncle Isaac and Aunt Deb – and the Lacons, our neighbours and work partners for so many years. For months my parents had sought spiritual guidance and waited on the inward light. Some Friends regarded emigration as a moral failure, a reluctance to stand up and face persecution. I knew my parents had wrestled with this.

"I think Dad is more certain," said Betty. "But when thou think how we have suffered, all of us – Dad has never really recovered from that time in New Prison, has he? – surely she must want to go?"

"Dost *thou* want to?"

Usually Betty likes to appear detached and worldly-wise. But not now. "Oh, yes!" Her eyes shone. "And thee?"

"Yes," I said. "*I* do."

The adventure drew me, and the vision of a society based on the gospel. But there was another reason: in Philadelphia the majority of people would be Friends.

We would not be living constantly among people who despised or mocked us; I would not need to pretend indifference to Friends' ideals, as I did when out with my butcher companions. Above all, we would not suffer for our faith. We need not fear arrest, imprisonment or fines.

I shall change when I am there, I thought. I'll show my father what I can do, and he'll be proud of me.

A new world, a new beginning. How could I not want to go?

Tokpa

A sound wakes me. A night bird? A footfall?

At first I don't think of danger.

The hut is dark, but I know in my body that dawn is not far off. My father and brother breathe steadily in sleep close by.

I stretch. My limbs ache from yesterday's dancing. Such dancing we had! Such drumming! All day clouds were building in purple masses above the hills. Soon they will burst and bring the rains. We young men painted our bodies, laughing as we turned about to decorate one another's backs and shoulders with patterns in coloured clay. Everyone came out to dance: mothers with babies, old men, old women, children who could scarcely walk, girls, bright-eyed and giggling. The spirit dancers appeared wearing masks. They were neighbours, men I knew, and yet the masks changed them. When *they danced, an ancestor's eyes looked out through the empty eye slits; the dried grass hair shook with the spirit's power.*

As I lie here, remembering the masks and the drumming, it comes again, that sound: a footstep; then muffled voices.

I leap up, heart pounding.

A scream pierces the night like a spear. I hear yells, wails, running feet. Smoke! The crackle of flames.

Outside, huts are ablaze; burning thatch lights up the night. My mother's hut is on fire. She bursts from the doorway, my young brother and sister clinging to her, screaming. People run and cry, trapped: my friend Manhtee, my aunt, my neighbours, running like ants when the nest is kicked open.

There are men here, strangers, not of our tribe; men with clubs who beat and seize us. My mother shrieks as they drag her away. Behind me I hear my father shout, then the sounds of a club and a groan.

I am caught. I struggle, but they bind my wrists, fix a collar around my neck, fasten me to a line of others. Yoked together, we stumble out into the dark forest, our homes blazing behind us.

I think of the masks, flames licking, devouring, shooting through the eye slits.

The forest is full of spirits. I cry out to them to help us.

Three

We left for Gravesend on the sixteenth day of sixth-month, the month the world calls August. This was the first stage of our journey. At Gravesend we would embark on the *Promise*, and sail to Deal, on the Kent coast, where we would take on stores and more passengers. Only when wind and tide were right would we begin our voyage to America.

The boat that conveyed us to Gravesend left Wapping soon after dawn. I stood on deck with my family, among a crowd of other passengers, mostly Friends, each of us alone with our thoughts as we gazed back at the London skyline. For me, it was the city where I had been born, the only home I had known. In the distance, gathering form and solidity as the light grew, I could see the scaffolding and half-built walls of the new steeple-house of Paul's – the old building having been destroyed in the Great Fire.

It was seventeen years since the fire that had blazed for four days and nights and left London in ruins. My parents had been caught up in that catastrophe, and as a child I'd loved to hear my mother tell how they escaped, with me in her belly, into the fields of Islington.

"We thought the fire would cleanse the city of its wickedness," she said once, "but it did not. The Truth is still unheard in the great Babylon."

The great Babylon: a place of luxury and corruption. How different would Philadelphia be? I wondered. My father, who had been brought up an Anglican and had learned Greek and Latin at school, had told me that the name Philadelphia meant "City of Brotherly Love". It could surely not yet be a city at all, for it was only last year that William Penn had sailed there with a hundred other Friends to found it.

When I remembered the alarms of my childhood – the meetings violently broken up by soldiers, my parents sentenced to prison, the bailiffs ransacking our house – I'd thought how good it would be to live in such a place as William Penn envisaged. And yet now I wondered if I might also miss some of the wickedness of the great Babylon.

The City receded from view, and in its place we passed through smaller docks and clusters of mean houses and brothels. The land was marshy and flat, and the river looped across it, slowly widening towards the estuary until we came in sight of Gravesend.

And there, at last, we saw the *Promise*. She was an old, round-bowed, weathered ship, her brown sails dirty and patched. My sisters and I were disappointed. We had imagined something more impressive – a vessel worthy of such a momentous voyage.

My father was watching anxiously for our chests and boxes, which were being removed from the boat by porters and transferred, along with everyone else's luggage, to the hold of the *Promise*. In addition to all our household goods, he'd brought a crate full of books for sale in Philadelphia, and cases of fonts, ink, paper, quills, notebooks and ledgers of all kinds. The bookshop and stationer's could be set up almost immediately on arrival, but the print works would take longer, for a press would need to be built and men hired. Once the decision was made to go he had spent weeks working out the packing and finances. The cost of our passage, he'd told me, was the smallest part.

"Look to the women, Jos," he chivvied me now. "And help find our cabin space."

A somewhat unseemly rush to claim the best spaces was in progress on the lower deck. We installed ourselves in a spot near the stern. When she saw the sleeping quarters we had been allocated, Betty was appalled. The so-called cabin the five of us would share for the next eight, twelve or perhaps even fourteen weeks, was an airless space, partitioned off from neighbours on either side by thin walls, and with just enough room for us all to lie down. A curtain screened it from the gangway.

"I won't be able to bear this!" she complained. "Mam! There's no privacy! We are all together – it's not decent. And where is the privy?"

My mother had no patience for her. "A little over-crowding is nothing to what Friends have suffered in their time," she said (at which Betty, turning away, rolled her eyes). "Dost thou imagine we had privacy in Newgate? We'll hang up a sheet if thou must pretend to such maidenly modesty…"

"It's not pretence!" protested Betty, but to no avail.

Our mother was more concerned about Sarah, whether the damp, malodorous air would harm her. Sarah was already coughing, but she was happy enough, helping Mam to unpack the few possessions we would use on the voyage.

There were several families on board whom we knew from Ratcliff and Stepney meetings, and the women soon began to help one another and to find ways of making their situation more comfortable. My mother brought out some sheeting and got us to help her make divisions in our space. "Catch hold of that end, Betty. Jos, can you reach up and fix it?"

I soon became tired of these domestic tasks and wanted to go ashore, but my mother forbade it; I think she was afraid I'd get into trouble again. Instead, I escaped by going up on deck. I breathed the salty, tarry air of the docks, and watched sailors and porters working on the quay, and seagulls swooping and crying. I had never seen the Thames estuary before, let alone the ocean. Later, lying on a thin mattress below decks at night, it was strange to feel the tide tugging the ship at its moorings. The cabin space was full of small sounds: a baby cried and was shushed; Sarah coughed and sighed; and my parents murmured together in low voices for a long time.

The next day we had to wait for a suitable tide and did not leave Gravesend till late afternoon; and then in Deal we were delayed for five days by contrary winds. Most people went ashore from time to time. A few, who could afford to pay for an extra passage, hired servants in the town, which was a rough sort of place, full of cheap lodgings and alehouses. We Friends kept together, and I caught the curious, sometimes unfriendly eyes of the inhabitants on us.

Our father gave each of us a small book in which to keep a journal. I knew he meant it for a spiritual journal – this being, for Friends, a voyage of the soul as much as of the body. He knew that Betty would write about everything she heard and saw; that Sarah would struggle with her letters, and lapse; and he knew that I would draw more than I wrote. But he left it to the spirit to guide us. Betty began writing that very day, with great enthusiasm. I tried dutifully to write about my hopes for our life in Philadelphia, but found myself daydreaming of forests and wilderness – vague imaginings that could not be put into words. Instead, I turned to drawing. I drew the harbour buildings, the quayside and the ship, paying careful attention to every detail of the rigging.

The night before we sailed, when all were aboard, we held a meeting for worship on deck: more than eighty people standing silent together. Even the crew fell quiet. The only sounds were the creak of the ship's timbers, the slap of waves on her sides, the cries of gulls. This meeting affected me more powerfully than any I had experienced before; and it was the silence itself that held me, for whenever a Friend spoke the wind carried away his words and I could not hear. It seemed to me, in the silence, that we felt and breathed as one, that we were all held in this great endeavour, this holy experiment.

Before mid-morning the tide began to turn. The master shouted orders, the seamen ran to their stations, and I watched the sails hauled up, belly-ing out as the wind caught and tugged them. Nearly everyone was on deck now, my family among them. My mother stood quietly, elbows on the rail, head lowered. She was praying. My father laid his arm about her shoulders. Betty and Sarah stood, intent and absorbed, as did I; I believe we all felt the seriousness of the moment.

The anchor was raised. And the *Promise* was under way.

Jokpa

M any days we walk through the forest, far from home, far from our ancestors. If there are spirits here, I don't know them. The rains have come. A roar of water fills the air, battering the leaves, drumming on the earth. Streams become torrents. We slip and slide in the mud.

My wrists are chafed and bleeding, my neck rubbed raw from the collar. The pace is fast. Our captors swear and beat us. My friend Manhtee is sick. When he falls and can't get up, they unfasten him and throw him to the side of the track. He lies still, the rain pounding his body.

"Manhtee!" I cry out. I want to help him, but they drive us on, on. Manhtee will die there, alone in the forest. Tears and rain run down my face and I can't brush them away.

Day after day we walk. We sleep at night in villages, still shackled. The rain lessens as we come out of the forest into a dry country. At last we arrive at a river. This river is so huge I can't see the other side. Boats like great birds with upraised wings float upon it. Our captors are gone. Demons surround us: pale-faced, thin-lipped, with noses like beaks and hair hanging down. They jabber together in a strange language. Many other captives are here, other tribes, other languages. I can't talk to them.

Two demons seize me, push me down, press red-hot iron into my flesh. I scream, then faint from the pain.

We are all made to strip naked, even the women, even my mother. The women and girls cry and try to cover themselves with their hands.

More demons come. They force open my mouth, look at my teeth, my anus, handle my genitals. I weep with shame.

We are all herded into a compound and kept there many days and fed like animals from big troughs of rice or cassava. The compound is foul and stinking. Every day people die.

At last they take some of us and row us out to one of the great winged boats they call ships. I am taken, but my mother, my brothers and my sister Musu are left behind. I see the water widening between us. I scream their names. All around me, people wail and cry out to those on shore. A man leaps overboard, but the demons catch him, haul him back in.

They force us up a ladder, make us board the ship. We are separated: women and girls; boys; men. I am placed with the men. All are strangers to me. They chain and shackle us, drive us down into the belly of the ship. A vile smell rushes up from its guts.

Four

Leaving Deal was a high point, a moment of hope, but it was not long before tedium and discomfort began to affect us all. Eighty passengers, a full crew: we had not enough room, no escape, no place to be alone. Friends do not engage much in outward quarrels, but there was friction and reproach and an undercurrent of constant irritation among the adults. Nevertheless, most people tried to help one another. My father suffered badly from seasickness at first, and Sarah coughed and wheezed and became very pale, causing much anxiety. Our neighbours were kind; one offered a ginger syrup for Sarah, another a calming herbal drink for my father.

Before long the overcrowded cabins began to smell bad. My mother had brought wormwood and rosemary to purify the air, and she cleaned regularly around the cabin with vinegar, but there was no freshening breeze to blow through it.

I went up on deck whenever I could, and spent much of my time looking out at the sea. Day after day I saw nothing but the ocean, its roll and swell, changing in colour from grey to green, to storm-dark, or flashing gold when the sun lit its surface. Only occasionally did I see a distant ship.

Sometimes my father or Betty joined me. My mother came up regularly to take the air, but the vastness of the ocean, and the knowledge that it would look the same for at least two months, and that every day took us further from England, overwhelmed and terrified her. My mother is not a timid woman; she has endured many hardships and has never been afraid to speak the truth and suffer for it; but this immensity of ocean between her home and America was too much for her.

I wrote in my journal, and made small sketches: coils of rope; the sails and rigging; and, secretly, people's faces – for I longed to learn how to capture a likeness, despite Friends' disapproval of such images. And I talked to the sailors and asked questions. One of the crew – not a sailor but the ship's cooper – was an older man who liked to talk. His name was Walt Burney and he had been at sea since he was fifteen. This was his third voyage on an immigrant ship. He told me we'd been lucky: only seasickness so far, no contagion such as the smallpox that had raged through the ship on his voyage last year, killing two dozen or so passengers. He reminisced about the places he'd visited, from Newfoundland to the Caribbean, and the islands off the coasts of Spain and Africa.

"We're sailing for Madeira now," he said, "for Funchal – that's the capital. "We'll take on water, fruit, vegetables, wine. Madeira's a beautiful island." He winked. "Lovely women."

When we reached Funchal the sea was blue, the sun shining, and the island a green, inviting place with forested mountain slopes rising above the harbour. We were able to disembark for a few hours and wander on unsteady sea-legs around the streets and markets, and marvel at the palm trees, the warm breeze, the brightness and colour. My mother was glad to be on land again; she seemed to open out like a flower and come alive in the sunshine.

We split into small groups, but such an influx of dark-clad, pale-faced Londoners could not go unnoticed, and people stared at us.

"You are Quakers?" a woman asked us in English. She was a stallholder, selling linen goods: cloths and caps – pretty, embroidered things set out to catch the eye. "You go to America?"

"We are plain folk, and need little to take with us," my mother said.

But the woman was persistent. I left her trying to interest my mother in caps for Betty and Sarah that had white embroidery: "Only a little stitching, see? So neat, so simple, for the young girls…"

I wandered off, around the nearby streets, drawn by the colour and warmth, the blossoming trees full of purple flowers, the white-painted houses with iron balconies, the strangeness of everything. A great square-towered fortress loomed above the town, and the houses were set all down the mountainside in a cascade of red-tiled roofs. I saw steeple-houses with brightly painted statues of saints and the Virgin Mary, which reminded me that this was a Catholic country; and although I had been brought up to worship God in simplicity, when I glanced in through the open door of one of these places I thought how beautiful and inviting the dim interior looked, glowing with candlelight and the gleam of gold.

I paused to listen to a blind man playing a flute – a pensive tune with rhythms strange but fascinating to my ear – and dropped a coin in his hat, though I didn't know whether an English penny could be of use to him.

The language I heard all around me was, I supposed, Portuguese, but the people were mixed. I saw many Negroes working as porters, as sailors, or haggling in the market; the women, dressed in scarlet, blue or yellow, walked like queens, balancing baskets of fruit or rolls of cloth on their heads. Who were these people, I wondered? Were they slaves of the Portuguese? Or settlers? Were they born here? My life in London had been narrow, I realized; there was so much I did not know.

I asked my parents about the people as we walked back to the ship.

"I'm told there are generations of Africans here," my father said. "Some are freedmen, many others born to slavery. It is a barbaric practice, the taking of slaves."

It shocked me to think that children could be born into slavery. We did not have time to discuss the matter further, for we had reached the ship and were about to board, but I felt glad to be going to a colony where the laws of England would prevail and where the light that is in all men would be recognized.

Within the hour we left Madeira, and soon were once again at sea with no sight of land. And now, from nowhere it seemed, came a series of great storms that buffeted the ship and caused all her timbers to creak and strain so that we feared she would be pulled apart. We stayed below and prayed as huge waves broke and streamed across the decks. Day and night the wind shrieked in the rigging. It was fearful, and yet exhilarating, and in a strange way I loved to feel its power.

But the storms kept me below, and I soon felt bored and restless. Occasionally I thought I heard, through the howling of the wind, strains of music – country tunes played on a flute and fiddle – coming from the deck beneath ours. This was the orlop deck, dark and low, where a few poorer immigrants and some of the crew slept. I have always been drawn to music, though Friends frown upon it ("a waste of time and an incitement to carnal passions", our schoolmaster had warned), and one day I ventured down there, and came into a low space among barrels and coils of rope. A lantern hung from a beam, and in its lurch and swing as the ship rolled I saw several people gathered, the fiddler sawing away, and others singing and clapping.

Someone laughed. "Good day, Quaker boy! Hast thou come to silence us?"

"No. To listen – if I may?" I wished people would not always mock Friends.

"Aye, well you won't hear much music in holy Pennsylvania!"

Their laughter was friendly enough. They let me stay, and one of them, a youth of about my own age, moved up to make space for me to sit next to him. He told me he was an indentured servant – one of several hired in Deal by the captain.

"See, the way it works, the captain pays for my passage, and in return I agree to work for him without wages for four years. So he goes to a notary and gets an indenture drawn up, all legal. Then, when we get to America, he'll sell the indenture to my new master. That'll be a settler, most likely, wanting labouring work."

"Four years without pay!"

I thought of my unhappy experience with Thomas Green. I was shocked. I had not heard of this system before.

"It's a chance, an adventure!" the youth said. "They say folk can make their fortunes in the New World…"

After that first encounter I went down several times to the orlop deck to listen to the music, or join in singing. The others often played at dice or cards, and were surprised that I knew how to play. But I was inexperienced, and though I won some money, in the end I lost more than I gained.

My mother asked, "Who are these companions thou hast met below?"

She was uneasy; and I knew she would not approve. My parents had warned me that I seemed to have an instinct for finding the wrong sort of company. And yet, I thought rebelliously, the light is in all of us.

Now, as suddenly as they had come, the storms subsided, and we were in calm seas. Everyone began spending more time on deck.

Betty and I often went up early in the mornings, before most people were about, to look out at the sea. Once we saw monstrous grey shapes rise, roll and sink in the distance. A plume of water shot skywards.

"Whales," said Betty, in a voice of wonder.

I had never thought to see the Leviathan with my own eyes; yet here he was, at play in the vastness of the ocean. We stared, amazed.

"We have been thirty-two days at sea," I said the next day, as we stood at the rail. I had been keeping a tally in my journal.

"Thirty-three," said Betty. It seemed she had been doing the same. She said I had missed a day; I thought she'd miscounted. We bickered amicably until Betty said, "Look! A ship!"

It was on our larboard side, coming out of the south towards us, but veering gradually west until we were on a parallel course.

Bound for the Caribbean, I thought; like us.

I supposed it to be a ship of a similar size to ours, but could see no detail, only its silhouette.

It was far off, but the wind blew from the south, bringing the faint sound of voices to us in gusts; and with the sound came a smell, a stench – foul, like nothing I'd ever smelt before, even in the shambles or the stinking rivers of London in summer. Excrement, blood, vomit: a smell of filth and fear. Appalled, I took a step back.

"What is it? What is that ship, Jos?" Betty's voice shook.

"I don't know," I said.

And yet I did know. Somehow I had known at once, instinctively.

Others were coming on deck now. Walt Burney was near by. We turned our faces to him.

"It's a slaver," he said. "With a cargo from Africa. You can smell a slave ship from five miles away. Better go below, the two of you. Wait till it passes."

Betty, hands over her nose, gagged and bolted down the gangway. The urge to follow her was strong, yet I held myself there. I thought of the Negroes I'd seen in Madeira. Since leaving England I had become more aware of slavery, and this ship was not something I felt I should run from.

"How many slaves could be on there?" I asked Walt.

He shrugged. "Two or three hundred – maybe more."

On a ship perhaps the size of ours. And we were cramped with eighty passengers.

"Where will it be going?"

"Jamaica? Barbados? Or Virginia."

"Hast thou ever sailed on a slaver?"

"Once, yes."

"An English ship?"

"Aye, we sailed from Bristol."

He seemed unwilling to say more, and I went below.

Many days later, when we approached Barbados, there was no sign of the slave ship. High winds and heavy seas kept us from making landfall in the Caribbean, but some traders rowed out to sell us fruit, wine and water.

My father bought a melon, fresh, cool-smelling, pale green and rosy inside. He cut it up and we shared it, laughing as the juice ran down our chins.

But the memory of the slave ship stayed in my mind.

The *Promise* turned north-east, and we came at last in sight of the coast of mainland America. It was distant – a thin grey line scarcely distinguishable from the sea until it was pointed out to us – but a source of great excitement and relief after so many weeks.

Now we became impatient. Our ship followed the coast northwards day after day, never drawing nearer, the only change being in the air, which grew cooler. But at last came an evening when we felt the ship begin to turn, towards the land.

The coast was far off. We would not reach it that night, and as darkness fell we retreated once more to our sleeping spaces. I woke from light sleep constantly throughout the night, felt the ship moving and imagined the land drawing nearer: the New World...

By dawn I was sleeping heavily, and it was Betty who woke me: "Jos! We're here!"

I pulled on my coat and breeches, pushed my feet into my shoes.

Betty shook our parents and Sarah. "Mam! Dad! Wake up!"

As they began to stir, we two hurried to be among the first, scrambling up the gangway, out of the stink and darkness into cold grey daylight.

"There!"

"It's huge!" I said. "Huge! I never imagined..."

Delaware Bay was an immense body of water. On either shore, in the far distance, low sandy hills rose up, covered with pine trees. We saw wooden buildings, and, beyond them, meadows and forest – endless forest, it seemed, that stretched as far as I could see. After London, with its low smoky sky and circling kites, the sky here was so big it seemed almost too much to bear. It reduced me to a speck on the ocean. And yet there was such a promise of freedom in that great sky, that wide water, that land of forests and grassy meadows that seemed to have no end.

We reached Philadelphia two days later, after a long wearying journey upriver during which we passed many towns and settlements. As we sailed into the harbour on the Delaware everyone was on deck, eager to see, and I thought the ship must be in danger of capsizing as we all crowded to the same side. Friends prayed and thanked God for our safe passage. Some fell to their knees. Many were in tears.

A steep bank, which appeared to be full of excavations, rose above the harbour. We anchored some way out and were taken in boats to the shore. As we drew nearer, I saw that the excavations were temporary homes. People were living in holes dug into the bank – some with roofs made of branches turfed over, and with chimneys of stone or clay. I saw whole families there with their goods around them. Above the bank, all along the waterfront, were buildings, mostly in brick, some still unfinished. Porters were carrying goods up the rough steps to the quay, where carts were waiting. All was new, raw, busy, and there were great quantities of mud. On the quay a party of Philadelphia Friends waited to welcome us.

A sailor tied up our boat at the jetty and people began to disembark.

I stepped forward, refused the helping hand of the crewman, and sprang ashore.

Jokpa

We lie chained together in pairs, naked, on the boards. The ship rolls and pitches, the boards scrape my flesh, and the shackles rub my wrists and ankles raw. It's dark, and a tumult of sound is in my ears: rattle of chains, creak of timbers, voices that scream and groan and cry out in despair. How many days we lie here I don't know. It feels like endless time, endless sound, endless pain. In our part of the deck there is one latrine tub for everyone. Many men are sick and can't climb across others to reach it. They relieve themselves where they are. We lie in our filth. Men quarrel and fight.

Once a day the demons drive us up on deck and make us dance to a drumbeat. They feed us rice. Some won't eat, and are forced with beatings. I am afraid, but I want to live. I eat.

I learn the demons' language. The captives from the coast already know it. Most of them were traders and fishermen, and they understand many tongues: Kru, Fula, Arabic,

English, French, Dutch, Portuguese. They also understand how to sail the ship.

This great water is called the sea. Some say it has no farther shore; they say we can never go home, that the demons will eat us. But there are men here who watch and learn. They stay strong in spirit and become our leaders. They say we will kill the demons and take this ship and sail it home. Others say that only through death can we go home. There is netting to stop us leaping into the sea, but some get under it. One day when the netting is lifted I see two women link hands, run, leap together. In an instant the sea churns and froths and turns red with blood. Sharks. They follow the ship.

We captives sing: songs of home, songs of sorrow. Songs travel throughout the belly of the ship; one starts, others join in, voices rise all around. We begin to learn one another's languages. We pass messages through the songs. The women, who are kept on deck, steal tools and pass them to the men. Our leaders have a plan. My heart fills with hope. I will find my family and we will return to our village and rebuild it.

But the demons catch the plotters and flog them with knotted whips. They cut off the heads of our leaders and throw the headless bodies into the sea. Now that their bodies are mutilated, the spirits of those men are lost; they can never go home. The ship sails on, and I lie grieving and fearful in its dark, stinking gut.

At last we see land. The sailors begin to clean the ship. They empty the slop tubs, scrub the boards where we have lain so long, scrub and sand the decks, sweeten the air with herbs. The stench of the ship's belly is masked. We captives are washed, oiled, our wounds tended or hidden. Some men are sick and have the runs; the crewmen plug their anuses with wads of linen. We are given loincloths to cover our nakedness.

I am afraid when they take us ashore. A great crowd of beak-nosed demons is waiting. We are put in groups, forced up onto a block. I stand there, chained, shaking with fear.

Five

The Friends who welcomed us were ready with the essentials: food and drink, comfort for those who were sick, blankets and tents for hire, a plan of the city-to-be with all the plots marked on it.

It felt strange to be walking on land after being so long at sea. I saw the unsteadiness of others, and how pale and tired many of them looked. A man directed my father to the agent's office, where details of our plot could be found. My mother and I watched for our trunks and the crate of books as sailors unloaded the hold.

"Jos, go and hire us a cart," my mother said. "Have the man wait over there – stay with him."

A large number of carters had congregated on the quay, eager for business. We had an address – a street and plot number; it was near the junction of Third and Sassafras Streets.

The man I found knew the place. He came to assist as my mother signalled that our goods were coming ashore. I helped heave everything onto the cart and wedge it securely in place; and then the five of us climbed aboard and sat on the plank seats, clinging and steadying ourselves as the wheels jolted over the rough ground. It was no distance: a few minutes' drive along the front and then two streets back from the river.

Along the waterfront we passed large brick buildings: merchants' houses and counting houses, I guessed; all new, and all occupied. Away from the harbour were a mix of such buildings and smaller ones – family homes and shops. Many of these were still under construction, and most were being built of wood. There were glimpses of gardens at the backs of them – a few cultivated, but a greater number still scrub or mud.

"See the log cabins?" My father pointed one out. "That's probably what we'll have to build first, to live in until we can build our house."

The log cabins looked heavy and crude, with jutting joints at the corners; but these were the simplest and quickest style to build, our carter agreed.

"Mam hopes our real house will be brick," Sarah told him.

"Only if we can afford it," my mother said.

The man glanced over his shoulder at her. "You're Londoners?"

"Yes."

"Thought so. Londoners always want a brick house. Afraid of fire. And who can blame them? Now the north-country folk, they don't mind. Timber's cheaper; and they're thrifty. Well, here's your plot!"

We had stopped at a long narrow rectangle of land, full of tangled grass and weeds and a few small trees.

"Ah…" My mother let out a breath. "At last."

I stared at the little strip of land. It was hard to believe we had come across an ocean for this; that we would build a new life here.

Next door on one side was a log cabin and a partially cleared garden, on the other an empty plot. Looking around, I saw a mixture of unclaimed plots, log cabins and houses – mostly built of wood, but some of brick. Building was going on apace, and workmen were everywhere, mixing lime, laying bricks, sawing wood; two men were setting small panes of glass into a window frame, others planing off the base of a door. There was much whistling and singing, and shouts rang from building site to street.

The carter left us, surrounded by our many boxes and crates – and the tent my father had hired at the waterfront. The first task was to find a suitable space to erect this. We chose the most level area, and began pulling up weeds and treading the ground flat. Then my father and I struggled with the tent. At last we had it up, the guy-ropes taut and pegs hammered in, and were able to move around, stooped, inside, and drag some of our belongings under cover. My mother cleared a space outside for a fireplace, and we fetched stones to enclose it and sticks to make a tripod so that we could cook.

My mother had recovered her authority. She had hated the voyage, but now I could see she felt secure again. She would take charge.

We had no need to go in search of firewood, water, beer or bread, for a neighbour appeared, bringing those necessities, along with a meat pie. She was the wife of a shoemaker from the cabin next door. While she talked to our parents and advised them about many practical matters, my sisters and I drank our beer, took slices of pie and wandered around the space that would become our home, workplace and garden.

A flock of birds flew up at our approach with a great rush of wings. They had been feeding on something in the grass. They looked rather like our English pigeons and yet there was something subtly different about them. At the far end of the plot were a few trees, some of them bright with autumn foliage. One in particular took my eye: its leaves glowed with radiant colours of yellow, deep gold, scarlet and purple.

My mother joined us. "Our neighbour says this is a sassafras tree. The street is named for them." She gazed up into its branches. "How beautiful the New World is! We shall keep these trees, but we must clear an area back there for planting vegetables. There is much to be done."

She looked at me, and I shrugged. I supposed I would be expected to help, at least until I could find work that would take me away from home. Gardening did not appeal to me. I was eager to explore this new land but not to be digging a garden under my parents' eyes.

Betty nudged me. "Who's Dad talking to?"

I looked round. Two men had appeared at the entrance to our plot and were in conversation with our father. Both were tall, fair-haired and strong-looking, wearing workaday clothing, leather jerkins and sturdy boots. We all made our way towards them over the rough ground.

My father drew my mother forward to meet the men. "Here is my wife, Susanna. Su, these men are Gunnar and Lars Andersson. They own a woodyard in the city and have been working here for a year, building cabins for English settlers. They say they can build us a simple cabin in less than a week."

"Four days. The more men, the better." The older

of the two looked at my father and me. "You can help. No need to be skilled."

"When can you start?" my mother asked.

"Monday, first light."

Today was sixth-day – Friday. My mother nodded approval.

"We have logs ready cut at the yard," the younger one said.

They appeared to be father and son. Lars was probably nineteen or twenty – tall, well-muscled, his hair the blondest I had ever seen, his eyes vivid blue in a tanned face. He seemed to belong in this new country, and made me feel pale and unmanly.

My father began discussing the price, and where the cabin should be built. The shoemaker from next door came over and offered to help.

Not long after they had all gone, while we were still contemplating the site of our cabin, two more visitors arrived: a man and a woman. The man – burly, with russet curls springing from under his hat – called out, "Will? Susanna? Is it you?"

My mother gave a gasp. She picked up her skirts and ran stumbling over the uneven ground into the street, followed by my father. We three hung back and watched. The woman turned to my mother, and with cries of joy the two of them flew into each other's arms and hugged as if they would never let go.

"That must be Judith," said Betty.

My mother and Judith stood back, gazed long at each other, wiped away tears, and embraced again. My father and the man who could only be Daniel Kite, the blacksmith, did less hugging, but they too seemed greatly moved to see each other.

I felt embarrassed by all the emotion; I did not expect such displays from my parents. But there was no escape. The four of them drew together and called to us to come.

My mother brought me forward; presented me to their friends. "This is our son, Josiah. Our eldest. And here are Elizabeth and Sarah."

They greeted us each in turn. Judith – a tall, spare woman with clear blue eyes – said to me, "Josiah! Su's first-born, after the Fire. Oh, thou hast such a look of Will!"

I grunted something I hoped was polite, and backed away, not wanting so much attention. I didn't know these people; they were my parents' friends, not mine, though I did not doubt that they must be good people. I was relieved when their attention shifted to the girls.

My father told Daniel about the builders, and Daniel said, "Oh, the Anderssons? They are skilled men. Fast, and honest. Gunnar showed me how to make my own outhouse with logs. I'll come and help."

My mother and Judith were talking about food

supplies, and medicines – my mother full of questions and Judith full of advice.

But our visitors did not stay long. "We won't hinder you," Judith said. She arranged for us to visit them the next day at their home. "Come early, and spend the day with us. Join us for dinner."

She would have had my mother and sisters go back with her immediately and sleep at their house, but my mother said no, we'd stay together in the tent, and make plans, and keep one another warm. And so we did. We were as close-packed as in the ship, but the air was sweeter, and we woke early to sunshine penetrating the canvas walls. My mother had lit the fire the night before, and now she revived it and heated water for washing. We found clean clothes in our trunk. These had been packed in wormwood, and we shook them out in the fresh air, wrinkling our noses at the smell.

We left mid-morning for the Kites' home. Their house and forge were little more than a mile away, but as soon as we left our street behind, the going became rougher. Fewer plots had yet been occupied further back from the harbour, and the roads were mere tracks through woodland. On the way we passed people busy with construction or planting. The day was bright, the air fresh and clean, and all around were the vivid reds and golds of autumn leaves. I had never seen such intensity of colour in England, and thought it must be the purity of the air that caused it.

We were all hot and dusty by the time we reached the forge.

Daniel was shoeing a horse – for he acted as farrier as well as blacksmith. Working with him was a young man, strongly built and auburn-haired, like him. This was his son, Ben.

Judith came out of the house, drying her hands on an apron, and after her came three younger children – a girl and two little boys, all blue-eyed and red-haired. I was told their names but instantly forgot them.

Judith had prepared dinner – the first large, proper meal we'd had for more than two months. It was a comforting meal, full of meaty sauce and dumplings and home-grown vegetables. And there was good beer, and afterwards a plum pudding served with cream from their cow. Judith Kite rose greatly in my estimation after that dinner.

Later I went for a walk with Ben and the Kites' dog, a brown and white mongrel. The dog ran ahead, forging his own tunnels through the grass, his passage marked by the alarm calls of birds. There were large clearings in the woods where the grass was shoulder-high and full of flowers and herbs, most of them turning brown or dropping seeds. I had no names for any of them. I felt surrounded by nature as never before, by the huge wildness of the woods. The smell of the grass and flowers, the feel of them brushing against me as we pushed through, made me realize that I had lived all my life till now separated from the natural world of God's creation. I was amazed and entranced by every plant, every smell, every bird sound.

"There's a little creek along here," said Ben. "Full of fish."

"Thou catch them?" I saw the shimmer of fish beneath the surface of the water.

"Yes. And trap birds and squirrels. Got traps at the house." He had a slow, shy smile. "Thou could come with me, if thou like."

I nodded. "Maybe I will."

We walked on, the meadow rustling, sunlight sparkling on the water, bird sounds all around us.

I liked Ben. He didn't talk too much, and he allowed me to feel equal to him, even though I was younger and a newcomer. We talked about what we'd come from, our lives in London and New England. He too came of radical stock, I realized. Daniel Kite had been continually in and out of prison. Ben seemed a milder person, less forthright, but certain in his faith; and he was happy in his work as a blacksmith alongside his father. I envied him that ease.

When it was time to leave we found that Dan and

Judith had loaded up a handcart with food, bedding, beer and other goods.

"Some provisions to start you off," said Judith.

"We can't take all this!" my mother protested.

"Indeed you can; it is merely some small comforts," insisted Judith. "And if you wish, when you are settled, you can do the same for other newcomers."

My parents thanked them, and we made ready to go. Ben turned to me and asked, "Will we see thee tomorrow, at Meeting?"

I nodded. "Yes, for sure," – and saw my father smile and give a little exasperated shake of his head.

The meeting was held at Front Street, in the house of one of the leading merchants.

People crowded into the room. Many were artisan families like ours; others looked like farmers. I saw a group of people in plain but costly clothes, and guessed them to be merchants or landowners – perhaps one was William Penn?

There were several children, a babe or two in arms, a few youths and girls who looked up as Betty and I passed. We saw the Kites and went to sit near them.

It was a relief to be in Meeting and not to fear the knock at the door, the soldiers marching in. I relaxed as the quality of the silence began to change and deepen. Those around me were centring down.

I tried to do the same, to become part of the meeting, but this cannot be achieved by any act of will, and my mind remained restless. So many new experiences crowded in on me. I thought of our long voyage; of the vast wild country we had come to. I wondered what work I might find; whether Ben might become a friend; whether, tomorrow, Lars would mock my cabin-building skills…

On second-day morning, early, Gunnar and Lars Andersson arrived in a large cart laden with logs and tools, and work began on our cabin. First, they staked out the length and breadth on the ground, and we pulled up shrubs, then beat and trampled the earth till it was level.

"Beat it down well," said Gunnar. "This will be the floor of your home."

When the space was ready, the two of them laid the first logs, making the longest sides of the rectangle. Next came two shorter logs. Gunnar measured twelve inches from each end, and cut a notch, and the notched logs were fitted over the longer sides, to make the shape of the cabin.

Now we continued laying logs, two on the long sides, two on the short sides, Gunnar making the notches. Our neighbour, the shoemaker Stephen Parkes, arrived, and then Daniel Kite joined us. We all worked at lifting and placing the logs in position. It was tiring work, and my father and I could not match the speed and strength of the others.

Gunnar reassured us. "Two months on a ship – it's no good. People come here weak – often sick. You rest now. Don't lift too much. Get strong slowly."

We all stopped work for a while. My mother and Betty brought out beer and pies, and Ellen Parkes provided more; then we sat on packing cases and ate together. The Anderssons told us they had come to Philadelphia from Upland on the Delaware ("Chester, you English call it now," said Gunnar) knowing there would be a need for their expertise and plenty of work in the new city as more and more settlers arrived. Betty moved among us, serving beer, offering more pies, making herself useful.

When the lifting became too high, we were obliged to work on trestles, and that slowed us down. Even so, by the end of the first day we had raised the walls and Lars and Gunnar had cut out the windows and doors. The next morning my father complained that every muscle in his body ached, and I too felt the strain in my shoulders. That day the two Swedes began building up the pitched roof. It was satisfying to see the house take shape. Betty wandered around, asking questions of the builders. She was looking prettier than usual, I noticed; she had done something to her hair, so that it escaped her cap, allowing loose dark curls to bounce against her cheeks. Lars, who was cutting shingles, let her help him sort them into piles. By the end of the second day we had a roof and a half-built chimney. I thought the cabin was all but done now, but the last two days were spent finishing the chimney and making doors, shutters, hinges and latches. The most tedious job was caulking all the gaps, something we would carry on with when the builders left.

My father paid them, and they loaded their tools onto the cart.

"Where will you work next?" Betty asked Lars.

"Across the way." Lars indicated a nearby plot. He smiled, teasing. "You want to come and count shingles, Betty?"

"Betty," said my mother, "find a broom and start sweeping out the cabin."

For the next two days I helped my father saw wood and make bed frames and shelves. We left the printing equipment in its packing case and used that as a table, to save space, but moved all the boxes of books and stationery to one end of the cabin. Lars and Gunnar had built our cabin larger than average, with a partition separating the living quarters from the shop. But the shop was a tiny room; it had no drop-down counter and little space to display goods, so shelves were essential.

"It'll be a start," my father said, when we paused for a rest. "We shall need to begin earning." I knew it was his inheritance from my grandfather Henry Heywood, along with his share in the business in Stepney, that had enabled him to bring us here to live without incurring debt; that, and a thrifty lifestyle. He would not want to be laying out too much with no return.

He smiled at me – a warm, unguarded smile with none of his usual hint of reproach. "Thou hast worked hard, Jos, and done well, these last few days. I would have struggled without thee."

His rare praise made me feel accepted, part of the family, in a way I so often did not. We were both covered in sawdust, our hands scarred with small cuts and splinters. Neither of us had any great skill at carpentry, but the shop was taking shape; it was satisfying work, and we were doing it together.

But I knew we would need more than the bookshop.

"I'll find a master," I said. "Start earning money again. That will help."

"Yes. We can ask Friends after Meeting tomorrow..."

"No! Well, yes, I thank thee, but I'll look around for myself first; try the shops and businesses on the waterfront. I'll go on second-day."

My father nodded. "Do that." He plucked a wood-shaving from my hair and gave me a gentle push on the head. "But not the butcher's this time."

We laughed.

But then he spoilt the moment by saying, "Thou will *come* to Meeting again? No more of thy backsliding?"

At once I felt resistance. I shrugged. "Maybe."

"I expect thee to come, Jos."

"I don't know anyone there," I said. The remark sounded childish, and I regretted it immediately.

"The purpose of meeting is not to chatter with acquaintances," he said. "Meeting is the assembly of God's people. Thou know the Kites, and will come to know others, in time."

It was in my mind to say that no one could force me to go, but I thought better of it. And in the end I went to Meeting, and the following day set off in search of work.

Six

*I*t was good to be out alone. From our cabin in Sassafras Street I walked down to Second Street, where several small businesses – a tailor, a hardware seller, a draper – had set up rudimentary shops. Everything looked new – fresh-painted wood, trodden dirt paths. I turned south, noting the names of the streets roughly painted on the sides of buildings: Cherry Street, Mulberry Street. The names amused me. They seemed unreal, not like the street names in London that had roots going down into history. Market Street was broader, and here I turned left and saw the harbour sparkling ahead of me: merchant ships anchored out in the river; brown sails furled; sunlight glinting on ripples.

All around was activity, the chance of work. Men were loading sacks into a waiting boat tied up at the jetty. An overseer on the dockside shouted orders, while a merchant and his clerk, list in hand, supervised the operation. I saw that they were sending goods out to be loaded onto one of the large ships waiting in the river. Further along the waterfront, men with shovels were emptying a cart of something that looked like gravel.

The shops along the front appeared more finished than those on Second Street. I noted a cooper's, a ship's chandler's, a large general store, an ironmonger's, a carpenter's – all with customers going in and out. An inn sign swung in the breeze – and I almost laughed aloud: the Blue Anchor. The same name as the inn I'd been in trouble for frequenting in Limehouse. Perhaps I should seek work there as a pot boy? Work of that kind should be easy enough to find. But I'd said I would try for something better. I supposed I should approach one of the shopkeepers – see if they needed a clerk. I hesitated, realizing now that it would have been sensible to have taken up my father's offer to talk to Friends at Meeting. An introduction would have made everything easier. And yet I wanted to be independent, not to rely on my father or to be restricted to working for Friends.

I became aware of a stir of movement and talk along the quayside. People were staring out across the water, where another large ship had come into view. I heard the name *"Chepstow"*. A man – the merchant

I'd seen earlier attending to the loading of his ship – called out to me, "Boy! Canst' take a message?"

"Yes – for sure!" I said.

He gave me a coin. "Dost thou know Walnut Street?" He pointed. "George Bainbrigg's house. Up there, near the corner of Second Street. Big house with a blue door. Tell George the *Chepstow*'s here."

I nodded, and turned to go. He called after me, "Tom Appleyard's my name!"

"I'll tell him."

I found George Bainbrigg's house easily, but its appearance daunted me. It was a large clapboard house of several storeys with a wide front and a balcony over the street. Should I grasp the sturdy brass knocker on the blue door, or go up the side passage, like a tradesman?

I decided on the door, and knocked. A maidservant opened it, but the master was already stepping into the hall. He was a man of middling age, not tall but sturdily built, his fair hair beginning to recede at the temples, his eyes sharp blue. I knew him for the master by his manner and his sober but well-cut grey coat.

"George Bainbrigg?" I asked.

"Aye, lad."

"Tom Appleyard sent me. He says to tell thee the *Chepstow*'s coming in."

At once he was alert.

"I must get down there! Mary!" The servant reappeared. "Ask Izzie to delay dinner. And tell Kate the ship from England is in, that I'll be in the counting house."

He opened the door, and we stepped out together.

"Thou work for Tom?" he asked.

"No. I was passing by. I'm fresh from England—"

"Oh, aye! I see that now. Thou hast those pale London looks." His own complexion was fair and ruddy, and he spoke with a north-country accent. "Thou came with thy parents?"

"Yes. They're printers—"

"Ah! I heard there was a printer come. That's good. What's thy name?"

"Josiah Heywood." I seized my opportunity, and added, "I'm looking for work. As a clerk, or some such."

He cast an appraising glance at me. "Art thou? Well, Josiah, I could do with an extra pair of hands right now for an hour or two, unpacking. I'll pay thee. It's not much, but I know what it's like when folks first arrive – especially folks like your father, with a family. Every penny helps."

"Yes! I thank thee," I said. Perhaps, if I showed willing and he liked me, he might offer me a permanent position, or recommend me to a friend. I'd taken to him already; I liked his straightforward way of talking.

"Here's my counting house."

We had walked only a few yards from his home, to the back entrance of a building on the west side of Second Street. George Bainbrigg led me in, calling, "Matt!"

We stepped into an office, where a young man was writing in a ledger. He got up, and I felt his gaze on me.

"The *Chepstow*'s been sighted," George Bainbrigg said. "We must get down to the quay."

"Ah! That's good!" The news seemed to energize the young man. He finished his note in the ledger, blotted it, snapped the book closed and stood up. He looked again at me, and his employer said, "This is Josiah Heywood. Josiah – my apprentice, Matthew Peel."

We nodded to each other warily.

"Josiah will help with the unpacking," George Bainbrigg told the other man. "He's newly come from England – from London – and looking for work."

The three of us walked the short distance to the quayside together, where a small crowd had gathered. Tom Appleyard's ship was now laden and ready to leave, and the sailors were raising the anchor. We all watched the ship move slowly out into the current as the wind took her sails.

"God speed," said George Bainbrigg.

The approaching *Chepstow* was much closer now. I could read her name on the side and see men on the decks moving about.

Tom Appleyard turned to George Bainbrigg. "She's made good time."

"Aye. Let's hope Arkwright's brought what we need. Folks I speak to are all after chisels, hacksaws, nails. And they'll be wanting woollens and sewing stuff with winter coming." He turned to me. "Thou might as well come back later, Josiah. It'll take them a while to unload the ship."

He explained that he'd had a part share in the trading voyage with Tom Appleyard, and I agreed to return when the goods had been transferred to his counting house to be divided up.

I used the intervening time to continue to look around for places where I might find work, but I did not search over-zealously. I wanted to be free to take up employment with George Bainbrigg if he should ask me. I liked the man, and knew my father would be impressed if I found myself work with a merchant.

Rather than go home, I went into the Blue Anchor and bought a measure of small beer and a pie. I sat in a corner watching the people around me – the Philadelphians. Not all the merchants and townsfolk were Friends, though most wore sober dress of one kind or another. I saw a man who looked like a trapper or backwoodsman, drinking slowly and steadily, alone except for a dog that lay across his feet. Two merchants were deep in conversation, a creased map spread out on the table in front of them. There were sailors of all nationalities – Dutch, Swedish, German, French. One of them winked at me, and I glanced hastily away.

When I emerged into the sunlight, the last of the crates from the *Chepstow*'s boats were being loaded onto a cart, supervised by Matthew Peel. I made my way to the front entrance of George Bainbrigg's counting house on Second Street. The doors were wide open, and the two merchants and Tom Appleyard's apprentice, David Severs, were inside, surrounded by crates, boxes and barrels. The only other person there was an older man, Zachary Rowe, who seemed to be employed as a general handyman.

Matthew arrived soon after with the final delivery, and we all set to work. The crates were roughly labelled, and Zachary and I prised them open so that the contents and quantities could be checked against the bill of lading. The two apprentices made lists, noting everything in detail, while the merchants discussed how it should all be divided up.

"No chisels," George Bainbrigg grumbled, "and I've been promising them to folk. But we have nails a-plenty. Thou'll take half, Tom?" He signalled to me.

"Push that crate over there, Josiah. We'll have Tom's stuff that side."

"There are four dozen scythes," said Matthew, scratching away with his quill.

George grunted approval. "They'll sell, with all these new folk coming in."

To my surprise there was not only woollen cloth and tableware but furniture in the consignment: a few dozen chairs and stools, finely finished and decorated, not like the furniture we'd had back home. We opened another crate and found thirty Bibles, several dozen ledgers and journals, some almanacs, ten reams of paper and a box full of jars of ink powder.

"Might thy father be interested in some of this?" George Bainbrigg asked me.

"I think so, yes. He wants to set up shop as soon as possible." I'd been looking around the storeroom upstairs, with its shelves stacked with goods. "Dost *thou* have a shop?"

"No. Some of the merchants do, but Tom and I, we both prefer to sell at public vendue. You can get rid of stuff fast, once word's gone out. And folk enjoy an auction. I sell wholesale to shops, though; tell thy father I can quote him a good price for stationery."

We continued our work, and I saw why extra help was needed, for there was a lot of lifting and stowing, and stacks of boxes to be carried upstairs. It was hard work, and my back and shoulders soon began to ache. We divided up the goods, loaded Tom Appleyard's share onto a cart, and stowed George Bainbrigg's away on shelves and in cupboards. Everyone worked together, even the masters. Matthew Peel was rather aloof, but David was friendly enough. Zachary, strong and quiet, chewed tobacco as he worked, and occasionally nudged me away from a particularly heavy box, saying, "I'll take this one."

It was early evening when I went home with money in my pocket and a feeling of satisfaction at work well done and connections made. My father would no doubt visit George Bainbrigg and buy stock from him. And the merchant had told me, when I left, that he might be able to offer me "something in the way of permanent work".

I walked back to Sassafras Street with a spring in my step.

Tokpa

M any more demons come. They surround us as we stand on the block. Their breath is foul; their eyes glare. They push and shout – all of them grabbing at us, jabbing fingers, pointing.

I shake with fear. What will they do? Will they kill us? Eat us? I call on the spirits to help me. I call loudly, for they are far away.

A crewman cuts me with a whip. He shouts words I've learned mean, "Shut your mouth!"

One of the demons jumps up onto the block, prods and handles me, forces my mouth open. He has a hairy, whiskery face and bad teeth. He keeps hold of me. Words fly between him and the captain.

I am taken off the block and made to climb into a cart. The driver is not of my people: he is Bassa. He wears clothes like the demons: trousers, shirt, straw hat. There are others in the cart: three men, two women. I smell their fear. The cart *is pulled by an animal of a kind I have never seen before. I watch its haunches moving as we follow the road. When I look over my shoulder I see the ship still rocking on the water. I feel afraid to be leaving it. It was a bad place, but a place I knew.*

Seven

I was hungry by the time I reached home. There was a smell of cooking in the cabin, and Betty exclaimed, "At last! Now we can eat! Mam! Jos is back!"

My mother had made a pottage of venison with onions and pumpkin, and we sat on boxes while she set out plates on the packing case. After we had given thanks in silence, everyone looked at me expectantly, but I made them wait until I had eaten a few spoonfuls. Then I told them about my afternoon's work and the people I had met. My parents were pleased, and I had the unusual experience of being both the centre of attention and the subject of their approval. I scooped up the rest of my pottage. "This is good! Is there any more?"

My mother refilled my plate. "I wonder, should thou continue to look around, or wait and see if the merchant comes back to thee?"

"I'd say wait a little," my father said. "Thou can help me set up the shop, Jos. The sooner that's done the sooner we'll make some return – though whether it'll be cash or barter I don't know. It seems there's very little money in the colony; it's all tied up in goods and land."

I was glad my father wanted me to wait, for I felt sure I'd hear more from George Bainbrigg.

Within a few days our bookshop and stationer's was stocked and open for business. We arranged some of the books by subject matter on the shelves: religion, science, medicine, history, poetry, books written in French or Latin. Many more remained in labelled boxes. We stood the pamphlets upright in boxes on the floor, and set out the stationery on a crate near the makeshift counter at the front.

I painted a sign saying WM. HEYWOOD – BOOK-SELLER & STATIONER and hammered it to a post on the roadside; and we hoped any customers would not mind tramping across our muddy plot to reach us.

George Bainbrigg was one of our first callers. When he came, my father was minding the shop. I was outside with my mother and sisters, helping to clear the ground for a hen house and some vegetable planting. Lars and Gunnar had cut down a couple of large trees for us, and Lars was showing me how to chop them up for firewood – something I had never done before and found surprisingly satisfying. Betty had paused to watch us – or rather, to watch Lars, for I suspected it was he she was interested in. My mother must have guessed too, for she called Betty away, back to the weeding; and Betty moved reluctantly, then brightened and exclaimed, "Oh! A customer!"

I looked up. "It's the merchant – George Bainbrigg!" I told my mother. I felt nervous at the thought that he might want to speak to me. "Should I go in?"

"Wait," she said. "They may call thee."

I brushed at my clothes. I was covered in a film of sawdust. It was in my hair, on my tongue – everywhere. "I feel dirty," I said.

"No matter. Thou look as if thou hast been working, and there is nothing to be ashamed of in that."

She herself was, as always, uncaring of her workaday appearance, her skirts caught up above the ankle so that she could dig, her hair tucked under a plain cap.

But they did not call me, though George Bainbrigg stayed some time. As soon as he left, carrying a small parcel, I put down my axe and hurried indoors.

My father was standing by the counter, looking thoughtful. I could tell nothing from his expression.

"Dad? What did… Did George Bainbrigg say anything…?"

He turned his attention to me. "Yes. He did. He

made me a proposition, and I must think on it. We all must. I'll talk to thee later, with thy mother."

"Oh, Dad! Tell me now – please. Did he offer me work? Thou didn't call me in," I added, reproachfully.

"Later!" he repeated – and went on to say how George Bainbrigg had looked all around and been impressed with the shop, and wished our venture well, and spoken of his terms for purchase of stationery, which sounded most reasonable.

"And he bought a book." My father smiled. "Our first book sale!"

"What did he buy?"

"Robert Barclay's *Apology*. Said his copy had been damaged by sea water on a voyage. I think he bought it mainly as a kindness – to encourage me in my venture."

I nodded – but I had grown impatient again. "Dad – when wilt thou say…?"

"This evening. When I've shut up shop."

I went back to report to my mother and sisters. Betty was laughing at something Lars had said and did not notice me. And my mother, with infuriating calmness, said, "In God's good time, then, Jos."

But after supper she put the dishes aside to wash later, and sent the girls up to the loft with a candle. "You may read, or write in your journals," she told them.

Betty protested; she wanted to know what was

going on; but my mother insisted, so she followed Sarah reluctantly up the ladder. I felt sure she would perch at the top, out of sight, and listen.

My parents and I sat down on boxes around the fireplace.

"Now, husband," my mother said.

"George Bainbrigg was pleased with Josiah, and would like to offer him work..." my father began; and I gave a little jolt of satisfaction.

He turned to me. "But it is not as simple as that, Jos. He has an apprentice, a young man of twenty-one, who is about to leave him at the end of his term. George Bainbrigg will then need another person to work for him. He could take on a clerk – a man of some experience – or he could take another apprentice..."

I saw where this was leading, and said, "I want—"

My father raised a hand to silence me. "George Bainbrigg's problem is cash. There is not much money in the colony. There is work, land, abundance of everything in nature; there are goods to be had cheaply enough. But the merchants – their wealth is tied up in goods. And, Jos, although George Bainbrigg took a liking to thee, thou'rt a youth, and inexperienced. He would prefer to take thee on as an apprentice."

I drew breath, desperate to speak; but he would not let me, and I was obliged to listen, clenching my fists, waiting, wanting only to interrupt.

"He offers a five-year bond," my father continued. "Thou would live in his house, with all found: clothing, food, drink, lodging – and he'd pay thee a small allowance. Thou would learn to do the accounts, write letters, and all the general work of the business. In addition, thou would accompany him on trading voyages and, after a year or two, be encouraged to undertake such ventures alone, trading on his behalf. There would also be the opportunity to trade for thyself and so begin to make some money of thine own."

My mother opened her mouth to speak – but I jumped up. "Father, this isn't what I want! I want to *earn* – now! I don't want to take thy money for the bond. I want to help the family – to be independent, to be a man! I went down to the waterfront on my own, to look for work for myself. Why didn't George Bainbrigg speak to *me*?"

To my embarrassment, I felt tears of frustration spring to my eyes, and dashed a hand across my face. "He treats me like a child!" I said.

My father put a hand on my arm. "Sit down, Jos. Sit down," he said, more gently than I'd expected. "George Bainbrigg came to me because he could not offer thee what thou wanted. An apprenticeship is different and must be arranged through the father. Thou know'st that."

"I had an apprenticeship before, and let thee down

over it," I said, scowling, as I sat down. I felt angry. I'd asked for honest work and they had gone over my head and wanted to tie me down to a bond. "You can't afford it," I said, looking at the two of them. "You need my wages."

My mother spoke then. "Jos is right, husband. We surely cannot afford to apprentice him to a *merchant*?"

"George Bainbrigg asks only for a bond of ninety guineas," said my father – and her eyes widened.

The sum was low. In London, to be apprenticed to a merchant, even one in a modest way of business, would cost four or five hundred guineas. Even the apprentice my father and Nat Lacon took on at their print shop in Stepney had been bound for two hundred.

My mother asked, "Is he – this man – a successful merchant? Does he thrive?"

"He does," my father reassured her. "He has been trading along the eastern seaboard for some twelve years or so and has many connections. Costs are lower in America. That's why people want to come here. Ninety guineas is a reasonable sum, and I believe we can find it. But only if it is what Josiah wants."

They both looked at me.

"I want to pay my own way," I said. "I want to be independent."

"That's as it should be," my father agreed. "But bear in mind thou hast no training and can only seek low-paid work – and that may become tedious. Thine only small experience has been in the printing and stationery business. Would'st thou prefer to work for me? I think not?" I shook my head. "A man who is not skilled has no real independence, Josiah. One day thou might want to marry, support a family…"

I felt uncertain and deflated. My plans for finding paid work for myself had come to nothing. And yet I saw that my father was right, and I would have better prospects with the apprenticeship. I ought to be glad of it. I'd hoped George Bainbrigg would offer to take me on, and he had, and in such a way as would set me up in a career of my own.

"I'd travel?" I said. "Trade on his behalf in a year or two?" That appealed to me. It might not be paid work, but he'd give me an allowance, and all found. And I'd be out in the world, away from home, as I'd wanted.

My father said, "That's right: New England, Maryland, the West Indies…"

My mother's face betrayed her anxiety. I knew the thought of me at sea must make her fearful; but she said nothing.

"We'd need to look into the cost," my father said. "It could be done, I'm sure. He would clothe and feed thee, and that would be a saving."

I tried to imagine becoming a merchant. Could I do

such a thing? Buying and selling, dealing with other traders, making decisions that could lead to wealth or ruin? Supposing I didn't succeed, and disappointed my father again?

"No need to decide right now," he said. "I told George Bainbrigg we'd give him an answer next week. That allows us all time to reflect and consider, and for me to talk to Friends who know him – for we must be sure that the two of you are suited."

"And we will wait in silence," my mother said, "and be guided by the inward light."

But there was to be no silence yet. Betty's slippered heels appeared at the top of the ladder, followed by her backside draped in a gathered skirt of brown wool with blue apron ties hanging down. She was already talking as she reached the floor and turned round. "Jos, thou must be mad to hesitate! Think what a life thou'll have! Sailing to the other colonies, to the West Indies, maybe to Portugal or Spain—"

"Betty—" my mother began, then caught my father's eye and let her run on.

"Thou might see Indians; they live in villages along the Delaware, Lars says. And there are trappers, and fur traders. Or thou might go to Boston, or New York, or Barbados. And thou'll live in the merchant's house, with space to thyself, and no insects coming in through knotholes in the planks, like we have here.

Thou'rt so lucky! *I'd* like to go!"

I listened to her with a grin on my face. She was only Betty, my silly, excitable sister, whom it was my duty to tease. And yet her words struck home. She knew me, and knew what I wished for, in my heart.

"Don't be too proud," she urged me later, as we talked together in low voices. "Let them spend the money on thee. They don't *want* thee sweeping floors for a living."

I did not sweep any floors, but for the rest of that week I dug the garden, stacked wood, and fetched provisions from the town, while my father waited in the shop for the few customers who came in. Clearly the shop would not make our fortune; many people could not read or write, and even those who could had little time for it.

"This is a young country," my mother said. "People want ploughs, spades, bricks ... not books."

But my father looked to the future. "Before long Philadelphia will be a city, and there will be a need for books and printing. And when that time comes we'll be here, set up and ready for them."

For that, I knew, we must make haste to build our permanent house and print shop, and that would cost money; and yet my parents had looked at their finances and agreed that they could afford to apprentice me to George Bainbrigg, if I wished it. When we met together in silence it seemed clear to all three of us that a way had opened for me and that I should follow it. My father sent word to the merchant and the bond was agreed. George Bainbrigg offered to accept the money in two instalments, the first part to be paid after the month's trial period, the second a year later. My parents were grateful; this would ease their burden considerably.

The following first-day, after Meeting, when people had risen and were talking to their friends, I saw George Bainbrigg moving towards us through the throng. At his side was a girl of about my own age.

He drew her forward. "My daughter, Katherine," he said.

She was a little below the middle height, not plump yet sweetly curved. Her gown was of plain dark grey wool, her fair hair tucked away under a linen cap, only a few curls brushing her cheeks, which had turned a faint, becoming pink on meeting us.

My father began making introductions. When he said my name, Katherine looked directly at me.

Her eyes were light in colour – green or grey – and they gave her face a liveliness and energy that instantly attracted me. I held her gaze, tongue-tied. I was taken by surprise. I had not thought that George Bainbrigg might be part of a family, like our own.

Now I envisaged a wife, perhaps younger children – a busy household into which I must fit. And this bright-eyed daughter, who was looking me over and no doubt thinking me a fool with nothing to say.

"Josiah," she said. "I am happy to meet thee. And thee, Elizabeth. And Sarah." She had the same broad north-country way of speaking as her father.

I thought her demeanour very womanly, with none of that shyness that girls usually show. Such confidence was intimidating. I stumbled over words of greeting, and asked, "Hast thou lived here long?" – a question I immediately regretted since Philadelphia had only been founded last year and no one could have lived here long. Out of the corner of my eye I saw Betty watching me and trying not to giggle.

Katherine answered, "Only a year. Though I have been three years in the New World; in Maryland. But you" – she turned and included my sisters in her question, and a note of eagerness came into her voice – "you are from London, aren't you? I should love to go to London."

This was more promising. But no sooner had we begun talking than the three girls were drawn away into a circle of women for more introductions.

George Bainbrigg turned to me.

"Kate is my only child," he said, his glance lingering on her. "She has no mother. It is good for her to meet other young people. Well, Josiah" – he gave me his full attention now – "to business. Matt Peel leaves me at the end of this week, and I propose that the following week thou come a-liking for a month, to see if we suit. Thy father agrees. How say thou?"

"I thank thee, George Bainbrigg," I said. "I shall be pleased to come."

Jokpa

*T*his place is strange. Tall huts are crowded together in rows. They have many windows like eyes and they watch us as we drive along the track.

I am near the driver, the Bassa man. He sees me trembling and says, in the demons' language that we all learned on the ship, "Don't be 'fraid, boy."

"What they do?" I ask him. "They kill us?"

He laughs. "Kill you? No! You worth too much. You slave. You work in fields."

In the fields. At home, it is women who work in the fields, planting and harvesting rice. Men hunt, or clear the ground for planting, or forage for nuts and berries in the forest.

But I would rather work like a woman than be killed.

And now we come out of the crowded village and see, all around, huge harvested fields full of chopped-off stalks — thick, heavy stalks that only strong men could have cut with great labour. Further on, we pass big huts with smoke and steam coming from them. There is a strange sweet smell, and a terrifying noise – thunder? or demons fighting? – like nothing I have heard before. This noise never stops. I think these huts must be full of evil spirits. The sides are open, and I see rows of people working. I don't know what they do, but the evil spirits roar and men with whips go up and down the rows, striking at any who slacken. Carts are lined up outside, and men load them with heavy boxes shaped like drums.

In the distance is a great hut – high, wide, with many doors and windows. It is a chief's hut, I think.

"What this place?" I ask. "What it call?"

"This island? It call Barbados."

Eight

And so, in the second week of November, I moved into George Bainbrigg's house in Walnut Street to begin my apprenticeship.

The household consisted of my master, his daughter and two servants: Isobel Judson, the cook and housekeeper, and a maid, Mary Sutcliff. I was surprised at first that there was no manservant for George Bainbrigg or lady's maid for Katherine – for the house was the size of a gentleman's house, though plainly furnished, and George Bainbrigg seemed to have a thriving business – but I soon realized he had no time for such vanity. He had made money, but he did not waste it; any excess would go to the charitable purposes of the meeting, to help poor settlers or Friends in need.

I left our cabin on Sassafras Street in the late afternoon of the day before I was to start work.

"I'll be home in my free time," I told my mother. George Bainbrigg's house was no more than ten minutes' walk away.

The novelty of our cabin, with its cramped space, had already begun to pall, and I was looking forward to having a room of my own again.

It was Isobel, the housekeeper, who took charge of me when I arrived.

"Mary's fettled up thy room," she said as she led me up two flights of stairs to the second floor, where candles in sconces were already lit against the early dark. "All swept and dusted, and the bed made ready. Here we are…"

She opened a door and led me into a small room containing a curtained bed, a table and chair and a fireplace where a fire had been lit to take off the chill.

The floorboards were new, clean and pale, the walls painted light blue. There was a red and grey rug by the bed, a chest and some shelves for clothes, a washstand in one corner.

I looked out of the window and saw an unfinished back garden and a small building I assumed was a privy or tool shed.

"There's nowt much of a view," said Isobel.

"It's a fine room," I said. "My sister will be jealous."

A hint of a smile softened her features. She was an

austere-looking north-country woman, wearing an old-fashioned large linen collar, her grey hair drawn back under a plain cap, her hands gnarled and red from much housework.

"They're in a log cabin, thy family?" she said.

"Yes."

"Aye, folks mostly start that way. It's hard if you're used to city life. Mind, those cabins can be fine and cosy if you get a good fire going… Well, I'll leave thee to settle thyself. I'll be in the kitchen if thou need aught – downstairs, at back. They'll have supper soon; I'll call thee."

Left to myself, I took out my few possessions and put them away. The room was almost dark, but I did not want to waste the candle, so I managed without light. My notebooks and journal I placed in the chest, under my clothes, my Bible on the shelf by the bed, next to the candlestick. I had brought little else with me. Since leaving Stepney I seemed to have been gradually divesting myself of worldly possessions, as if in preparation for finding Eden.

There was no trace in the room of Matthew Peel, who had presumably slept here before me. I had found the former apprentice somewhat unfriendly, but now I reflected that he seemed also to be a capable and hard-working man, and I guessed that George Bain-brigg must have been pleased with him. I wondered whether he would be equally satisfied with me.

I sat on the bed a while. I meant to wait on the inward light, but was too restless, and instead thought of my new undertaking, my new master and this new home – and the presence of Katherine. She disturbed my thoughts, as she had done ever since I met her.

It was now quite dark in the room. I rose, opened the door, and stepped out onto the landing. I supposed Isobel and Mary must also sleep up here. There were several doors. One was open onto what was clearly a linen cupboard. A narrow stair led to the attic.

I went down to the first floor, wondering which of the rooms there was Katherine's.

The house was quiet, though I detected a murmur of voices and movement from somewhere below. Then I heard a door open downstairs, and Katherine's voice, saying, "I'll do that, Izzie!" – and the next moment she was on the bend of the stairs, looking up at me.

"Josiah, will thou join us for supper?"

She spoke formally, but there was a playful note to her voice that I found inviting. I smiled and thanked her, and followed her downstairs, admiring the tendrils of blonde hair that had escaped her cap and hung on the nape of her neck.

My master was waiting for us in the parlour, where a log fire was burning. The table was set for three with bread, cheese, cold meat and pottage. As we went in, I heard a swift rattle of claws on the wooden floor and a dog – a leggy, rough-haired hound – appeared. It sniffed me thoroughly, wagging its tail. I patted its head and felt a wet nose pushed against my hand.

"Ah, Josiah! Welcome!" George Bainbrigg said. "Hob, sit!" The dog settled by the fire. "Sit thyself down, too, Josiah. Thou hast everything thou need in the room, I hope?"

"It is all most convenient, I thank thee," I said.

I felt extraordinarily shy and unsure of myself. Even pulling out a chair to sit down was an ordeal; I was aware of its scrape on the floor, my own awkwardness, the feeling that father and daughter were watching me, sizing me up. I had been much more confident when working in the counting house.

When we were all seated we bowed our heads in the customary pause for shared silence. I breathed slowly and tried to steady my nerves.

We ate mainly in silence, as I was accustomed to at home, speaking only to pass dishes around the table; but this made me more aware of the sounds I made swallowing or picking up cutlery. Then I reached and cut off a piece of cheese, which, to my horror, shot off the table. I went to retrieve it, but the dog was there first, moving in one swift bound to intercept and swallow the morsel almost before it hit the ground.

Katherine gave a little yelp of laughter and put a hand to her mouth. I burned with embarrassment.

"Hob doesn't miss a trick," George Bainbrigg said. He pushed the cheese dish nearer to me. I felt more at ease, and managed to smile in return. The dog had moved to sit beside my chair and now had his hopeful gaze trained on me. An occasional sigh escaped him.

"I bought him as a puppy from an Indian," George Bainbrigg said, "back in seventy-four. We've travelled a fair way together since then." He sent the dog back to the fireplace, where it lay down.

When we had eaten, my master and I sat by the fire, the dog between us, lying half on George's feet. Katherine took a seat by the table, moved a couple of candles closer, and brought out some sewing. She was near enough to hear everything that was said.

Her father asked me about my family and our former life in London. We spoke of the sufferings of the English meetings – ours in east London; his, fifteen years or more ago, in Skipton, Settle and Halifax, places I had heard of, though my sense of where they were was vague.

He was the son of a wool dealer in Skipton and had been convinced of the truth at the age of eighteen in the 1650s and become one of the earliest Friends. When he spoke of the persecution and the struggles, I was reminded of my parents and how they too seemed to be forged of stronger metal than I, without doubts or fears. Even this journey to America they saw not as flight but as a new endeavour.

"When did thou come to America?" I asked.

"Sixteen sixty-nine," he said. "Fourteen years ago." I saw that Katherine was alert now, and listening. "My wife died the year before, in the spring of sixty-eight, when Kate was born. I felt, at that time, that everything was lost. My wife gone, my daughter puny and ailing – aye, I know" – he looked fondly at Katherine – "you'd not think it now. And I heard of Friends, many of them, going to America: to Maryland, New Jersey, New York – to a new life. I left the baby with my sister – she was a widow without children – and went off to the New World."

I wanted to know more about Katherine, but he began to ask me about my own childhood in London, and what our lives were like; what work I'd done, and what my interests were. I told him the things I thought he'd like to hear, leaving out the failed apprenticeship and the dockyard alehouses. All the time I was conscious of Katherine, listening as she sewed, the candlelight soft on her bowed head, the swift stab and pull of her needle.

I told George Bainbrigg I'd always liked the docks, seeing the great ships come in; that I'd loved the river and the great city; had scarcely ever been into the country, though there was farmland around Stepney.

"Thou'll see wilder places here," he promised. "And different folks. Trappers. Indians. Dutch, Swedes and Germans. I have a schooner, the *Frances* – thou hast perhaps seen her earlier, out in the river, though she's away right now. The captain is Richard Grey. He trades on my behalf in Delaware and New Jersey, and up to New York and Boston. He's not a Friend, but I like him well; we have worked together for years."

"I should like to travel," I said.

Katherine said suddenly, "Dad? Will we go to Barbados next year?"

It was the first time she had spoken since supper.

"Aye, I hope so," her father said. He turned to me. "I have friends in Barbados, in Michael's Town. Most years I go out there for a few weeks. It's trade and pleasure mixed. And support for the meetings, of course. Barbados Friends are under duress."

Nine

$\mathcal{N}$ext morning I began work. I'd hoped to see Katherine again before we went out, but my master roused me early and we left, without breakfast, before she came down.

He showed me around the counting house. Downstairs, at the front, was the sales area with its huge set of scales and tables for weighing out dry goods or displaying cloth. Barrels of dried fish and several great casks of sugar stood along one wall.

"I'm low in sugar," he said. "Most of my stock went to England on the *Chepstow*. Grain, other perishables, they move through quickly. I hope to shift the wool soon. Come upstairs. I'll show thee the storeroom."

The stairs were wide and open. On the upper floor were stored paper, tobacco, timber and household goods. Shelves were stacked high with bales of cloth, each one wrapped in paper, stamped with the width, type, quality and place of origin. Most of it was shipped from Liverpool or Bristol. George Bainbrigg pulled out a bale of flecked grey wool and partially unrolled it.

"Feel that – go on, get hold of it, lad! That's a good warm homespun, from Yorkshire. Now this" – he hauled out another bale – "this is kersey. And that's broadcloth. And here's fustian – feel how soft that is. Thou'll need to get a feel for all these fabrics. I've got linens, too, but I deal mainly in wool. I grew up with it; still have contacts in old England."

Some of the cloth would go to auction, he said, the rest to the new shops that were opening up in the city. The boxes of nails I'd unpacked the week before had been split up into more manageable amounts for sale.

"A lot of the tools – the scythes and saws – have been sold already. Tell thy father there's a good hardware shop on Second Street: Gerrit Bakker's."

"We already found it," I said.

"Good, good. Come down to the offices now." He led the way. "I'll show thee the books. That'll be thy task, much of the time. Thy father said thou'rt skilled at reckoning?"

"I am," I said. It was something I felt confident about. I knew I was quick and rarely made mistakes.

"But thou won't have learned double-entry book-keeping? I'll have to teach thee that."

He pulled out one of the ledgers and showed me the pages of neatly-written entries in red and black ink – Matt Peel's work, I supposed.

I saw that most payments were in goods. "So much sugar!" I said.

"Aye, the sugar! We get huge quantities in exchange for grain and meat. Most of it goes to England. Now, this room here is my own office…"

He led me into an adjoining room where there was a large table spread with books and papers. All around the walls were maps.

"Ah, I see thou'rt drawn to the maps," he said, as I moved to look at the largest one. It was disappointingly lacking in detail. Philadelphia was marked and, leading from it, several long-distance tracks that he said were Indian trails – the only roads. Along the river, he pointed out Burlington, Chester and New-castle. "I'll begin to teach thee something of navigation later," he said.

The sea on the map was decorated with drawings of spouting whales, dragon-like sea monsters, and cherubs blowing ships across the ocean. I followed the coastline north to New York and Boston, and south to Maryland and Virginia. I'd seen smaller versions of such maps at home in London, but they held more meaning for me now that I had the prospect of travelling to some of these places.

There was a safe in the room, and a tall bookcase, curtains at the windows, and a rug in front of the fire. Clearly this was George Bainbrigg's haven when he was at work.

"Here are the keys." He took a bunch of keys from his belt and checked them off for me: "The outer doors, back and front; the two offices; the storerooms." He put them into my hand. "Thou'll need them in the morning. From now on I'll expect thee to come down and open up first thing, and lock up in the evening if I'm not here. It'll be thy job to keep the wood stock topped up, light the fires, fetch water and beer, fill the inkwells, sweep the floors and keep the sales area looking spruce."

I nodded. There would be a weight of responsibility: the accounts, the keys, all the things I must remember and take care of. I looked forward to it – relished it, even.

In the adjoining office he set me to copying some entries from the ledgers. I saw that he wanted to test my accuracy, so I concentrated on the task.

After about an hour he sent me back to the house to fetch breakfast for us: beer and warm pies, fresh from the oven. Mary put them into a basket for me.

Isobel slipped in an extra pie. "Thou won't go hungry here, lad. Thou'rt as thin as a lath, any road; could do with putting on a bit of weight – eh, Mary?"

Mary looked up at me diffidently as she handed me the jug and basket. She was probably seventeen at least, but very short – stunted, as the poor often are. Her hands were red and calloused from hard work. When I took the jug she made a slight involuntary bobbing movement, a hint of a curtsey, although I was sure George Bainbrigg would not expect such deference, even for himself.

I left by the garden gate and walked along the short path that led to the back of the counting house. Zachary joined us for breakfast, and we sat on benches by the fire in the outer office, where there was a shelf with tankards and a bowl for washing dishes. The pies were good, but it was a short break; I saw that George Bainbrigg liked to get most of his work done in the morning. I returned to my copying, and later wrote out an invoice for a customer under my master's supervision.

I did not see Katherine again until dinner, which was the main meal of the day and eaten soon after noon. This time the table was set for five, and both the house servants were there. My master sat at the head of the table; Isobel was at the end and Mary nearest the door, from where Isobel despatched her from time to time to fetch another dish.

The meal began with silent waiting on God and continued in silence except for necessary speech, and

George Bainbrigg's thanks to Isobel and Mary for the food. Mary looked subdued, and I guessed she would have preferred to eat in the kitchen. I was opposite Katherine, acutely aware of her, of her gaze connecting with mine when I looked up, of the colour coming and going in her fair complexion, of her hands, white and smooth-skinned, not roughened like Mary's. The dog, Hob, once again stationed himself beside my chair, so close that he leaned against my leg. When I reached and put a piece of meat on my plate he gave a sigh with a whimpered enquiry in it. I caught Katherine's eye and we both shook with suppressed laughter.

I longed for a chance to talk to Katherine alone, but there seemed to be no way that this could be achieved with any propriety. I wondered how she occupied herself. Sewing, perhaps? Or studying? She was too old for school.

In the afternoon George Bainbrigg expressed himself pleased with the accuracy of my copying. He seemed relieved at this, remarking, "Some lads can't copy owt but they litter it with errors." I felt I had passed a test. Later in the week, he said, he would begin to explain to me the system of bookkeeping he used. "But for now, thou can take a break from the books and give Zach a hand upstairs. We'll hold the public vendue next week; thou'll see how that works." Then he looked at me sharply, as if a thought had struck him. "Dost' have any skill at lettering, by chance? Design, I mean. We'll need a poster or two, and some handbills, to get the word out."

"I could do that," I said. I felt pleased and interested. "I'd enjoy it."

"Good. I'll give thee the details. Do a draft, and show me. Keep it simple. We've no printer yet – as thou know – so each one must be drawn by hand."

I set to with enthusiasm, and spent the next hour designing a poster. I used bold lettering for the words "GOODS FROM ENGLAND", and made the letters stand out like solid objects; then added, "from the ship *Chepstow*, lately come from Bristol. To be sold at Public Vendue on seventh-day the 20th of ninth-month, called November, at 12 noon at the premises of George Bainbrigg and Thos. Appleyard, merchants."

I went up to the storeroom and sketched some of the objects for sale. The furniture was decorative, so I put a drawing of one of the chairs in one corner, and a bale of cloth in the opposite one. I placed a simple drawing of a ship at the top. For a frame to contain everything I simply drew two straight parallel lines.

George Bainbrigg came in while I was putting the finishing touches to my work.

"This is excellent!" he said. "I see thou like to draw. Do two or three of these, and we'll put them up

around Front Street. The handbills can be smaller" –
he sketched a size in the air.

"Octavo," I said.

"That's the one! No drawings on the handbills.
Date, time, place, 'goods from England'. That'll be
enough. Folk coming into town will take them back
to the outlying areas and the news will pass around."

The next morning he left me in the counting house
while he went to a meeting of the Society of Traders.
I worked steadily at copying the handbills. It was
mindless work, once the designing was done, but I
knew he needed them as soon as possible, since the
sale was fixed for next week.

I was working, head down, when I heard someone
come into the outer office.

I jumped up and went to the door, thinking it might
be a customer, but it was Katherine. My heartbeat
quickened. She seemed to be alone.

"I'm helping Izzie," she said, and I saw that she had
brought a jug of beer and a folded napkin containing
something that smelt fragrant.

"I'm sorry, I should have come to fetch that! I
forgot." I could not believe my good fortune.

"No matter. These are caraway-seed buns. Izzie
and I made them this morning. Try one."

I took a bun, and bit into it, aware of her watching
me, half smiling, waiting for a response.

"It's good," I said, trying not to spray crumbs. "Won't thou have one?"

"No. They are for thee – and Zachary."

"Thy father is at the Society…" I began.

"I know. He told me thou had designed a poster. He seemed very pleased with it."

I showed her a copy. "Thy father has taken one to the Society's hall today. This one will go outside, on the street door."

"Thou can draw well," she said.

I felt pleased. It was rarely that I was praised for drawing, and from Katherine praise was especially welcome.

"They are just sketches. But I like to draw. My mother disapproves." I put on a mock frown. "No drawing. No dancing. No singing."

She giggled.

"Is thy father strict?" I asked.

"He has no time for singing or dancing, but I think that would be the same whatever his beliefs. But Aunt Jane, who brought me up, *she* sang. She never became a Friend, although she was close to them. She was a draper's widow, and ran the business in Settle after her husband's death. She used to sing around the house" – she smiled – "stirring hymns, that sort of thing! And she liked stories. She'd tell me stories about the family: the day her grandfather bought a donkey at the fair; how my uncle Marmaduke courted the notary's daughter; the winter of the big snow that her grandmother remembered, when they couldn't get out for weeks. And of course stories about me ... all sorts of things. I loved Aunt Jane."

"But thou left her?"

"She died. She got ill, and for a year I looked after her and ran the shop and dealt with customers —"

"At – what? – eleven years old?"

"Yes. I had help from neighbours, of course, and from another aunt. Then, when Aunt Jane died and all the family started talking about who would take me in, I thought, None of them shall – I'm going to America to be with my father."

"So thou knew him? He wrote to thee?"

"He visited when I was five, and again four years later. But he wrote letters to me all the time, and sent me little gifts, and I wrote back (Aunt Jane had sent me to school and I learnt to write). So we knew each other, and I loved him, even though he'd only been back twice. Of course he set off for England when the news reached him that Aunt Jane was dying, and when I heard he was on his way I decided I'd go back with him." She smiled. "I wasn't going to take no for an answer. I had a bag packed and ready to take with me."

"And was it what he wanted, too?"

"He came round to the idea. He was worried about

his home life not being settled. Said he needed a wife, to be a mother to me; and a bigger house, and servants. I said I didn't need all those things! Any road, he hired Izzie in Langcliffe, and Mary from the orphanage at Skipton, and we four sailed out together, and stayed with Friends in Maryland until he found a house."

"And thou hast not regretted it?"

"No! I love being with him at last. I was sorry to leave the people I knew in Maryland and come *here*. I don't love Philadelphia yet – especially the muddy roads – ugh!" We both laughed. "But thee?" she said. "Don't thou miss London? *I* would."

I replied, teasing, "How can thou *know* thou would?"

"Oh! Because London is such a great city, and so famous, so much to see – and the king lives there! What was it like, where thou lived? Did thou work in thy father's shop?"

"I worked in the shambles, as a butcher's boy," I said.

She pulled a face of disgust, and I laughed and said, "Not for long. I took the job to annoy my father—"

"Oh! Why?"

She was wide-eyed now. I was enjoying her attention, but at that moment we heard Zachary moving about in the storeroom overhead, and that reminded me that I was keeping him from his breakfast and wasting my master's time.

"I'll tell thee later," I promised.

And Katherine said, "Thou must! But for now I'll leave thee to thy work."

In a moment she was gone.

I called Zachary, and poured beer into two tankards. She's a chatterer, I thought – worse than Betty. Well, I'd encouraged her. I'd wanted to keep her there. She had such a sparkle about her, such liveliness. And she seemed to like me. She had come down here alone – and she had known her father was away; she said so. I wondered if Isobel had known that, when she let her bring the food and drink; I guessed not.

I felt pleased with life and full of hopeful anticipation. In this mood I went home on seventh-day, which was my half-day off.

It felt strange to be back in the log cabin – like being in a dolls' house, I joked to Sarah. I had forgotten already how cramped it was. There was news. My mother had found that a school had been started in a Friend's house, and Sarah had been enrolled in it; Betty, however, would help with the house and shop. Betty bombarded me with questions about the Bainbriggs, my room, what my master was like, what Katherine was like, whether the servants were friendly. Sarah asked whether there was a dog, or a cat; she was hankering after a pet herself, but our mother had said no – "Not till we have a proper house."

"Both," I said, in answer to Sarah. I told her about Hob and made her laugh.

Betty was jealous of my room. And she questioned me closely about Katherine – almost, I felt, as if she could read my thoughts. "I wish *I* could meet her again," she said. "I don't know any girls here, except Esther Kite. No one to *talk* to."

I could see that my parents were also anxious to hear about my first week – the first week of their investment, I thought wryly – but they did not press me for news; that is not their way. Only, when I had been back a while, and we had eaten, my mother, passing by, touched my cheek and said, "Well, thou look happy, son."

I smiled. "Yes. My master is good to me. They all are." I told them who lived there; that Isobel was keeping me well fed; that I would be learning a complex form of accounting. I told them about the poster for the auction. My mother was pleased. "I hoped thou'd find a proper use for thy drawing," she said.

"And George Bainbrigg is pleased with thee?" my father asked.

"Yes. And I work hard, Dad. Thou need not fear. It'll be different to Thomas Green's. The work is interesting, and I like George Bainbrigg well."

"Good." And then his eyes brightened like a boy's, and he said, "We had some excitement of our own this week. The Proprietor – William Penn – came to the shop!"

"Thou *met* him?"

"I did! And introduced him to thy mother and sisters. I had never met him before, though I was more than once at a meeting in London when he spoke; and of course we used to sell his books and pamphlets. Ours is the first bookshop in the colony, so he was interested to see it."

His words were restrained, but I knew it must have been a great occasion for him, William Penn having been such a hero of his for as long as I could remember.

"He is a very learned man," my father said. "His mind is extraordinarily agile and wide-ranging. He is full of ideas – has great plans for the colony."

"And did he buy any books?" I asked, grinning.

"He did! And ordered some. And was most encouraging about the prospects for a printer's. And he told me he had met the leader of the German Friends, Francis Daniel Pastorius – another scholarly man – and would recommend me to him. Those people have set up their own township, Germantown – nearly all of them live there, some way north of Philadelphia."

I listened, but was not much interested in scholarly Germans.

He saw this, and said, "We heard news of the public vendue. A week today, isn't it?"

"Yes. You must come early, if you want to see the goods."

But he knew that. He'd been to auctions in his youth, he said, with his father. My grandfather Henry Heywood had been a wool merchant in Shropshire.

I said, "Betty and I thought we'd walk up to the Kites' – find out if word of the auction has got around."

I felt sure it had, but I needed a walk, and wanted to tell Ben my news, and I knew Betty wanted to escape before our mother found some task for her. "She's always so busy on seventh-days," she said, "rushing about working so that she can rest on first-day. If you can call it resting: sitting in Meeting all morning, and then hours more in the afternoon…"

As we set off, she asked, "Will Katherine come to Meeting tomorrow?"

"I suppose so."

"Dost thou like her?"

"Yes … yes, I do." I hoped she wouldn't tease me. I was so caught up in my fascination with Katherine that I didn't think I could tolerate it.

But Betty wasn't thinking about me. "I shall go and talk to her again after Meeting," she said. "Mam says if I want to make friends I must speak to other girls. And Katherine will be with thee, so that will make it easier."

Betty was right. From now on, as George Bainbrigg's apprentice, I was obliged to go to Meeting with him and his family and servants. It felt strange not to be sitting with my family, but to see them across the room: my father, tall, lean and scholarly-looking, with an open Bible in his hands; my mother, held in that calmness that hides her impulsive nature; Sarah lolling against her, chewing a strand of hair and gazing up at the roof beams. And Betty, dark-haired and slim, and already taller than our mother, looking around and watching people. She caught my glance at her and gave a discreet wave.

Isobel, next to me, who I'd thought was immersed in her Bible, murmured, "Thy sister?"

"Yes. That's Betty."

I saw Isobel studying the rest of my family and wondered if Katherine was doing the same. We could not look at each other, for her father sat between us – and, besides, the meeting was beginning to draw together.

Much later, when Meeting was over and people had begun to move about, and my master was engaged with another merchant, I saw Betty standing alone and trying to catch my eye. Betty talks a lot and seems confident, but deep down she is shy. I saw that she would not approach Katherine herself, so I called her over and brought them together.

"Betty!" Katherine exclaimed. "I'm glad to see thee again!"

Betty brightened at this; and the three of us, released from the long silence of Meeting, began to talk animatedly to one another. Soon we were chatting and laughing so much that older Friends near by turned round and frowned at us in disapproval.

We lowered our voices a little, but continued to talk about London and Maryland, our families, our new life in Philadelphia. When Katherine heard that Betty was to be employed in our father's print shop, she was envious.

"I wish I could work! Paid work, I mean, not household things. I like to be busy. I can do accounts. And I'm studying languages – French and German – but it's hard on my own. I help in the kitchen—"

"She makes excellent caraway buns," I told Betty.

We all laughed. We would laugh at anything now; the long meeting had left us full of high spirits, and it felt good to be in a youthful group together. The diffidence I usually felt when I was alone with Katherine disappeared.

Katherine asked Betty about the bookshop, and

Betty began describing it: "the smallest bookshop in the world", she called it, squeezed into the end of our log cabin, with books piled in heaps – and all the family living in such a small space. She made it seem much funnier than it really was. "We can just about edge past one another now Jos has gone and isn't sitting there with his big feet sticking out."

Katherine, giggling, said, "I must come and see it. No, don't laugh – I mean it! I like books, and we don't have many in our house."

"Oh, yes, do! We're on Sassafras Street, near the corner of Third. Jos can show thee the way…"

Ten

"*Y*ou young ones were merry after Meeting," my master said, when we came down for dinner.

At once I was anxious. "The fault was mine—" I began, but Katherine said, "Oh, Dad! It was not unseemly, surely? I did enjoy meeting Josiah's sister."

Her father looked at the two of us in puzzled amusement. "I said you were merry – nothing more. Why so much guilt? I was glad to see it. Thou *need* to be among young people, Kate. Oh, I'm sure a few older Friends thought you were too noisy, but I like to hear youngsters laughing together."

I felt relief. He looked from one to the other of us, and I think perhaps it was at that moment that he began to realize something between us that we had not yet acknowledged ourselves. I hastened to add, "My sister misses her London friends. I sought to bring her and Katherine together. She is a little younger, but more grown-up than many girls of her age – though thou might not have thought so this morning…"

"She wants me to visit their bookshop," Katherine said. "She reads a great deal and can advise me what to try."

He smiled. "I think it a grand idea, Kate. The walk will do thee good and you can talk about books or whatever else girls talk about."

I felt pleased with this outcome, and could see that Katherine did, too. Perhaps, I thought, I might offer to take her there on my half-day off.

But I knew none of us would be free for some time. The public vendue was to be held next seventh-day, and preparations would keep us busy all week.

"I'll give thee time off in lieu the week after," my master promised when we began work the next day.

Tom Appleyard, whose counting house was next door, was also involved in the auction. We made more leaflets, and Tom's apprentice, David, and I took them around the town, and talked to shopkeepers and artisans. The town crier went about, and word was sent to Germantown and the older settlements along the rivers.

I worked hard. The day before the sale, all the

goods had to be brought down and laid out for display in the sales area. I helped Zachary with this work, the two of us carrying boxes and furniture down the stairs, and George Bainbrigg directing where each item was to go. Under his orders we partially unrolled a few lengths of cloth and pegged them so that they draped and showed to advantage. The chairs, stools and cabinets were set out as if in a house, the china in an open box. I made a numbered ticket for each lot and entered the numbers and details in a book.

Katherine and Isobel, under the guise of bringing us refreshments, came to look at what was on offer. Even Mary came to see. The women were particularly interested in the woollen cloth, having a mind to make winter gowns. Katherine was drawn to the pretty painted china, but her father dismissed it as "vanity" and doubted whether any Friends would buy it. He had been disappointed in that part of the consignment; it was not what he'd expected. "But these things happen when folk act on your behalf," he said.

Next morning I rose before dawn and went to the counting house to open up and make ready. I swept the floors and checked that everything was clean and orderly. Zachary and my master arrived soon after. The event was to take place outside, run by an auctioneer hired by the two merchants. I was to be employed with Zachary in bringing our lots forward, while my master would keep the tally.

It seemed that the notices I'd made, and the voice of the town crier, had done their work, for in no time the first customers began to arrive. The auction would not begin until noon, but many people wanted to look around first and decide what to bid for. My family and the Kites were among them, but we scarcely spoke because I was kept busy talking to customers, showing them the goods and keeping an eye open for thieves. Soon people from further afield began to arrive: farmers in dusty clothes who must have driven or walked in from the outlying areas; men who looked like trappers or hunters; a group of Pietists from Germantown in their black hats and sober clothes, similar to those of Friends.

A wooden platform had been placed outside, between the two counting houses. At twelve o'clock the auctioneer's boy climbed onto it and rang a bell to open the proceedings. Immediately a tide of people surged towards us. I could feel their eagerness for the sale to begin.

Now I had to be quick on my feet and responsive to my master's orders. Zachary and I brought up some of the furniture and placed it on the platform, and the auctioneer began the bidding. He was a sharp-eyed, energetic man with a voice like gunfire, and he never missed a hand, a call or even, it seemed, the lift of an eyebrow. The crowd soon became excited, jostling and pushing, hands shooting up, hats waving, voices striving to outbid one another. I trudged to and fro all afternoon, along with Zachary and David, bringing up lots to the stand. The tools and hardware items were especially wanted, as was the woollen cloth, and people were set one against another to obtain them. Towards the end of the bidding a frenzy seemed to grip those involved, and I felt something frightening in the power of the crowd – the clamour of voices and the fierce looks – and it seemed to me almost as if the auctioneer were possessed by some malign spirit, whipping up souls to covetousness and envy. I knew this was a normal way of selling, and yet I did not like it.

At last all – or nearly all – was sold. Even the furniture, the paper and the box of Bibles had gone; and one of the wealthy merchants had bought the painted china dishes. My master and the auctioneer went off to the office to settle accounts, while Zachary and I helped some of the buyers to load up their carts, then returned to the counting house to sweep the floors. My whole body ached. I stretched and groaned, and Zachary laughed and said, "You'll get used to it, lad." He was an old man of perhaps fifty, yet he seemed less tired than I.

When I walked back to the house with George Bainbrigg, he said, "Thou did well, Josiah. We'll go through the transactions on second-day and I'll show thee how everything is entered twice. I'm hungry now! And thou?"

"Starving," I said, with feeling. We'd had nothing but a pie and a mug of beer at dinnertime.

"Isobel will have an early supper ready," he said.

He gave me the afternoon off on third-day. Katherine was there when he told me, and I saw her take a small breath, and then look from one to the other of us.

I seized my opportunity. "I'm going home, and could escort Katherine," I said, "if she wishes to visit my sister and see the bookshop."

"I do," said Katherine.

"If you both wish it, then I agree."

He approves of me, I thought; and he trusts me with his daughter. It made me feel more determined than ever to do well in this new situation.

On third-day afternoon I took the china jug from my washstand down to the kitchen and asked Mary for more water for washing. I was glad Isobel was not around; she would have commented on such unusual cleanliness. Back in my room, I not only washed, but dressed more carefully than usual. I put on fresh linen, cleaned my shoes and brushed my coat. There was a small mirror in the room, intended for shaving. I looked at my face, and combed my hair, which hung to my shoulders, and put on my hat, carefully adjusting the angle. I liked this hat, the extra height it gave me, and its dark colour that matched my eyes and hair.

When Katherine appeared she was wearing a sage-green gown, a cloak, and a hood of fine wool, simple in style but becoming. Beneath its soft folds her face was fair and smiling.

We stepped outside into a cold north wind, the first breath of winter.

"I thank thee for thy company, Josiah," she said.

"It's a pleasure."

We were both shy, and now that we had this little space of time together, we did not know what to say and took refuge in formalities. I tried to slow my pace to spin out the walk, but it was too cold to dawdle.

As we turned the corner into Third Street, the wind hit us with full force. Katherine squealed as her hood flew back. Strands of loose hair whipped across her face and she struggled, laughing, to tuck them away under her cap, then pulled up the hood and rearranged it.

She turned to me. "Is my hair tidy? I cannot meet thy mother looking wild."

"Thou don't look wild. Thou look…"

She pulled the hood close. "Plain?"

"Plain. The *hood* is plain. My mother will approve."

We both laughed.

"My father is pleased with thee," she said, holding on to the hood as we walked on.

"I'm glad. I like him well. He is a good master. And the work interests me."

"So thou'll stay on when thy trial time is over?"

"I think so, yes … if he'll have me."

"Oh, he will! But thou sound unsure?"

"No. Only… It was not what I *thought* I wanted…" I tried to explain to her my longing to be independent, to find work on my own, without the help of my father. "But my parents persuaded me. And now" – I glanced at her upturned face – "I find that I want to stay."

"That's good." She looked down, as if embarrassed at revealing her thoughts, then said, "Thou never told me why thou sought work in the shambles in London to annoy thy father."

"And I won't tell thee now!"

"Why not?"

"Because we have arrived. Our plot is there – see the log cabin?"

I led her into the yard, where my mother and Sarah were clearing stones from what would be the garden. Near by, I saw several chickens pecking among the weeds.

"Those birds are new," I said.

"Jos!" My mother sprang to her feet. Her face was pink from the wind. "We didn't expect thee today! And Katherine, too! Thou should have told us." She brushed at her dirty apron. "I'd have made puddings…"

"It doesn't matter," I said. I looked around. "All these chickens…"

Sarah caught one of the hens and brought it to us. "This one is called Mercy." She offered the bird to Katherine, who took and held it.

"She is tame, this hen," Katherine said, "not frightened of me at all. I like hens. What are the others called?"

Sarah scurried around after them. "This is Speckle; that's Faith; that's Dot…"

"We bought them from a neighbour of Judith's," my mother said. "Six hens and a cockerel. Katherine, welcome to our home. Will thou take small beer? I'll warm some for us… Sarah, take the hen from Katherine and let her come in."

She ushered us into the house, glancing between Katherine and me. I knew she was wondering about the two of us here together, what it signified.

Betty appeared from behind the bookshop screen. "Jos! You've brought Katherine!" She stood there, shy and pleased.

"I wanted to see thee again," said Katherine,

"and Josiah had the afternoon off."

My mother took our coats and hats and hung them up, and set a jug of beer to warm near the fire.

"Will thou come into the bookshop, Katherine?" Betty asked. "I'm minding it. We haven't had many customers but I need to be there. Dad's gone to look at house plans."

They disappeared together.

"Thou look very fine today, Jos," my mother said, as I took off my hat. "Is it Katherine who has wrought this change in thee?"

I would not rise to this, and said, "I thought thou'd *like* it."

At once she was contrite. "Oh, I do! I'm sorry. I should not tease thee."

We sat down, and she began questioning me about my work, how the household was run, whether George Bainbrigg read to us all from the Bible each evening, as my father always did. Was I attending to the inward light? Keeping my journal? Was Isobel feeding me well? I reassured her on all these points.

"We have chosen a house plan," she said. "It's a house with workshop and saleroom – and we hope at least to get the post holes dug before the ground freezes solid. It'll be a wooden house – clapboard…" She looked pleased and yet anxious. I knew she was remembering the Great Fire.

"Clapboard is good," I said. "George Bainbrigg's house is clapboard. It's strong, well-built, comfortable."

She nodded. "Well, it will be cheaper. God has given us wood in abundance, so we will use it and trust in him."

"The houses won't be as close-packed as in old London."

"No. It will be safer. We shall flourish here."

She poured beer for me, listened to the voices of the girls behind the screen, and said, "They'll come for theirs when they want it. Let's leave them be." She touched my hand. "I see thou hast a liking for Katherine."

"We are friendly – as we should be."

"She seems a good girl, without pretence or worldly ways."

"She is." And yet I was glad Katherine was not one of those who think continually of God. In her the spirit seemed to find expression in a cheerful busyness – she was always looking for something useful to do. "Thou would approve of her housekeeping skills," I said. "She's most capable…"

"And merry," said my mother, as a burst of laughter came from behind the screen.

"That, too." I grinned.

"Be sure thou treat her with proper respect—"

"Mam!"

"I know. I know thou will. I need not tell thee. But, living in the same house…"

"Mam, we are not… We have scarcely exchanged more than a few words."

She smiled. "Oh, words don't matter. It is all there in thy looks."

She was right, of course. I tried to pretend otherwise, but Katherine came to absorb much of my thought. We walked back that afternoon, talking easily together about our families, our friends, about books.

"Betty is reading Herodotus," she said, in some surprise.

"Oh, she'll read anything. She likes history especially."

"Thy father has a great many books there – some I would not have expected: poetry and drama, and music."

"He learned such things at school," I said. "He was not brought up a Friend. His father was an Anglican – and a merchant, like thine. Our bookshop in London was large; you could wander in it and make discoveries. I liked the maps, and the books about voyages. There was a book of travels we used to look at, Betty and I, that had pictures of strange beasts, and men whose heads were below their shoulders…"

"Ugh!" She laughed. "At home in Yorkshire we had only the Bible and some almanacs and recipe books. But in Maryland I had lessons with our friends' daughters and we read more. I liked *The Pilgrim's Progress* best."

"I have that book at home! *'As I walked through the wilderness of this world…'*"

She smiled in recognition.

The wind was behind us now, and we hurried before it, driven by the cold blast.

Once inside, the door shut, we recovered our breath. Mary appeared and took our coats, and asked in her timid way if we wished for anything to eat.

"No, Mary, we'll wait for supper," said Katherine. "Is my father back?"

"Not yet…" – Mary knew not to call Katherine "Miss", but she made that little bobbing movement I'd seen before, as if subservience had been bred into her. "The fire's lit in the parlour – and the old dog's in there."

"Let's go and get warm," Katherine said to me.

There was only one candle burning in the parlour, and as we entered our shadows leapt about the walls. I should have liked to stay and talk in the half-dark, but Katherine – conscious, no doubt, of propriety – took a spill and lit a few more candles.

Hob occupied most of the hearthrug. He stirred

and gave a brief wag of his tail. I patted him, then sat down on the bench by the fire, thinking Katherine would sit in her father's chair opposite. But instead she dropped to her knees beside the dog and began stroking and playing with him. A quiet settled between us. I heard only the crackle of flames and the contented sighs of the dog. Hob rolled in restrained ecstasy and allowed Katherine to tickle his belly. The firelight glowed and flickered on her face and her moving hands; she looked up at me and smiled. I was shaken by a desire to kneel beside her, to take her in my arms and kiss her.

"Katherine…" I said – and was on the brink of following my impulse when Isobel came in with a jug of warm beer and three tankards.

"Thou'll scorch thyself, Kate," she said, setting the tray down on the sideboard. "I'll leave this here and you can help yourselves. The master should be home any minute."

The moment was gone. Katherine tried to stand up, but the dog was lying on her skirt. "Let me go, old boy," she said, giving him a shove. "I want to pour Jos some beer."

It was the first time she had called me Jos.

"I can do it," I said, standing up.

"No! I shall."

She pulled herself free of the dog, and was up and

standing at the sideboard when her father came into the room.

He greeted us. Katherine handed out tankards of beer, and we all talked together of small things until Isobel and Mary brought in the supper.

My moment of quiet, alone with Katherine, had been brief, and yet I knew something had happened between us. We were no longer merely friends.

Eleven

During the remaining two weeks before my bond with George Bainbrigg was to be decided, I was in a heightened state of feeling, constantly aware of the presence of Katherine and seeking out ways to be alone with her, if only for a few moments. I was sure she felt the same. Whenever we encountered each other we talked and listened to one another's deepest concerns. And all the time we were talking I was aware of her physical presence: her eyes, her body, her voice. She was like a magnet, irresistibly attractive to me.

Along with my pursuit of Katherine, I worked hard at mastering the system of double accounting and familiarized myself with the names and locations of the merchants my master dealt with in New Jersey, Maryland, Boston, New York and the Caribbean. I studied the account books and bills of lading, and began to read about the principles of navigation.

By the end of the month the weather had turned colder still. It was not the chill damp and fog of an English November, but a fierce, clear cold that swept down from the mountains in the north. In the mornings the windows of my bedchamber were transformed with sharp-etched star patterns of frost. Deep frosts whitened the trees and shrubs, and the churned-up mud of the roads turned silvery and crisp to walk upon. There were a few light falls of snow.

Katherine and Betty had met a few times more, usually at my master's house, where they could sit in the parlour and talk and sew. But one day Katherine said she would go that afternoon to the bookshop and call on Betty, and I offered to go there after work and escort her back to Walnut Street.

It was already dark when we left my family's home. We walked back along Third Street, where the lamps above people's doorways cast pools of light and the snow sparkled underfoot, and as we talked we drew closer and our gloved hands brushed briefly together. I caught Katherine's hand and held it. She did not resist, though she fell silent. We walked on slowly, our hands clasped, and I felt a bloom of happiness and expectancy unfolding within me.

When we reached the turn into Walnut Street

I saw the house only a short way off, the lantern shining above its door. From now on there might be eyes watching us.

"Kate," I said – and I stepped back into the shadows and turned her towards me. And it happened easily, as if by instinct; her face lifted to mine, our noses bumped, and then my lips were on hers, and I felt her respond and soften against me. We dropped hands and our arms went round each other. I kissed her again, and pulled her closer. I didn't want this to stop.

But we heard footsteps coming nearer, and voices. We drew apart and moved on, linking hands again, and only let go as we approached the house.

Once inside, I felt that everyone – Mary, Isobel, my master, even the dog – must be able to see the glow that came from us. I wished them all a quick "good evening", and went up to my room, my heart soaring.

The next day I was kept busy. The *Frances* returned from New England, and when she dropped anchor in the river my master took me out there in a boat and showed me around. There was plenty of storage space in the schooner's hold, which at that time was laden with a cargo of fish and about to be unloaded. I saw the captain's cabin, and the one my master would use if he travelled with the ship. These were plain, but comfortably furnished with bunks, tables, chairs and writing materials. The sailors – and no doubt any apprentice who accompanied the merchant – would make do with whatever space they could find.

On board I met the captain, Richard Grey. He was a Bristol man, someone George Bainbrigg put much trust in; and we had his company later at dinner, and heard news of Boston and Rhode Island merchants – many of them fellow Friends or Yorkshiremen – of my master's acquaintance. I listened with attention to all the talk of his travels and dealings.

The *Frances* would not now undertake another voyage until the spring, for at the beginning of December the snow began in earnest and the weather grew much colder.

We heard that William Penn was shortly to leave Philadelphia and set off with a group of Friends for an area of wilderness in the north of the province to negotiate the acquisition of more land from the Delaware Indians. He was gradually buying up tracts of land in this way – for although the king of England had granted him ownership of Pennsylvania, the Indians who lived there knew nothing of this; and William Penn would take no land unless it had been fairly purchased from the Indians and agreements drawn up and signed by all parties.

I looked at the map in my master's office and saw that the area called Pennsylvania was immense, most of it unmarked by any settlements.

"The settlers occupy only a small part of this great wilderness," George Bainbrigg said. "There is room for all."

We occasionally saw Indians in Philadelphia. They would arrive with furs for sale – beaver, fox, otter. These Delaware Indians were strong, hardy men, their skins brown and greased with bear's fat against the cold. They wore trousers of animal skins, and mantles of duffel, and their hair fell straight to their shoulders, much like ours. Many strings of beads hung about them, and feathers, and little skin bags, and other heathen objects like bones and animal skulls. They wanted metal goods, kettles, tools, blankets and duffel cloth, and when they were bargaining they kept their faces very still and expressionless and showed no emotion, no clue to what they were thinking.

I watched how my master dealt with them.

"Never smile," he warned me. "They don't like to be smiled at."

He bought furs and sent them to the tanners to be cured. When they came back they were soft and pliable, and we hung some of them for display in the sales area, where Kate came to admire and stroke them.

The time had come for a decision about my future. Was I willing to be bound as an apprentice to George Bainbrigg for five years? He had made it plain that he wanted to keep me.

"I'm pleased with thee, Josiah," he said. "And pleased with myself, too, for judging well. I thought, that day when thou knocked on my door, that thou seemed a suitable lad. Thou must talk to thy parents, but I'll be glad to sign the bond."

There seemed no reason to refuse. I'd wanted freedom – but to do what? To pick up rubbish? To swill floors? Every job worth doing needed a time of learning. I liked my work here; and my parents would be pleased.

And there was Kate.

"I shall tell them I am happy, and want to stay," I said.

"Good! Then I'll arrange for the agreement to be drawn up."

The contract was signed in the second week of December. I read it through, and agreed to the conditions; then my father and George Bainbrigg signed it. And so my life for the next five years was settled for me. I'd be nearly twenty-two at the end of my apprenticeship: old enough to set up in business on my own, to marry, to rent or build a house. Such things seemed far off.

Later that day I walked over to the forge to see Ben Kite and tell him my news.

"Thou hast done well!" he said. He was beating

a rod of iron into a hook shape, the hammer blows ringing in the cold air. "A lot of conditions, aren't there, for apprentices?" He paused. The hook was finished. He set it aside to cool, and grinned at me. "So – what is forbidden thee? I know there's fornication."

I laughed, and began ticking them off on my fingers: "I must not fornicate. I must not marry. I must not frequent playhouses or taverns, or play at cards, dice or any other form of gambling. I must faithfully serve my master, and obey his lawful commands. I must not buy or sell without his licence. I must do no damage to my master and his business, nor steal his goods, nor lend them unlawfully to anyone…"

"Well, that lot should keep thee out of trouble!" Ben said. "Which dost thou think will be hardest to keep?"

"Fornication," I said, grinning – for it seemed the thing to say.

But I was resolved to keep all these commandments. There were no playhouses for me to frequent in Philadelphia; and taverns and gambling seemed to me part of my old London life. I thought about Kate, and the feelings I had for her, and believed I could – indeed, must – resist temptation, or at least postpone it until I was of age. As for the promise to obey my master's lawful commands and to protect his goods and interests: not to do those things seemed so alien to my nature that I never gave it a thought.

Tokpa

We are in the great hut, in a room at the back. The whiskery man, the one who bought me when I stood on the block, brings clothes: trousers and shirts like those the Bassa man wears, and skirts and blouses for the women. We put them on. The trousers feel strange on my legs; I feel as if I am caught in a net.

When we are dressed they take us into a kitchen, where a black woman is cooking over a fire. She offers us food and water. I am so thirsty I gulp the water down. There is stuff she calls corn in a dish with beans and spices. I eat some and begin to feel stronger.

The chief comes into the room. I know at once he is chief because the whiskery man and the cook both show respect to him. He talks to the man and they gather us together – those of us who came in the cart. They count us, look us over and begin to send us out into the yard.

But then the chief puts a hand on my shoulder, holds me back.

At once I am afraid. What have I done? Why can't I go with the others? He will whip me, I think.

But no one seems angry. The whiskery man goes out with the captives from the ship. The chief begins to talk to the cook, and then to me. He seems to be speaking English, but there are too many words; I can't follow them.

But I understand when he points at me and says, "Antony. Thy name is Antony." I want to cry out, "No. My name is Tokpa!" But the words are afraid to leave my mouth.

He goes away, and I stay with the woman. She is a Vai woman, but she speaks to me in English, like the chief. She speaks slowly, so that I understand, and her voice is kind.

"Don't be afraid," she says. "Master is a good man. Thou'rt lucky."

I ask, "Why others go, I stay?"

"He wants thee for a house slave, not to work in the fields."

"What I do?"

"Look after Master's clothes. Clean boots and shoes. Wait at table. Chop wood. Light fires. Many things. But not cutting cane. Not under the overseer with his whip."

She takes away my empty cup and plate.

"Thou'rt lucky," she says again.

Twelve

That winter was one of the coldest that people in Delaware and West Jersey remembered. By the end of tenth-month – the month the world calls December – the Delaware and Schuylkill rivers were frozen over and the snow was several feet deep. The builders stopped work on my parents' house, leaving posts set in holes ready for when the thaw came. The Swedes who had been building log cabins went home. The cold was intense, but bright and clear, and I enjoyed being out in it and active about my master's business.

I seized every moment when I was not at work to be with Kate. My master must have been aware of our attachment, but he said nothing about it, only to remind me generally that my behaviour must be proper at all times and that I must never be idle but always have his interests in mind. I think he was pleased that

Kate was happy and had made a friend of my sister.

Although Kate and I lived in the same house we were rarely alone together. In the evenings we sat with her father, and if he was away from home Isobel made it her business to keep an eye on Kate and not to leave us unchaperoned for long. But there were moments: chance meetings in the kitchen, in the storeroom, on the stairs, or in the counting house. There were times of day when such encounters were more likely and we soon got to know how to achieve them. Then we would move swiftly into each other's arms to kiss and whisper endearments.

Betty began visiting more frequently, driven by the cramped conditions in the cabin now that people were mostly staying indoors. "And it's warmer here!" she'd say, holding out her hands to the parlour fire. She and Kate would sit in the parlour with their books or sewing and talk.

Later, when I had finished work, I would walk Betty home along the snowy roads, taking Hob with us for exercise. One dark afternoon, on my return, I came in through the back door into the lobby, stamped off the snow from my boots, and began drying the dog with a cloth.

Kate met me there. It was one of our trysting-places. We knelt together, rubbing the dog and smoothing his coat.

"Betty seemed a little low in spirits today," I said. "I don't know why, unless it's being cooped up in the cabin so much."

"No," said Kate. "It's because of Lars."

"Lars? The one who built our cabin?"

"Yes. The builders can't work in this weather, so they have gone home – and Betty is pining."

"She never told me."

"She never told *me* until I asked her." She frowned. "I hope she will forget him over the winter. He is too old, and too handsome, and sure to have a girl already. He is not suitable for her."

I laughed. "How shrewish thou art, Kate! Am I unsuitable for *thee*?"

"Thou'rt entirely suitable and know it."

I leaned across Hob and kissed her. The dog became excited and licked us both enthusiastically. "And not too handsome?" I persisted. "Get off, dog! I want Kate, not thee!"

"Not at all!"

"That's the wrong answer," I said, and we tussled, laughing, until Hob began to bark at us, and we broke apart before Isobel came.

"Thou hast grown, Jos," my master said. "We must see to thy wardrobe."

He paid for a set of new clothes to be made for

me, in dark grey wool, and two new linen shirts and new shoes.

Kate approved. "The dark colour suits thee," she said. She herself had a new gown of grey-blue wool.

My appearance impressed my father when I went home.

"Be sure thou work hard and justify George Bainbrigg's confidence in thee," he said. "And Jos – take care of thy behaviour with his daughter."

I resented this last remark, and glowered at him. "I know how to behave," I said.

On the sixth day of February I reached my seventeenth birthday, and on the second of April, Kate turned sixteen. During the intervening weeks the ice melted on the rivers and creeks and we heard again the sound of water running. Spring came quickly. The river began to fill with ships, and Betty was made happy by the return of Lars Andersson. The builders began work again on our house and shop. My parents had a letter from Nat and Rachel Lacon telling them that the winter in London had been hard and the Thames had frozen over. They also sent news of Florian Marshall, a London typesetter, who had said he would be emigrating to Pennsylvania in the summer.

"This is excellent news," my father said. "We

should soon be able to open the print shop."

Meanwhile, George Bainbrigg made plans for a voyage to Barbados.

Jokpa

The chief looks like the demons on the ship, with a sharp nose and hanging hair. He wears a great black hat like the ship's captain and many layers of clothing that smell stale. There is a spring in the garden but no one bathes in it. All the beak-nosed demons smell of unwashed clothes. The chief is thin and sad-eyed. His wife is thin too, and ugly, and has a voice that always brings trouble. This is a big house but the chief has only one wife.

I am afraid in this house. There are bad spirits here; I feel them all around. But the chief is kind. He does not beat me. He shows me what to do in the house and yard, and he tells me I am in a good place, where no one will hurt me.

The house has many rooms. In one room the chief keeps box things called books. He opens one and shows me. It is full of trapped wings or leaves which are covered with little black marks. He says that when I understand his language better he will teach me to read, and then the black marks will turn into words and the words will speak to me and tell me things I need to know.

I want to ask the books: Why have I been brought here, to this demon-land? Who has done this to me? By what right? Who is my enemy and how can I fight him? I want to shout at the books: Let me go home!

But I am here and my home is across the great water. The other house slaves help me to settle. Lucie, the Vai woman, takes charge of me. I learn English. I learn to call the chief "Master". I clean shoes and cut wood and draw water and serve food high up, on a wooden platform called a table. I work. I learn how to live in this house.

And there is one here, a girl – a girl with soft round arms, whose hips sway as she walks; she is Kpelle, like me. When she speaks to me I hear the sounds of home. We talk together in our own language. We talk of our families, the songs, the forest, the spirits of our ancestors. We talk of going home.

This girl is called Patience, but she tells me her true name is Miata.

Thirteen

We sailed to Barbados in April. By that time I had learned enough about how George Bainbrigg's business was run to be able to deal with customers and do accounts without supervision. But although I had become useful to him, he would not risk leaving me in sole charge for the month or more he would be away. To my relief he decided to take me with him.

"I'll ask Tom Appleyard to keep an eye on things for me," he said, "and it'll be good for thee to see Barbados. It's a whole different world for Friends, out there in the Caribbean."

I was pleased. I wanted to travel, and I also wanted to be wherever Kate was – and she would be with her father, for this was partly a social visit.

We loaded the *Frances* with a cargo of meat, grain, wood and hardware. My master was able to estimate almost exactly how much of each commodity the hold would take. He called this "gauging".

"Thou'll learn how to do it," he said. "It comes with practice."

We would return with sugar and rum.

"Sugar is the currency there," George Bainbrigg said. "Everything is valued in pounds of sugar: goods bought, fines levied – all in sugar."

As I'd guessed, I did not have a cabin. Instead, I found a space on the lower deck between some coils of rope, and laid my bedding there. Kate had a tiny cabin next to her father's.

We made slow progress as we battled the prevailing winds down the coasts of Virginia and Florida, following the reverse route that the *Promise* had taken when I came to America. The early spring weather had been cold when we left Philadelphia, but now, as we entered the Caribbean Sea, we began to feel a change in the temperature. The sailors told me the names of the islands we passed: Porto Rico, St Kitts, Martinique, St Lucia… We saw, in the distance, pale sandy beaches, palm trees, green wooded heights. These islands, I thought, looked like Eden – an Eden of the senses, if not the soul.

Barbados is to the east of the outermost crescent of islands. In the old days, my master told me, ships found it difficult to land on Barbados because the prevailing winds were against them and there were few natural harbours.

But that must have been long ago. As we approached the island from the west – the three of us leaning on the rail, looking out – I saw towns, houses, churches, all the signs of a settled place. I noticed also many forts standing all along the shore. One guarded the entrance to the port of St Michael's Town (which Friends simply call Michael's Town, since we do not use the word "saint"). This port was where we were headed, and further inland I could see another huge fort on a hill.

"That's the garrison," my master said.

"They must greatly fear attack, to be so well fortified."

"Yes. First Oliver Cromwell, then the war with France. But all these Caribbean islands are prizes, to be taken. Barbados has a very active militia. Friends here bear witness against it, to their cost."

We saw evidence of this soon after we disembarked.

We walked up the careenage, where ships lay with their hulls uppermost and men were at work, scraping them clean of barnacles and seaweed. The air felt hot and the sun burned like a brand. It was a relief to enter the town and the shade of the streets; but Michael's Town is low-lying and swampy, and foul odours waft from the sewers. I took an instant dislike to the place, with its heat and stink.

My master had hoped to go to the home of a merchant friend, Nicholas Yates, where we were to stay for a night or two. But the streets began to fill with soldiers and people, pushing and shouting, and we saw that the soldiers were attempting to drive along a cow, and behind it a Negro man with his wrists bound who stared about him with angry, frightened eyes.

As the soldiers forced a passage through, we drew back, for the cow was skittish. A man in sober clothes – a Friend, I guessed – ran alongside, shouting, "This is an injustice! The cow alone would more than pay the fine! I demand recompense! I shall go to the Governor…"

"Huh! Good luck to you!" a soldier jeered.

Several Friends now joined the owner of the cow and began remonstrating with the soldiers. My master recognized one of them and called out, "Nick Yates!"

The man turned, and the two greeted each other warmly. My master introduced us. Nicholas Yates was a man of my master's age with a businesslike air and a look of keen intelligence – the kind of man I'd want on my side in a dispute, I thought.

He indicated the Negro and the cow, now moving away. "It's outrageous. The fine was fifteen hundred pounds of sugar and they have taken a cow in calf, worth two thousand pounds, and one of his best Negroes. That Negro alone is worth three thousand pounds of sugar."

I felt a profound sense of shock at these words. All my beliefs about what it meant to be a Friend were thrown into confusion. I looked at Kate, to see if she had felt the same, but her expression was merely one of sympathy for the Friend who had been fined; and my master said, without any sign of surprise, "Fines for not serving in the militia?"

"Yes. And the musters are frequent, every few weeks. Every man has to serve, and if he has the means he must also send horses, servants, apprentices. Oh, and lances! For every twenty acres of land a man owns, he must provide one lance with a steel head and an eight-foot shaft. Of course Friends send none of these things, and are fined; and the authorities always take goods to a value far in excess of the fine." He looked at the aggrieved Friend, who was walking back towards us. "That's Gilbert Bell. He has been steadfast in his testimony against outward weapons. Refuses to bear arms or to send men for the militia, and has suffered for it – even to imprisonment and being tied neck to heels. We will protest this case. But thou know, George, we have constant harassment here. This Governor is very hostile to Friends. He would like to prevent us meeting altogether, but the law does not allow him. Well" – he extended an arm to indicate all three of us – "come to my house! Eleanor has been expecting you any day this past week. And Agnes will be glad to have thy company, Kate. Josiah, all this will remind thee of London, I think?"

It was much later, when I was alone with my master, walking back to the ship to fetch some goods, that I said – still in shock, "They have *slaves*? Barbados Friends have *slaves*?"

He looked at me in surprise. "Yes, of course. Everywhere in the Americas people have slaves – those who can afford them."

"*Thou* don't."

"I don't want or need them. I like my Yorkshire servants."

"But I've seen no slaves in Philadelphia."

"There are not many in Pennsylvania. Indentured labour is plentiful there. But Barbados is all sugar plantations. They need slaves here – a constant supply. They could not run the plantations without them."

"I never thought of that," I said.

"Thou wouldn't, living in England. But it's the way things are, out here. And Friends look after their slaves, treat them well – good housing, good food.

And most promise manumission after fifteen years."

"What's that? Manumission?"

"Freedom. They set them free. And look after them in old age. The truth is, Jos, many of these people would have had much worse lives in Africa: disease, and wars, and ungodly practices."

Back at the merchant's house, I saw evidence of what my master had said. Nicholas Yates had several Negro slaves who seemed to be treated much as Isobel and Mary were in my master's house.

And yet it worried me. I wanted to talk to Kate about it, for everything was new to me and I wondered how much she already knew of this and what her thoughts were. But it was difficult to find time to be together. All my hopes about spending time with Kate, on the voyage and now, in the merchant's house, had so far come to nothing. On the ship we were never alone, and now, in the merchant's crowded home, I could only gaze at her across a room or exchange quick glances from time to time. The next day the merchant's wife took her to a meeting of women Friends in the town, while I was out and about with my master and Richard Grey at the Merchants' Exchange, involved in business and being introduced to other traders and apprentices. Many of these were Friends, so I heard much about the troubles they were experiencing in Barbados.

"It's worse for the poor," Nicholas Yates said. "They often have the tools of their trade taken, or even their household pots and furniture. Thou will know what it's like, Josiah, being lately come from London. And no doubt thy father, too, has suffered because of his refusal to swear on the Bible?"

I agreed. He told me also that Barbados Friends were forbidden to bring their Negroes to Meeting – or even to hold meetings in their own homes at which Negroes were present.

I was bewildered. "Why?" I asked.

"No one is allowed to teach slaves the Christian religion," he explained. "The authorities fear it will give them a sense of being equal to us, and cause them to rise up and demand freedom."

I thought this not unreasonable, that they should wish to be free.

"But they live in spiritual darkness," he said, "without moral purpose. They are loose in their behaviour; the men take more than one wife; they lie, steal, and fight. We need to bring them to see the evil of their ways and to find the light within. This is God's work. Because of this we must suffer fines and imprisonment."

"Do they imprison the slaves, too?"

"They take and sell them unless we pay a ten pound fine for each one."

I thought about this. "And when they come to the

light, if they do, *are* they equal to us?"

He frowned. "They always were equal, for the light is in everyone."

"And yet they are slaves."

"Slavery has been a condition of mankind since earliest times. We are required to treat our slaves well, to educate and care for them, and bring them to God."

He must have seen the uncertainty in my face, for he said, "If thou'rt to become a merchant in the Americas, Josiah, thou will find thyself dealing with slaves."

The next day being first-day we went to the meeting house in Tudor Street. A large number of Friends were expected since there had been so much repression of late, and the highly charged atmosphere reminded me of some London meetings I had attended. I sensed that trouble was anticipated. Friends began filling the room, bringing with them their servants and apprentices and, in some cases, slaves. Nicholas Yates was there with his house slaves – two maids and a young girl, the daughter of one of them. The Negroes sat scattered around the room among their owners, and whereas some of them wore a look of apprehension, as if they knew what might happen and feared it, others appeared resolute. It was hot. A few small high windows were open, but the room was stifling.

George Bainbrigg looked anxious. As we sat down, he turned to Kate and said, "I think I should have left thee at the house."

"Dad, I'm not a child!" she retorted.

"I know, lass. That's why I fear for thee, now thou'rt over sixteen. Stay quiet if the Governor's men come. Don't speak out, even if the spirit urges thee. Remember, it's against the law for anyone not resident here to preach at Friends' meetings – and they'd call it preaching no matter how little we said."

I had a tight knot in my stomach. This reminded me too much of meetings in Stepney and Ratcliff. Why must my master put himself at risk? Surely he could support local Friends without involving himself in this provocative meeting?

Kate was sitting on the other side of her father. She looked across at me and gave me a small, tight smile. I wished I could take her hand.

Soon, a deep silence fell, and as it continued I felt its power. A Friend stood and began to speak of the many trials members had suffered, and of the need to be faithful and patient. He drew in the Negroes, and welcomed them – and was developing this theme when the door was flung open so hard it hit the wall behind. Soldiers armed with swords and cudgels burst into the room and moved quickly in among us. Their leader read out the prohibition on bringing Negroes to Meeting, and ordered the arrest of all present who were in breach of the law and the confiscation of their Negroes.

All but a few stalwart Friends rose and began to move as the soldiers broke up the meeting, thrusting them aside and seizing the slaves. My master spoke to me urgently: "Take Kate – move over there, out of the way" – and I caught Kate's hand as we struggled to avoid the soldiers, who swore at us all as they pushed through: "Quaking dogs – out of the way, you rogues!" "Sons of whores! *Move!*"

A bench toppled over, and a woman screamed as she was thrown down. The soldiers knew who they were looking for. They rounded up several ringleaders, together with the Negroes who belonged to them, and pushed them into a group. The elder of Nicholas Yates' maids clutched her daughter to her side, crying out to them not to take her child away. My master moved in to remonstrate with the soldiers.

I drew Kate to the edge of the room, and came upon a young Negro man the soldiers had missed. He was shrinking towards the wall, trying to avoid their notice, and there was a look of fear in his eyes.

I knew at once how he felt, for I must have worn the same look many times during my childhood in London. And he had good reason to be afraid, for he might be taken away and beaten and sold to another master. Instinctively I moved, with my arm around Kate, to stand in front of him, blocking the soldiers' approach and, with luck, hiding him from them. We three remained still and quiet, and did nothing to draw attention to ourselves.

I could feel Kate trembling and knew she was anxious about her father, who was now in the thick of the tumult. By this time, it seemed, the soldiers had laid hands on sufficient prisoners to justify having stormed the building, and their leader was noting names of slaves and owners.

"A ten pound fine is required for each one taken," he said. "If you can't pay, they will be sold."

Voices erupted all around.

"I can't pay!"

"Nor I! I am a poor carpenter, trying to make a living. My shop, my rent—"

"Friends," one of the merchants said, "we will find a way to pay for all…"

Several Friends were arrested and sent out under guard. More soldiers left with the slaves. I felt indignation on behalf of these Negroes, who'd had no choice but to be there, and now must take the consequences. My sympathy was more for them than for their owners, no matter how poor. Behind me I sensed rather than heard the breathing of the young man I had hidden. People began to assemble and talk, to pick up fallen benches and gather their families and servants around them. I turned, and caught a look of gratitude from the youth before he slipped away, presumably to join his owner.

My master was making his way towards us, and I reluctantly let go of Kate, who went to him.

"Well done, lad," he said. "It could have been worse. They'll bring our Friends to court in the morning, most likely, and the Negroes will be released on payment of the fines. I told the soldiers I was from Philadelphia. The Governor needs to know that Friends here have our support..." He caught the eye of someone beyond me and smiled a greeting. "There's John Crosbie! I hadn't realized he was here. He was lucky not to be arrested, for I see he's brought at least one of his Negroes with him."

I turned to see a tall, fair man, younger than George Bainbrigg. With him were two white men, apparently his servants, and the black youth I had helped to hide.

"Come and meet him," George Bainbrigg said. "He's a friend of mine – another Yorkshire man. We'll be going out to his plantation soon."

That evening I managed to find a moment alone with Kate. My master and other Friends were talking downstairs – too taken up with the day's events to concern themselves with us. Kate and I met on the upstairs landing, by a shuttered window, and clung together for several moments without speaking.

"Oh, I've missed thee!" I said at last.

"It's always like this, travelling with my father. He knows so many people, and we visit and talk…"

"I've wanted to talk to *thee*," I said. "Didst thou know – I suppose thou *must* have known – that Friends here have slaves?"

"Oh, yes. Didn't thou realize?"

"Not till we came here. Not till I saw that man being taken as payment for a fine. A *man*!"

She looked up at me anxiously. "Thou should not be concerned, Jos. None of our Friends here would ill-treat their slaves. They care for them, encourage them to marry, educate their children. You've seen the servants in this house, Dinah and Tilly, how contented they are; they are house slaves."

I said hotly, "I saw how that woman – Dinah, is it? – was terrified when the soldiers came, begging them not to take her child!"

"It was the soldiers who terrified her."

"But it was our Friends who brought her to Meeting!"

I had spoken more loudly than I intended, and she flinched. "Jos! People will hear…"

She looked hurt, as if I accused her, and I felt sorry and gathered her into my arms and apologized with kisses.

The colonial way of life had not been such a shock to her, I supposed. She had come to the New World as a child of twelve and would have become accustomed to it more gradually.

She leaned in against me. "We'll have more time together at the Crosbies', I think. And more chances to meet."

"Is it a big place?"

"Not as plantations go. But the house is a rambling sort of place, lots of rooms; verandas... Thou'll like it there."

Jokpa

When my master says he will take me to the big meeting of Friends in town I want to hide away. Why me? Why not all the other house slaves? I have been to the Friends' meeting before, and demons with guns and loud fierce voices came and dragged me and the other slaves away and locked us up and beat us. They said we would be sold, but the next day my master came and paid money and the demons gave me back to him. The Friends sit long hours waiting for the Light, but they are always troubled by these bad spirits with guns. I don't want to go, but my master says I must.

"He likes thee and wants to teach thee," Miata says. "He is taking thee under his wing."

I know this is true. My master often talks to me about the Light. I tell him I think the Light is like Yala, and he agrees, but he says I must not believe the things I was taught as a child; I must not believe in spirits and evil spells. He says the Light is inside me; inside everyone; the Light is all we need.

In the meeting house silence falls and we sit still – as still as hunters who wait for their prey. At last one of the Friends stands up and talks long, long, about God, and the Seed, and the Light.

Then the demons with guns come in and people move and cry out and the smell of fear rises. I shrink back against the wall. There is a man there, a man of the Friends. He is young, like me, and has a girl with him. They move in front of me so that I am hidden from the demons. The young man says nothing, but I know he has done this to help me.

Fourteen

About a week later we drove to
the Crosbie plantation in a wagon, Kate and I sitting
together and her father opposite. All the way I was
aware of Kate beside me, our arms almost touching,
her thigh – under its layers of skirts and shift – next to
mine. It was frustrating to be so close and yet unable
even to hold hands.

I had not liked Michael's Town, but now, as we
drove towards the centre of the island and up through
the plantations, I thought this high ground would
surely be healthier. For as far as I could see the hill-
sides were covered with tall green plants, swathes of
stubble and lines of black people cutting the cane.
Almost the whole island, it seemed, was given over
to the production of sugar. As we drove closer, I saw
what arduous work this was. The men were using
huge curved knives – billhooks, my master called

them – to hack at the canes, which were thicker than a man's arm. They cut them a short way above the base and threw them down, while women and older men moved along the rows, bending and gathering, and loading them onto carts, leaving a field of thick stubble. The sun beat down, and overseers – also black, some of them – patrolled the rows. Several times I saw a whip curl through the air and strike a worker. Once this happened so close to us that I heard the smack of the plaited leather on the man's flesh. He staggered, but did not cry out, stoically continuing his work.

"Planters who are Friends discourage such cruelty," my master said. He glanced out. "The land up ahead is Crosbie's. See those buildings? That's where they process the canes for sugar." He explained the method, and said John Crosbie would be sure to give me a tour of the works. He also told me about the Crosbie family: John, who had come to the New World from Halifax in Yorkshire five years before; his wife Ann; and their two small children. It seemed that all was not well with the Crosbies. They had suffered greatly from fines for not sending men and horses to the militia and for bringing Negroes to Meeting; last year's harvest had been bad; and recently a fire had destroyed some of the plantation buildings.

"John needs help," George Bainbrigg said. "He

spoke in his last letter to me of selling up and going back to England. His wife's health is not good and she has no love for the island."

I murmured sympathy, but in truth I thought little about the Crosbies' plight except to wonder whether my master's absorption in their affairs might allow me more time with Kate. I spared a passing thought, also, for the black youth I had encountered at the meeting; no words had been exchanged between us, and yet I had felt a connection with him. I wondered who he was and whether he was one of these who laboured in the fields. The wagon jolted over the rutted path and the hot wind blew dust over us. Sweat trickled down my forehead and between my shoulder blades; I felt ludicrously overdressed in my woollen clothes. Kate, whose face looked pink and shiny, brought out a small fan and wafted the air between us.

Now we were approaching the house, which was set apart from the plantation buildings and fields, and had a garden around it. It was a large white stone house with a veranda all along the front and balconies above.

"John Crosbie must have been wealthy," I said, "to have bought this place."

"Aye – but business is always risky," my master said. "Bad luck can happen to anyone. Well – here we are."

Our hosts came out to greet us. John Crosbie was

a tall, scholarly-looking person with a slight stoop, not the sort I would have expected to find running a plantation. He looked tired; his eyes were bloodshot and his fair skin was reddened by the sun. His wife was much younger (a second marriage, Kate told me later). She appeared unhappy and resentful, though she was civil to us. Her eldest child, a boy of about three, held the hand of a black nursemaid – a slave, I supposed – and hid his face in her skirts when Kate tried to talk to him.

Their house was cool and spacious, with airy rooms and windows open to the veranda and a breeze blowing through from front to back. I was given a room to myself with a door onto a balcony and shutters that could be closed at night. A black girl brought a jug of water, towels and soap. She was soft-footed and submissive, with a downward glance, but when I thanked her she looked up with a flash of eyes darker and more brilliant than any I had seen before.

I washed and changed my linen and then, hearing a door open, stepped out onto the landing, hoping to see Kate. But it was her father, who had the room next to mine. Kate appeared from a room further along, looking cool and smelling of rosewater.

We ate fresh fish – flying fish, our host told me – for dinner; and breadfruit, and beef from New Jersey. Two slaves served us – a woman and a young man;

their names were Lucie and Antony. I recognized Antony as the youth from the meeting. For an instant our eyes met, and I knew he remembered me, but he gave no other sign. Like the girl, both he and Lucie were quiet and unobtrusive. I watched his hands as he set down the dishes for me, and noticed roughened weals from old scars around both his wrists. Shackles. I had seen such scars on the wrists of Friends who had suffered in London's prisons. It struck me forcibly how he must have been brought to this island, bound and shackled; and I remembered the slave ship I had seen on our voyage to America, and the unspeakable smell that came from it; and Walt Burney telling me how that ship would be carrying three or four times the number of souls as ours.

And yet, here, this young man seemed to have a good life. He was a house slave, clearly well treated. Maybe Nicholas Yates was right, and the slaves were better off here than in the moral darkness of their lives in Africa? Capture and transportation seemed unbearably cruel – but perhaps, I thought, for the sake of their souls, it was a necessary evil.

That evening, after supper, I stayed for a short while with my master and John Crosbie as they talked of earlier times and John's present troubles. But they were old friends, and I felt I was inhibiting their conversation. I soon excused myself. Kate had already disappeared with the wife and children; I could hear the little boy's voice from somewhere on the floor above as I left the room.

I went upstairs, to my room, opened the door onto the balcony, and stepped out into the embrace of the warm evening air. It was dark, the breeze blowing streamers of cloud across the moon. In the shifting patches of clear sky I glimpsed stars that shone with a wondrous brightness. There was a scent of flowers. And from all around came a high persistent shrilling of insects. This I knew to be the sound of cicadas, for Kate had told me about it. I wished she was here to share the sound with me now.

The balcony overlooked the side of the house, and a little way off I could see what looked like a village, with huts set in a straight line as if along a street. Fires flickered there, and in their light I glimpsed people moving about. Beneath the sound of cicadas I heard other sounds: voices, and an intermittent drum beat. I realized that these must be the homes of the slaves who worked on the plantation.

Curiosity led me downstairs again, and I found my way out through a back door and onto a dirt path that led to the slaves' village.

Here, the sounds of human activity were much clearer: children's voices; women calling to one another; babies crying, water splashing; two men arguing or, perhaps, merely talking loudly – I could not tell which. There was a smell of cooking and woodsmoke – homely smells.

And still I heard the drumbeats – not loud, not persistent; it was the sound, perhaps, of two friends idly picking out a rhythm together. Now and then it stopped; occasionally a few men sang – one calling, others responding; sometimes the song broke up in laughter. It sounded companionable. These were men who were tired after a long day's work, sitting at ease together, making music.

I did not dare go any closer. I guessed I would be unwelcome in the village. I stopped in the shade of a large tree and listened.

There were two drums, I realized, a larger and a smaller, and some kind of twanging stringed instrument. Blended with these was the sound of voices. Their music seemed strange at first, but after a while I began to hear different rhythms, criss-crossing and changing in a complex way. The sound got inside me; it caught and fascinated me. I'd been told these people were savages, but when they sang and played they made a pattern of harmonies as subtle as any I'd heard in England.

The moon was high now, and the wind had risen and was rattling the leaves of the palm trees; yet the air was still warm – a sticky heat. A lamp had been lit above the door where I had come out.

I turned back, and had almost reached the door when I heard whispering voices, a scamper of quick feet – and then someone came around the side of the house and started at the sight of me.

It was Antony.

"Sorry, master – sorry," he said. "I did not see thee…"

"It doesn't matter. And don't call me 'master'. I am only an apprentice. My name is Josiah."

He looked wary. I remembered the whispering; one of the voices had been female. Had he been returning from a tryst with someone, out there in the dark under the palms? The thought made me shiver with envy and desire.

"I came out to listen to the music," I said. "The drums and singing." He did not respond; and I sensed that he was nervous, that he feared trouble. "I'd have thought thou might be there, among them?"

"No. I am a house servant. I wait on the master." And he lowered his gaze and half-turned towards the door.

"That drumming!" I said. "I never heard such music before! It – it *speaks* to me. I can feel it in my bones."

He paused then, and I knew I had his attention. "Some nights I go down there," he said. "The drumming takes me home to my village. I remember my friends. I remember songs, dances, making music together." There was longing in his voice.

"And that is lost to thee now. I am sorry."

He hesitated; then said, "I made a drum… Thou won't tell my master?"

"No!"

"My master is a good man. He does not beat his people. He teaches me to speak English, tells me about the Light. But in his house we must not sing or dance."

"It is the Friends' way," I admitted.

And it struck me, not for the first time but more strongly than ever, how strange it was to deny the urge to make music that God had given us. But I knew Friends would say that God gives us many desires that must be reined in or denied.

I tried to explain, to myself as much as to him. "Other people – worldly people – dance and sing. But Friends believe music takes up time that should be spent in prayer, or reading the Bible, or in silent waiting on the spirit."

"In my village the spirits dance," said Antony.

I wanted to ask him about his country, about his life there, how he was taken from it, how he came to be in Barbados; but the questions seemed too big, too painful. Instead, I asked him, "May I see the drum thou made?"

He looked uncertain, and began to retreat. "I should go in now. My master…"

"He's talking with *my* master. They won't need us."

"Come, then." He opened the door, stood back for me to enter, then led me along the passage to a small room containing three pallet beds on a wooden floor, a bench and a washstand. I noticed a Bible lying on the bench. The room was plain, but not so very different from my own room at George Bainbrigg's house – except that this was a dormitory.

"Others sleep here?" I asked.

"Yes. Reuben, the groom; and the boy, Paul – Lucie's son."

He reached into the space between his bed and the wall and brought out the drum and handed it to me. It was small, made from a hollowed-out gourd, and covered top and bottom with a membrane of hide, tied in place and adjusted with pegs set around the rim. I tapped the skin experimentally and felt a satisfying resonance.

When I gave it back to him he squatted on the bed, set it between his knees, and began to play. It was a repetitive, mesmerizing beat, simple at first; but then he began to add different rhythms, building up one on another. After a while he stopped drumming and started to sing, quite unselfconsciously, almost as if he had forgotten I was there. I did not need to be told it was a sad song; all the pain of separation and loss was in it.

I sat on the bench and listened, and observed him. He was as tall as I was, but bigger and stronger-looking. What was his life, his work, in Africa? I wondered. It was beyond my imagining. But I understood that this drum was a work of love. I thought of him making the instrument himself, finding the materials and tools, and having the skill to do it.

The song finished – or rather, it stopped, because the music was too unfamiliar for me to hear the approach of an ending. He offered the drum to me again.

I tapped a simple rhythm, childish in its simplicity. What a joy it must be, I thought, to be skilled at this, to play and sing with others.

"I can't play," I said.

"Thou could learn."

He had learned many things. How to endure the terrible Atlantic crossing; how to survive in a strange land; how to speak English – and Friends' English, at that.

"Thou speak English well," I said.

He looked pleased. "I learned many languages since I left my village – I did not know there *were* so many, or so many different people in the world. When I went on board the ship there was no one else who spoke my language."

"But" – I was puzzled – "surely the ship was full of other slaves?"

"Yes. But none who spoke Kpelle. I learned Kru,

Bassa, Asante, Temne, Fulbe…"

"Those are all African languages?" I felt ashamed of my ignorance. I'd had no idea. I'd assumed the slaves were all the same; all spoke the same tongue.

"Yes," he said. "We all learned the English the white slavers spoke to us too. But my master taught me to speak English like the Friends. He said I should also learn to read. But now … I don't know if he will teach me. My master is not happy. His wife is not happy. Things are wrong in this house. Someone has put a spell on John Crosbie."

"No, no." Now I felt confident, certain of my superior understanding. "He has suffered for his witness against weapons and for teaching Christianity to thee and the other slaves. The authorities have fined him. And there was a bad harvest, I heard, and a fire. These are misfortunes, not witchcraft."

He looked at me sombrely, and I saw that my words had had no effect. "An enemy of my master has done these things," he said. "An enemy has paid a sorceror to make these bad things happen."

"That is all darkness and superstition," I insisted. "Thou should cast away such beliefs. Friends will try to help John Crosbie, and we will hold him and his wife in the light."

He agreed with me then. "The Light is good, strong. Maybe stronger than the sorceror's spell."

Fifteen

"I fear I must neglect thee a little, while we are here," my master said next morning.

And when I began to protest that it didn't matter, he added, "Kate, too. She's complaining already about being left with Ann Crosbie. The poor woman is in low spirits and wants only to go home to England. She is no company for a young girl."

"And will the Crosbies go?" I asked. I felt a lift at the realization that I might be able to spend more time with Kate.

"I think so. John already has a buyer for the plantation, but there is much to consider and arrange. He needs my advice. So – if thou can keep Kate company now and then in a seemly manner…"

"I will." I tried not to look too eager, but I think he knew.

"John's plantation manager will take the two of

you around the works today," he said. "Thou ought to learn as much as possible while we are here, and it will do no harm for Kate to know about these things, too. And thou must keep up with thy studies, Jos, and ask questions and stay alert."

The tour of the sugar works was much enlivened for me by Kate's presence, though I found the process – the beating and crushing of the canes, the boiling and extracting, all performed by an army of slaves – horrible and unnatural. I was accustomed to working with machinery in my father's print shop, but I had never witnessed machinery and labour on this scale. Almost the whole island, it seemed, was given over to the sugar crop. I should never want to be a planter, I told Kate afterwards. It seemed to me a vision of Hell, such as the papists believe in.

The next day, with the woman of the house a-bed and tended by servants, and George Bainbrigg and John Crosbie deep in prayer and consultation, Kate and I spent the morning on the veranda, which we had been told we could use for our studies. Lucie brought us pineapple juice to drink. It was the colour of sunshine and tasted like nothing I had ever drunk before: fresh and sweet, with a delicate fragrance.

"Adam and Eve must have drunk this in the Garden of Eden," I said.

Kate was struggling, with the aid of a dictionary, to read a book in German, while I was studying a manual on navigation, and making notes. We worked hard for about two hours, before I sighed and stretched, and Kate said, "It's hot!" and we stopped work and walked up and down the length of the veranda.

I told Kate about hearing the music from the slaves' village, and about my meeting with Antony.

Kate said, "Antony is the one Patience is in love with."

"Patience?"

"The maidservant who cleans the bedchambers."

I remembered the soft-footed girl, the flash of dark eyes. So it was she Antony had been meeting that night.

Patience seemed a strangely English, Protestant name for such a girl. Of course it would not be her own name, any more than Antony's was his. Ann Crosbie, or some former owner, would have given it to her. And I wondered about those other names the slaves must have, their real names, that were never used.

"Thou hast talked to Patience, then?" I said.

"Yes. I knew her because we'd visited before, but we'd never spoken much until now – not about anything important. But this time I saw her with Antony. It was only a glance that passed between them – but

I understood. And it made me realize that we were the same. They are like us, Jos, those two, snatching moments together…"

I took her hand, and we drew closer.

"So I asked her about him," Kate continued. "She said she had not met anyone of her tribe – the Kpelle – until he came to this house; and when he spoke to her in her own language she was filled with joy, so happy that she broke down in tears."

"This is making *thee* cry," I said – and the tears glistening in Kate's eyes spilled over.

She brushed them away. "Oh, Jos! She told me how she was captured and brought here! She was working with the women in the rice fields, some way from the village, when raiders came and seized them all – children, too. They screamed and shouted for help but no one came. Patience believes the men had already been taken, but they never found out; never saw them again. The slavers fixed a collar around her neck, and yoked her to another woman, and they were forced to walk like that, in pairs – linked in a line – for several moons, she said; and then they were herded into a compound, a place that stank of fear and death. And she was branded with a red-hot iron. How can anyone *endure* that?"

"I don't know," I said. "And yet Friends have endured torture and branding as punishment. And some have been transported here, to the Caribbean."

"But those people *chose* martyrdom. They had faith in God. And they were not separated from everything they knew. Patience had never seen a ship before. She had lived all her life in the forest. She didn't understand what was happening to her."

The weight of such suffering oppressed us. We leaned on the balustrade and looked out. From here we could see mile after mile of sugar plantations – the destination of so many captive people. And yet this was a place of beauty. In the far distance was a blink of sea, blue as sapphire; and below us lay a garden with palm trees, vivid scarlet and yellow flowers, and walks shaded by rose-covered arcades. Kate told me there was a pool at its centre.

"Let's go down there," I said. "We can study again later."

We took the books inside and went out into the garden. It was larger than I had first thought. On one side was a herb garden, and on the other an area of fruit trees and bushes, with some vegetables growing in rows. We encountered a black gardener at work there, weeding. Near the house Kate showed me what she called the "coral drip".

"This is how they purify water for drinking. It comes through cooled and clean."

I was interested in this. I saw that the coral was

porous and the water was filtered through it. All my life, in England, I had drunk small beer because water was not fit to drink. Here, it seemed, the purity of God's creation had not been spoiled.

The formal garden stretched across the whole front of the house. There was an English-style lawn made of some springy herb, surrounded on all sides by straight paths and beds full of flowering shrubs; and beyond it were stone steps leading down to a lower level.

We saw a child's bat and ball lying on the lawn and played with it for a while. I had the bat and kept Kate running and diving after the ball until she was hot and giggling and complained that it was not fair.

"Thou can't catch!" I said.

"Thou hit it too hard, that's why." She wrestled the bat from me. "It's *my* turn."

But she managed no better, and before long she sent the ball deep into the bushes, and I had to crawl in and find it and emerged covered in earth and twigs.

"Oh, Jos!" She brushed at me, laughing.

"It's thy fault." I wanted to grab and kiss her, dirt and all, but we were in view of the house. "Let's go into the shade, then, and cool down." I began moving towards the steps. "Shall I dive into the pool?"

"No!"

She was laughing as she followed me.

Down here the garden was shadier, with palms and tall trees ringing with bird calls and alive with their movement. Bushes laden with scarlet or white waxy-petalled flowers gave off a sweet, overpowering scent, and some of the paths were arched-over with trellises entwined with roses. Here we could not be seen from the house, so I put my arm around Kate and we walked close together and several times stopped and kissed.

The pool lay at the lowest level, but even here sunlight broke through the canopy of leaves and made the water sparkle. A stone edge surrounded it, and at one end stood a statue of a nymph in a wisp of drapery; a surprising ornament for a Friend's garden, I thought, but I supposed a former owner had chosen it.

"Look!" Kate touched my arm and pointed.

A jewel-green lizard was poised on the rim of the pool. We crouched to watch it. I was entranced by the gleaming perfection of its scales, by the tiny splayed feet gripping the stone, the unblinking eye. This garden seemed to me a place of wonder, full of the works of God and yet a place that stirred the senses.

At the other end of the pool was a stone seat in an arbour, and here Kate and I sat and kissed and embraced each other, hidden from the world. I knew our behaviour was not what my master would consider seemly, but there was no one to see. Kate's gown was lightweight wool, with a linen kerchief covering the neckline, but under it she wore stays, and under them a shift. As we kissed and my hands found their way to her breasts, despite all the clothing, I thought of the nymph across the pool in her slipping draperies, and imagined Kate in such a garment, how it would slide to the floor and she would step away from it, naked and lissom.

"These stays…" I teased.

"Don't!" she said. "Someone might come." But she didn't look as if she minded.

Suddenly she cried out.

"What is it?"

She had a hand to her chest, below the collarbone. "Something stung me!" Tears of pain sprang to her eyes.

"Let me see." I moved her hand, and saw a red mark. A wasp, perhaps, or bee? Or some strange Caribbean insect that might do harm?

The redness was beginning to spread. Clearly our time here together was over.

"We'd best go back to the house," I said. "They'll have some salve or remedy."

She was struggling to rearrange her clothing. "I can't show anyone! It's low down – below where my kerchief should have been covering me."

I chided her, laughing. "No one in the kitchen will care about that!"

I helped tidy her up and we walked back to the house together.

In the kitchen the servants were preparing dinner. A woman I hadn't seen before was frying something over the fire in a skillet; the serving-woman Lucie and the girl called Patience were chopping herbs.

They must have been surprised by our sudden entrance, but they became instantly attentive and respectful. I found this unsettling. Their total submission made it difficult for me to appeal to them for help. But as we began to explain, I saw a look pass between Lucie and Patience and knew they understood the cause of Kate's embarrassment and were perhaps amused by it.

Patience left her work and took Kate along the passage to another room. I followed behind. The two girls were similar in height and build, both curvy, with round bottoms and slim waists. But there were no stays on Patience, and I found myself watching her, wondering whether Kate's hips, too, would sway in that enticing manner if left unrestrained.

When we reached the room, which seemed to be a stillroom or pantry, Patience led Kate inside and – with a little smile – closed the door on me. From behind it I heard their soft voices, ripples of stifled laughter. What were they talking about? I felt shut out from their feminine chatter.

When they emerged, Kate was smiling and smelt of some herbal preparation.

"Better?" I asked.

"Yes. They have a stock of salves and other remedies in there that Ann and the maids have made up."

I saw that Lucie was preparing glasses of pineapple juice.

She turned to me. "The young mistress should go and rest on the veranda. Patience will bring some juice."

We were being dismissed from their domain. We left obediently and went to our place on the veranda, taking our books and papers with us.

After dinner, my master and John Crosbie spent time with me, talking to me about the management of plantations and the financial risks, while from outside I heard Kate and Ann Crosbie playing with the little boy. I did not have any time with Kate again until the evening, when we met briefly on the landing.

The warm night air, the events of the day, and the memory of the garden with its pool and nymph, its arbours and fragrant blossoms, made me bolder than usual; and as I kissed Kate I felt her drawing back a little, startled and perhaps alarmed by my ardour. I released her, and looked down into the shadowy yard beneath the balcony.

Someone was there, by the bushes. Antony. He stood as if waiting. The high thrum of cicadas filled the air, but beneath their sound I heard a faint click: the back door opening. Patience flitted across the yard and into Antony's arms.

Their bodies seemed to blend together. Her arms slid around his neck, his head came down, his hands were on her hips, pressing her against him. Sighs and murmurs escaped them as they withdrew into the darkness of the bushes, out of sight.

I felt a surge of longing. They were slaves and yet they were free in ways that Kate and I were not. I glanced at Kate and knew she had seen them too.

I turned away from the balcony. "We should go to our own chambers."

"Yes." Her face was burning.

The next day my master and John Crosbie drove into Michael's Town to visit a Friend who was a notary. Once again Kate and I were left to our studies.

"Patience tried to give me a ... *thing*, an amulet," she said, as we set out our books.

"When?"

"This morning, when she brought my washing water. She said it would keep me safe from the bad magic in this place. She blames the bee sting on magic."

"What nonsense!" I said. "It was an accident."

"I know. I told her she should not use such things, that it was ungodly, horrible…"

"What was it like?"

"Oh ... feathers and" – she shuddered – "thou know the sort of thing the Indians wear? Like that. These people are caught in such darkness, Jos, for all they join us for prayers and meetings."

"But ... didn't country folk in Yorkshire put faith in similar things?" I asked. "My mother said they did in Shropshire. Rabbits' feet, and horseshoes on the door, and touching wood and suchlike."

"Yes, they did. I hadn't thought of it like that. But of course Friends don't do those things. Or shouldn't."

"I suppose," I said, "the Negroes are much like the Indians in their way of life and their beliefs?" I realized I knew little about them, except what a man was worth in pounds of sugar.

"We should find out," said Kate. "We are here to learn, my father says."

When Patience came with juice and sweetmeats for us, we detained her, and asked her about Africa, about the place she had come from. She seemed relieved not to be chastised any more about the amulet, and the words spilled out of her as she recalled her family home: the village in a clearing in the forest, the thatched huts, the people working together in the rice fields, her sisters and friends. But soon, as she talked of them, she began to gulp and cry, and great tears rolled down her cheeks as she sobbed, "I don't know where they are! I was separated from them long before we reached the coast. My littlest sister – she was torn away from me; she reached out her arms and screamed to me not to let them take her... I don't know if she is alive or dead – if I will ever see her again! I don't know if I will see any of them again." And she curled her arms around her body and rocked in grief.

We watched her, appalled at what we had unleashed. At last Kate put a tentative hand on her shoulder and said, "Don't cry! We should not have asked thee. We will not speak of it again."

"No!" Patience brushed away her tears. "I *want* to speak of it. It hurts, but I want to remember. One day, I hope, I will go home and my family will come together again – those who are still alive. I am the eldest. My father was – is – an important man in our village. My mother is his first wife and I am her eldest daughter." She spoke with pride. "I will fetch a high bride-price."

"Thy father has other wives?" Kate's voice did not betray the disapproval she undoubtedly felt.

"Two. Bindu is young; I like her; she has a nice baby. But the second wife – Koto – hah!" She made a gesture of dismissal.

"And you all live in the same house?" I asked, thinking of the quarrels that must ensue.

"No!" She burst out laughing, despite the tears still

wet on her cheeks. "Each woman has her own hut, and her children live with her. But we cook and eat together."

She began to talk more calmly, reliving her childhood in the forest. She told us about the rainy season which lasted around five months, when the forest steamed and squelched as they waded through deep mud, and everything rotted in the wet; and about the dry months when the hot winds brought dust from the desert and they all suffered from cracked lips. She told how she used to help her mother at home and in the fields, growing rice, yams and beans, looking after the chickens and goats, and caring for the younger children. She regarded the forest as dangerous, full of snakes and scorpions, and spirits who must be given gifts to keep them friendly: rice on a plate of fresh leaves; a chicken or two.

"But sometimes the men catch monkeys or deer in the forest. They are good eating. And we collect giant snails for the cooking pot." She showed us their size against her hand and forearm.

Kate winced. "How long hast thou been in Barbados?" she asked.

But Patience did not know. "Three years? Four? I was in a bad place first, working in the fields a long time, loading cane onto carts. It was hard. But here the master and mistress are good. And there is Antony…

When I am with Antony I remember my other life –
my home – and I believe we can go there again."

Neither Kate nor I spoke in answer to this. It seemed
to me impossible that they could ever go home.

The next day was seventh-day, and I went into town,
to the Merchants' Exchange, with my master. We
met up with several of the people he traded with, and
he made deals and showed me how everything was
done. I gathered that we were coming to the end of
our stay on the island.

On first-day John Crosbie did not go to Meeting in Michael's Town, but gathered together all the
house slaves and several of those who worked on the
plantation, and held a meeting in his house, which we
three also attended.

As I looked around the circle of faces – John and
Ann Crosbie, George Bainbrigg and Kate, a dozen or
so slaves, including the black nursemaid holding the
little boy on her lap – I had a sense that beneath the
shared silence there was something unspoken. John
Crosbie looked weary, drained, yet determined. His
wife looked almost happy. The Negroes appeared
variously respectful, serious, bored or fidgety accord-
ing to their temperaments.

The meeting settled, but I do not think it ever
became gathered. When it was over, John shook

hands not only with his wife and my master, who sat on either side of him, but afterwards with many of the Negroes; and some – Antony and Lucie among them – he even embraced. It seemed an unusually emotional way to end Meeting, and at the time I was surprised.

But the following day I understood, because that day everything changed.

Tokpa

I am surprised when my master embraces me. I feel a sadness in it, like a farewell. But the Light in the meeting is powerful. It banishes the spells his enemies have laid on the house, and the mistress looks well again.

That night I hear the drumming from the plantation village. It is strong and lively, and I know the people will be dancing. On first-day there is no work, so they dress up, they sing, they dance as they did at home. I go with Miata, Lucie, Reuben and Paul to the village. We join the dancing. There are people here from many places and we make new songs and new dances. When I dance my spirit comes alive in me; I feel free.

Later I meet Miata in the yard. We go into the woodland and lie down together and make love. Miata will be my wife, even though I cannot offer bride-service to her father and have no home for her.

We talk in whispers in our own language.

Miata says, "They are up there on the balcony again – the young ones."

"Kiss and cuddle?"

"Mmm…" She giggles.

"Do you think they do what we do?"

"You mean…?" She touches me.

I pull her closer. "Yes. That's what I mean."

She laughs softly in my ear. "I don't think so. Too many clothes. He can't get in."

"But he'd like to!"

"Oh, yes. They are looking and touching all the time. But they must wait. It's the way with their people. I think they can have no joy in it."

"We have joy," I say, "even here, in this demon-land. Miata?"

"Mmm?"

"One day we'll be free."

"Mmm."

"We'll go home."

"Mmm."

"Go home to our people."

"Our people."

We rock with the rhythm of the words. We've said them before, many times. It's like a song we sing together.

"Miata, when we go home, when we find your father, I will offer him bride-service; I will work for him. You will be my wife, and we will have a celebration in your village."

"I wait for that day. I keep it in my heart."

Sixteen

*O*n second-day morning my master and I went over the books together, looking at the trade we had done at the Exchange in Michael's Town; how many hogsheads of sugar, rum and molasses were to be stowed in the hold of the *Frances*; how much profit he had made.

"And there's more to come," he said, closing the account book. "John and I have some business to settle. Once that's done we'll sail for Philadelphia."

I attached no significance to that remark at the time. But all too soon I came to understand the nature of the business he was referring to. That afternoon, when I was on my way to join him and Kate on the veranda on the cool side of the house, there came a sudden cry – a woman's voice, raised in a wail that shook me to the heart.

The sound came from the kitchen. I raced down

there, and burst in to see Lucie on her knees, her hands raised to John Crosbie, who stood looking awkward and unhappy. Tears were rolling down Lucie's face. Antony stood as if in shock. Patience and a kitchen maid were crying with their arms around each other.

The moment I came into the room Patience broke away, ran to me and threw herself at my feet, lifting her tear-blotched face to mine. "Oh, please, young master," she begged, "don't take us away!"

"What...?" I was bewildered. "Patience, get up, please!"

But she stayed there. "Master says ... we must go ... go in the ship..." She became inarticulate, gulping back tears.

I caught John Crosbie's eye, but he was taken up with trying to calm Lucie, who seemed almost hysterical. Overwhelmed by all this, I backed away, and fled to the upper part of the house. Kate was already with her father on the veranda. I knew they had heard the sounds, for Kate was standing up and looked alarmed, and I guessed he had prevented her from running to the kitchen.

"What's happening?" I demanded. In my turmoil I forgot to address my master in the usual respectful manner. "Patience says we are taking her away, and Lucie is on her knees, crying, and John—"

"Sit down, Josiah," he said – so sternly that I

obeyed and was silent. "Thou should not have gone down there."

Although the wails had subsided, we could still hear sobbing and pleading, mixed with John Crosbie's calm, placatory voice.

"Pay no attention," my master said. "It is not for us to interfere."

"But – what is happening?" I demanded again.

"John has sold the plantation and will return to England within the month – as I told thee he probably would. The new owner has bought the plantation slaves and one or two of the house slaves, but he does not want them all. John needs to sell the others separately. Naturally they are distressed."

"Sell them?" And then I understood. "This is that other business thou spoke of? Thou agreed to buy them?"

"Yes."

"But – I thought thou did not *want* slaves."

"I'm buying them to sell. It relieves John of the burden, and since slaves are scarce in Pennsylvania I can sell them easily there, and make a profit."

"A profit?" I felt sickened. These were *people*. "Who? Which ones?"

He ticked them off on his fingers: "Lucie; her son, Paul; Antony; the nursemaid, Rebecca; and the chambermaid, Patience. Five in all."

I thought of Antony, his look of utter shock, and imagined how bereft and frightened he must feel now.

"How can John sell Antony?" I said. "He is fond of him, I know. He was teaching him…"

"There will be no place for Antony in England," my master said. "It's for the best. I will find them all new masters in Pennsylvania. If they stayed here they would probably end up as plantation slaves, working in the fields. John wanted to avoid that. And he wants Lucie and her son to be sold together. He will be trying to reassure her of that now."

"Dad," Kate said urgently, "thou must not split up Patience and Antony, either. They love each other."

"I will not split up any of them if I can help it. If I can sell them all to one wealthy settler I will be pleased."

I sat down. I felt shaken.

"The Negroes are easily stirred up," my master said, "but it will soon pass. They are bound to be afraid of change. John has been a good master and they are happy here. But he won't stay, so there is nothing else to be done." His manner became brisk. "I went on board the ship when I was in Michael's Town the other day, and saw Richard Grey and checked the wind and tides. We can leave at noon on fourth-day."

The day after tomorrow. It had all been planned. While Kate and I dallied in the garden, our elders were making arrangements to stow slaves among the hogsheads of sugar on board the *Frances*.

Our last two days on the island were busy; and I was glad of it, for the atmosphere in the house was strained – both the Crosbies and the slaves subdued and unhappy, and my master aware of my dismay at the turn of events.

"I hate this business," I told him, when we were private together. "I want no part in it."

I thought he'd be angry, but he merely sighed and said, "Thy compassion does thee credit, Jos. But thou must understand that from both John Crosbie's and the Negroes' point of view this is the lesser of two evils."

"Thou agree it is an evil trade, then?"

"No! I spoke loosely. I meant only the choice between servitude in Pennsylvania or in Barbados." He walked to the window and looked out at the landscape. On this side the view was of trees partially screening the sheds and boiling-house of the manufactory; and, beyond it, fields of sugar cane and row after row of distant figures cutting and binding. "The slave trade is both necessary and lawful. My conscience is clear that I may engage in it as long as I deal fairly with others."

"I did not mean to question thy honour," I said.

"I know that. And thou'rt right to think about these

matters, for we are all answerable before God for our own actions. But as to the business in hand: remember that thou'rt bound apprentice to me and must obey my lawful commands."

"I will," I said. But although I respected my master I was no happier about the trade.

The next day, the two of us went to Michael's Town, to the harbour, and I became once again involved in the process of gauging – assessing by eye and experience how much could be stowed in the hold. But this time it was different: space was needed for five Negroes to sleep below, "in due decency", as my master put it, which meant there must be a screened latrine bucket for the women, and a bowl for washing, and males and females must be separated.

I remembered the slave ship Betty and I had seen from the deck of the *Promise*; remembered the smell that came from it on the wind. The people we were to carry on the *Frances* had all experienced that unimaginable passage across the Atlantic Ocean. They must dread setting foot on a ship again.

"We won't keep them below?" I asked; and was much relieved when he exclaimed, "Of course not! What we have here is space for them to sleep. During the day they may remain on deck as much as they wish, provided they give no trouble. But in any case, we have only one man. Women are generally docile and are always allowed on deck."

Despite this, I noticed that some of the crew had fixed netting around the sides of the ship, above the rail, and guessed that this was to foil any attempt at escape – or suicide.

Having helped make space for the Negroes, I was then set to gauging the remaining capacity, and performed quite well, my master said, given my inexperience. I could see that the addition of five slaves considerably decreased the storage space. It was clear that we could have bought more goods if this sale had not arisen, and I understood why my master was concerned to make maximum profit from the slaves: they were an expensive and troublesome cargo.

I found the whole process disturbing, and said so to Kate when I managed to meet her in the garden on the last evening at the Crosbie house. We walked around among the sweet-scented flowers and English roses, but I was no longer in the mood to idle away our time in the arbour seat by the pool. And as if the weather caught my mood, a wind sprang up and ruffled the surface of the water and made the arbour an uncomfortable place to linger. We both felt low-spirited. Perhaps it was simply that the charm of the house and garden was broken now that its foundation in slavery was revealed. The weight of the coming voyage, with the Negroes we had befriended held captive on board, hung over us.

"It's *wrong,* Kate," I said. "Against the whole spirit of Pennsylvania, surely?"

"But Dad is not like the slave-drivers who beat and shackle Negroes. He is always kind and careful of their welfare."

"Yes – because if he was not, his profit would be less."

"That's unfair!" She looked hurt. "My father does not think only of profit. He wants to help his friend John Crosbie, and he is the best person to do it because he can take the Negroes away from Barbados and the plantations and find them better masters in Pennsylvania."

"Thou'rt blinded by love for him," I said – and immediately regretted my words, for her eyes flashed and she retorted, "I am *not*! He is a good man. Thou'rt wrong, Jos. This is for the best – the best thing he can do."

I put my arms around her. "I'm sorry, Kate – sorry. I know he's a good man. Don't let's quarrel. Only it's hard – the gauging, the nets going up around the ship's sides…"

She was stiff at first, still angry; but then she said, "I hate it, too. I knew it happened, but until now my father has always kept it out of my sight. He never carried slaves on the ship when I was with him."

"And thou didn't *know* the slaves."

"No. I feel now how wrong it is. I've been talking to Patience. She's afraid Dad will separate her and Antony, but I told her he would not do such a thing. I'm sure he will not."

"I must speak to Antony," I said.

We walked back together, and I left her at the door and went around the side of the house to the yard, where Antony was chopping wood. The blows of the axe fell steadily and his gaze was fixed on the job in hand. There had been no tears, no outcry from him.

"Antony…" I said.

"Master…" – he corrected himself – "Josiah…"

His look was sombre. He put down the axe.

"I am sorry," I said. "Sorry thou must leave this place. I didn't know what my master intended. I … I had no idea of it."

"John Crosbie tells me not to be afraid," he said. "He tells me it is good that Friend George takes us away from this island."

"I believe he may be right."

"Josiah, the place thou come from…"

"Pennsylvania."

"No, not there. England. My master says all of you – himself, his wife, Friend George, you – come from England?"

"Yes. England is our home."

"And there are no slaves in England? Some of the

people in the plantation village say when a man sets foot on English soil he is free."

"That may be true," I said. "I believe no Englishman can be a slave." I had a feeling it might be written in law, one of the ancient laws of England, though I had no proof.

He nodded agreement. "I want to go to England. John Crosbie showed me your island on his picture that he says is an image of the world. I know if I step ashore on that island I will be free – free to go home." To my distress I saw that his eyes had filled with tears. "I asked John Crosbie to take me back with him to England," he said. "Me, and Patience, to be his servants. I begged him. I fell on my knees…"

"Antony…" I felt his despair as if it were my own.

"He says he can take none of us with him – that there is no place for us there. But I will find a way. I will become free, and then I will go home."

I knew it could not be that simple. Surely he'd be captured and sent back? It was true, I felt sure, that no one was allowed to keep slaves in England, but who knew what went on in the docks, in the big ports where the ships of the Atlantic trade came in? Slavery was hidden in my country. I'd known almost nothing of it, and yet I realized now that all my life English ships had been taking slaves from Africa to America and sailing home laden with sugar, rum and molasses:

a seemingly innocent cargo.

"Antony," I said, " I don't know how this can be done; I don't know if it's possible. But I will be thy friend; I'll stand by thee. I won't let any harm come to thee or Patience."

It was a rash promise, since I had no power, and he must guess that. But it made a bond between us.

Seventeen

On the day of our departure George Bainbrigg and I were at the harbour early to oversee the lading. My master gave directions to the crew about how the goods should be stowed, while I checked each cask and hogshead and noted its weight and value. Last in were some straw-filled palliasses for the Negroes to sleep on, and cloths to hang up as screens.

I would have enjoyed this work had it not been for my misgivings about transporting the Negroes, for my master allowed me to take charge under his supervision and trusted me to make accurate records, and I was encouraged by his confidence in me.

Our human cargo arrived later, brought by the estate manager in a cart driven by Reuben, who was to be sold later with the plantation. They looked a sorry little group: forlorn and apprehensive – Antony and Patience close together, Lucie holding on to her son as if afraid he could be snatched from her at any moment, and the sad-faced nursemaid, Rebecca. Rebecca had been distraught at the prospect of leaving the children, Kate had said, and begged to be taken to England with the family, but they had refused her; they wanted no reminder of their unhappy Caribbean venture.

We sent the Negroes on board, where Richard Grey and the crew took charge of them. While my master went aboard, I was despatched to the Yates' house near by to fetch Kate, who had been waiting there while our preparations were made.

"How are things on the ship?" she asked, in a low, urgent voice, as soon as we were alone on the street.

"Very well. We are fully laden and will leave within the hour—"

"Thou know that's not what I mean. How are Patience … Lucie…?"

"They all look anxious," I said, "except Paul. He's interested in the ship, running about, asking questions. The crew have taken to him already."

"That's good. Oh, I hope there will be no trouble! I wish *we* could keep Patience. I like her well. But we have Mary, so I suppose there is no need for another girl. And of course she must not be separated from Antony."

Her remarks grated on me somewhat. I felt that her objections to the sale were immediate and personal –

as if keeping Patience would make everything right, whereas it seemed to me that the buying and selling of human beings was wrong in itself. And yet – hadn't *I* made a promise to stand by Antony, who was merely one of thousands?

We arrived at the harbour, and all seemed well on board the *Frances*. Lucie and Rebecca had gone below; Paul was with one of the sailors, learning to tie knots. Antony and Patience leaned on the side, against the netting, talking together in low voices. I noticed that Antony had brought his little drum, fastened to a belt around his waist. The two of them turned round as Kate and I came by, and we exchanged cautious glances. It was going to be difficult, I thought, on a small crowded vessel, to maintain distance between master, crew and cargo.

It was time to go. The mooring ropes were cast off, and the sails filled as the tide took us. Blue Caribbean sea opened between our ship and the dock. Antony and Patience watched it widening, the island seeming to slip away into the distance. But Paul ran to the forward rail and looked out to see the way we were going.

We made good time on our return voyage, allowing the trade winds to take us up the coasts of Virginia and Maryland. We might easily have sold some of our Negroes in those colonies, but my master made no attempt to do so. He had promised John Crosbie he would sell them in New Jersey or Pennsylvania, where they might expect to have a better life and avoid working on a plantation. We anchored for a day or two at Chester on the Delaware, and here he put the word about that he had slaves for sale. In no time at all he had sold Rebecca to a respectable merchant of his acquaintance – a Friend – whose family were in need of a nursemaid. He was well pleased with this transaction.

"I don't want to sell them to dealers if I can avoid it," he told me. "A direct sale is best."

Patience and Lucie embraced Rebecca and talked to her in low, soothing voices, and they all wept together a little when the time came to part. Rebecca looked apprehensive as she was taken away.

Kate drew close to me. "She will soon settle," she said. "I know the family. They will be kind to her."

I hoped she was right.

It was difficult for me to find place or time to talk to Antony. I was aware that my master preferred to keep distance between us and the Negroes so that selling them would be less distressing. But there were moments; and that evening, when we were at anchor in Chester, was one of them. I met Antony on the lower deck and told him, "We will soon be in Philadelphia."

He had a brooding look about him, no doubt caused by the sight of Rebecca being led away.

"Are there other slaves there?" he asked.

"I don't know. I haven't seen any, but they say some of the big landowners in the colony have slaves."

"In Barbados," he said, "the slaves hold markets. If they have a good master they can grow their own food and have some left over to sell. So we used to mingle and talk; make friends; maybe ask about lost families – brothers and sisters; people would get news if they were lucky."

"Did thou ever hear news of thy family?"

"No. But there are many slaves, many islands in the Caribbean. I always had hope…"

He looked at me and I saw his fear of the unknown and his powerlessness. I wanted to reassure him that all would be well – but how could I know that? I could only offer Christian platitudes, and so I was silent.

The next day we had several enquiries about Lucie and Paul. Lucie was a cook and housekeeper and therefore of considerable value; and her son was not necessarily a disadvantage since he was old enough to work. I began to realize how easy it might be to sell our people here in New Jersey and Pennsylvania.

Lucie and Paul went to a gentleman landowner who was en route to his estate near Trenton. Parting with them, especially with the child, was hard. The crewman who had been teaching Paul to tie knots gave him a toy wooden dog he'd been whittling away at during the last few days. The Negroes made their farewells to one another below deck, but we all heard their lamentations.

It was my job to write up the accounts. This focused my mind on the iniquity of what we were doing. Mother and child were sold together, and might well be going to a good place; but they were slaves, and what was to stop their new master, at some later time, selling Paul away from his mother, if it suited him? Nothing can justify this business, I thought.

We left Chester, and arrived at last at Philadelphia. My master and Richard Grey congratulated each other on a successful trading voyage – one, moreover, achieved with no trouble from the Negroes, for Patience and Antony had remained tractable, and there had been no need to confine Antony below decks.

"And it has been an enlarging experience for Kate, and even more so for Josiah," my master said, turning to include me. "Thou hast done well, lad; been a great help to me and shown thyself willing and able and interested in everything. I did not expect thou would be so directly involved in the sale of slaves on thy first voyage; but it is all experience, and the sales in Chester turned out well."

I thanked him for his praise. And it was true, I thought: this voyage was not an experience I would have missed, for it had given me much to think about. I felt that I had entered the Garden of Eden and found the serpent coiled at its heart.

Eighteen

"Should I add, *'To be sold together'*?" I asked.

My master read through the notice. "No. No restrictions. Buyers must be free to negotiate. Thy notices are well drawn, Jos. I'm pleased with thee. It's a useful skill."

I felt far less happy about the notice than he did. Last night, on board the *Frances*, I had been writing up my journal. I wrote at length about my concerns, and how I had never imagined, when I left London to be part of a better future in this city of brotherly love, that I would be involved in the buying and selling of human beings.

It surprised me that I appeared to be alone in my objections. Even Kate took the situation for granted, as being normal – though the more we talked together I realized that she was beginning to feel, as I did, that for Friends to own slaves was wrong in itself. But she loved her father, and would not believe ill of him. I too liked him well, but I believed I saw more clearly.

"This trade is evil through and through," I told her, "and therefore anyone who takes part in it is tainted by it. Can't thou see that?"

"Yes ... but there will always be slaves, so isn't it better that they should go to Friends rather than those who might abuse them? It is how we behave towards our servants that is important. Friends treat them well and encourage the light within them."

"Thou'rt simply parroting what thy father says—"

"No! It's true!"

"It's what thou hast been taught to believe – not what thou hast experienced thyself."

She looked troubled. I knew I was forcing her to

think in ways that were unsettling for her, but I persisted in it, for I needed her to understand. I needed her to agree with me, to be on my side.

My mother had been waiting on the quay when we arrived at Philadelphia, word having come to her that the *Frances* had been sighted. I waved, and she waved back eagerly, with a little girlish bounce of delight; I knew the sight of me, safely home, must be a huge relief to her.

"Go greet thy mother," George Bainbrigg said, with a smile, as we clambered ashore, the mud clinging to our shoes.

My mother hugged me hard. "Thou'rt well, son?"

"Yes. And I'll come soon, and see you all – on seventh-day, if not before."

"And tell us thy adventures?"

"Of course."

She moved away, content with that.

Now the ship had to be unloaded, the crates and hogsheads brought off in boats and checked against the bills of lading. And there were Antony and Patience to be attended to. They came ashore last and stood on the quay, wide-eyed, close together, glancing all around, and shivering – for although it was summer and the sunshine was bright, the air struck cool after the heat of the Caribbean.

"What will we do with them now?" I asked my master.

"We must find somewhere to put them while they await sale. They need to be watched at all times and restrained if necessary." He sighed. "I never know how best to accommodate slaves. They are a trouble to deal in. The sooner they are sold the better. But for now Antony can help move the goods into the counting house. I'll take charge of him. Thou can take the wench up to the house with Kate and ask Izzie to find her some work to do and somewhere to sleep – there's a room upstairs that can be locked. I doubt she'll give any trouble; she seems a good, quiet girl. Come back to the counting house when thou'rt done."

"Right."

Antony and Patience immediately appeared anxious as we came to separate them, and clung to each other. But my master had no time for any nonsense, as he called it. He directed Antony towards Zachary and the crates and barrels that the seamen had unloaded onto the quay.

"Thou must come to the house," Kate told Patience. "Don't be afraid."

And so Patience walked up Walnut Street between the two of us, holding herself proudly, even though we knew she must feel frightened and out of place in this unfamiliar country where there were no other slaves to be seen, no one like her at all.

Mary answered the door, and I saw her eyes widen at the sight of Patience.

"Oh!" she exclaimed – and seemed unsure whether or not to allow us all in. "Isobel! Here's Kate, and Josiah, and a Caribee wench with them!"

Isobel appeared, drying her hands on a cloth. I saw that she had the measure of the situation and was not pleased.

"Isobel," said Kate – and I was impressed by her authoritative manner – "my father has with him two Negroes, bought from John Crosbie of Barbados. They must stay here until they are sold. This is Patience. She will need one of the top floor rooms."

"I'll see to it," said Isobel. "Mary, fetch beer! And some meat and pickle. Does the girl drink beer?"

"Yes, I thank thee," Patience murmured, lowering her eyes.

I saw Isobel's surprise at this direct response. "And there's another, thou say?" she asked.

"A man," I said, "Antony" – and caught Patience's bright glance on me at the mention of his name. "I don't know where he is to be housed."

"In the counting house, I'd guess," said Isobel, evidently in some relief.

I took a jug of beer and a basket of bread and cold meat back with me to the counting house, leaving the women to deal with Patience.

Antony was at work with Zachary, manoeuvring hogsheads of sugar into position at the back of the building.

"He's a good worker," my master said. "Some of these Negroes can be sullen and deliberately slow. But John always treated his people fairly – that makes a difference."

He called a break, and I poured beer into tankards.

My master took a swift draught of beer and went off to settle accounts with Richard Grey and the crew, leaving me in charge.

I helped Antony roll one of the barrels of rum into place.

"Where is Patience?" he asked me in a low voice.

"At my master's house. Up the street."

I spoke shortly, for Antony now belonged to George Bainbrigg and I had been left in charge of him and felt a need to establish my authority.

When my master came back he left the other two at work and called me upstairs, where he unlocked one of the small storerooms – a closet rather than a room, except that it had a tiny high window covered by a grating. Inside were a few pallets stacked against the wall, and a large chest which he opened to reveal a stock of well-worn blankets and clothes.

"Thou can make this space ready for Antony," he said. "Put down a pallet and some blankets, and fetch a bucket from the yard – that'll serve as a chamber pot. I hope he won't be here long. With luck I'll sell the two of them together to one of the settlers from upcountry."

I too hoped it would not be long. The room was like a cell, dismal and dark, and my master told me that Antony was to be locked in there overnight and watched at all times during the day.

"They get nervous when they're to be sold," he said. "There's no knowing what they might do. He could make a run for it, or drown or hang himself. So keep him in your sights."

I thought it unlikely that Antony would be in such despair while Patience was close by, but I did as I was told. It was that afternoon that I drafted the sale notices. I despised myself for doing it, but could see no way to avoid the task. In the evening, when we had closed for business, I was obliged to lock Antony into the little room without a candle (for my master had a great fear of fire destroying the counting house). I felt sorry for Antony, but did not know what to say, for after all he was a slave and might have to endure much worse when my master sold him on. I guessed that many slaves slept in barns and outhouses all year round.

"There is food for thee here," I told him, setting down a trencher and a tankard of beer. "I'll come early in the morning to open up. And I'll bring thee word of Patience."

"I thank thee." But he looked dejected. It occurred to me that he might never have slept alone before.

"Eat now," I said, "out here, where we have light. I'll sit with thee." My master was in his office, working; he would not mind, I knew.

We sat on the top step of the stairs. Antony wanted to share the bread and meat, and I took a little to please him, though I explained that I'd be eating later.

"At home, in the forest," he said, "my name was Tokpa. Then John Crosbie bought me and named me Antony. Maybe soon I will have another name. But Tokpa is my true name."

"Tokpa," I said, trying it out. I felt that a gift had been given me, but one I knew I must keep secret. "And Patience?" I asked. "What is her true name?"

"Her name is Miata. Her father is kinsman to a chief and she is his eldest daughter. The bride-price for such a girl is high. I could not have paid it, even with the help of my family. Instead, I would have offered bride-service. Her father would accept my labour in return for his daughter."

I thought about this. The idea of buying a wife seemed to me strange – and demeaning to the girl. And yet Tokpa seemed to hold Miata in high honour. A thought that had been at the back of my mind for a while came more clearly to me, and I wondered if Kate and I would marry – whether she'd wish it, as I felt I would. It would suit both our families very well, I realized. Everyone would be pleased. The route from apprentice to son-in-law was so common it was almost to be expected if the young people were of the right age and inclination. But not yet. I was still an apprentice; I could not marry yet, and did not feel ready to do so.

Unlike Tokpa.

"Could thou and Miata have a Friends' wedding?" I asked. "Would John Crosbie have allowed it?"

"I don't know. We didn't ask. We would not have wanted to be married in that house. It had bad magic in it. And Friends' weddings are not joyful. We want to go home, to our people, and be married among them."

"What *should* thy wedding be like?" I asked.

He gazed out into the sales area, as if he were seeing the event. "It will be celebrated in her village. Miata will be waiting for me in a headdress of beads and white cowrie shells that shake and shine around her face. The women and men will sing and dance, and the little children will copy them; and we will laugh, and talk, and the elders will advise us about married life. We will eat goat and chicken, and rice with pepper sauce, and beans, and slices of mango…" He paused. "One day this will happen. We will go home. We will be free. And Miata will be my wife."

My master called up from the outer office, "Jos! Art thou ready to leave?"

Antony and I looked at each other, then rose together; and he did not resist when I locked him into the tiny room. I took the keys and went downstairs.

Nineteen

*T*he following morning I got up, as always, before my master, took the keys from their box on the parlour wall, and went to open up the counting house. Once there, I ran upstairs and freed Antony from the storeroom. He was awake; I saw the whites of his eyes flash in the gloom.

"Help me fetch the kindling and lay the fire," I said. "That's my first job in the mornings. And then we'll eat. I've brought beer and bread for us both."

As he rose I added, "Patience – Miata – is well cared for at the house. Kate says she'll try and bring her here later so that thou can speak to her."

I did not tell him that my task that morning, after my usual chores, would be to make two fair copies of the sale notices I had drafted the day before. These were to be displayed outside the counting house and at the Society of Traders' hall, in the hope of generating a quick response.

This, and the coming and going of customers who had seen the *Frances* arrive and came to see what goods were for sale, took up all my time. I had thought I might be given permission to go home that evening and see my family, but my master kept me busy and did not mention it; and in a way I was glad, for my mind was so full of conflicting thoughts and ideas to be talked over with Betty and my parents that I knew an hour in the evening would not suffice.

My master arrived, and went into his office, and I started work on the notices. Halfway through the morning Kate appeared. Instead of Mary she had brought Patience with her to carry the jug of beer. As soon as she saw Antony, Patience ran to his arms and they began talking together in soft, urgent tones in their own language.

I saw that they made George Bainbrigg uneasy. "Kate," he said, "take Patience back to the house. And don't bring her again unless I ask thee."

Later that day, when I had finished the notices, he took one of them and went out to meet other traders and spread the word that he had slaves for sale as well as sugar and rum.

Almost immediately we had enquiries. A trader called the next morning, and my master sent me up to the house to fetch Patience so that she and Antony were available for viewing together.

There was a steady flow of customers throughout the morning for the sugar and rum we had brought back from Barbados, and I was left to deal with these and other routine sales while George Bainbrigg showed Patience and Antony to prospective buyers and answered questions.

In the afternoon, when Patience was back at the house, he called me to him. "Jos, I want thee to draw up bills of sale for Antony and Patience. Come into the office and I'll give thee the names and figures."

At once I felt breathless with anxiety.

"It is all settled, then?" I tried to sound business-like, but he must have heard the tremor in my voice, for his glance at me was sympathetic.

"Yes. As I thought, there is a need in Pennsylvania for Negro labour. It will be a growing need, I reckon, as the colony develops. I had no trouble finding buyers, and both will pay in coin, which is excellent."

"Both?" I felt a sinking in my stomach. "There are two? They are to be sold separately?"

"Yes. Yes, I know, Jos, it's not what thou and Kate hoped. But it was unavoidable. I found a buyer for Patience straight away who agreed to my price. I tried hard to interest him in Antony – told him the two were attached and would work well together and probably breed – but he wanted only the girl, as a house servant for his wife; said he had bonded labourers for the land. He has a plot eight miles or so from town, west of the Schuylkill, near Darby Creek." He showed me where on the map of Pennsylvania on the wall.

"But – Antony?" I said. The blood beat in my ears.

"He is to be sold to a settler on one of the plots north of the city."

"This man wouldn't take Patience?"

"I didn't ask. By that time I'd already agreed the sale with the other."

"Couldn't you tell him you'd changed your mind?"

He gave me a sharp look. "I'm a Friend, Josiah. My word is my bond."

"But" – I stared at the map – "they'll be far apart, and across rough country! They may never see each other again."

"I doubt they will. It's a pity, but it can't be helped. Friends don't haggle, as thou know. I asked a fixed price, and the man offered it."

"I should have put '*To be sold together*' on the notices!" I said. I felt furious, both with him and with myself.

"Thou did as I told thee." His voice was stern. "Enough of this, Jos. It does thee credit that thou care about the Negroes, but the sales are agreed, at a good price, and after tomorrow we shall not be troubled with this matter any longer. Now, go and draw up those invoices. The girl's buyer will be here within the hour."

So soon! How could I prevent this? There seemed no way.

I took the note he'd written for me.

"When is Antony's buyer coming for him?" I asked.

"Tomorrow morning."

I went to my desk and sharpened a quill and looked at the details of the sales. Patience's buyer was John Outram of Darby Creek, and her price was thirty pounds; Antony's was Isaac Shore, who would pay forty-two for him. Sick at heart, I wrote out the invoices, making two copies of each one so that my master had a record.

I could hear Antony and Zachary talking as they packed goods in the storage area. If Antony had guessed he was sold, he clearly knew nothing for certain.

But there was no suppressing such news, once out. Kate appeared suddenly in the outer office, saw my door open and hurried to me, demanding, "Is it done? Are they sold? Patience says several merchants came…"

She must have seen from my face that something was amiss. "Jos? What's happened?"

"Thou had best ask thy father," I said.

She stared at me, alarmed.

"Ask him, Kate." I nodded towards the closed connecting door between the two offices. If anyone could move him, I thought, it would be Kate.

She knocked, and went in at his call.

I heard their voices, then a cry from Kate. My fingers tightened on the quill. Kate's voice rose, angry and tearful; her father's, soothing at first, became increasingly exasperated.

"But thou *promised*!" I heard her say.

"I promised nothing."

There came the sound of his other door opening – the one that led directly into the outer office. He was ushering her out.

"Back to the house now, Kate. No – don't go to Josiah! Go straight home. Say nothing of this to Patience – it will only frighten the girl – but tell Izzie to have her ready to bring here when I send for her."

"Dad, thou can't do this!"

As she passed my open door I saw Kate wiping tears from her face. She looked angry as well as distressed. We exchanged a quick glance. "Later!" I mouthed – and she nodded.

"Go *now*, Kate!" her father called. "And don't come again. Thou hast no business here."

She left. But then Antony appeared, and I knew he must have caught enough of the argument to cause him alarm. George Bainbrigg came out, and Antony confronted him. He stood taut, fists clenched. I sprang up and went to stand beside my master, ready to defend him if necessary.

Antony stared at us. "Master? Josiah? What's happening?"

"Antony, thou must be locked up now," George Bainbrigg said.

"No!"

"Jos! Zach! Hold him!"

"No!" He was bigger than any of us, and desperate. I seized one arm while Zachary took the other, but I doubted if even the three of us could restrain him.

"Where is Patience?" he demanded. "Is she hurt? Why was Kate crying?"

"Patience is safe in the house," I said. "Don't fear — "

"You sold her? They come for her?"

We tried to manhandle him towards the stairs, but he fought us all the way, knocking me, with a great blow, against the balustrade. Zachary, though the eldest, was strong and handy, and got him into an arm lock. He then produced a short length of rope. My master nodded, and the two of them bound Antony's wrists behind his back. Once his arms were immobilized we were able to push him up the stairs.

"Thou had best go quietly, lad," my master told him. "The wench is safe at the house, and thou will not be harmed here. The two of you have been sold and will leave soon."

Antony still struggled. "Together? We go *together*?" he shouted, as we wrestled at the door of the room. Zachary forced him inside.

We closed the door on him and my master locked it. The door shook as Antony hurled himself against it, over and over again.

I hated myself at that moment. How could I have become part of this, when I'd called myself his friend?

My master sighed. "Well done, men. I wish Kate had not come and stirred things up. Did he hurt thee, Jos?"

"No," I said, though I could feel a painful bruising in my ribs starting to make itself felt.

It was no more than I deserved, I thought.

And now I had more foul work to do. John Outram arrived to collect and pay for his purchase, and my master sent me to the house to fetch Patience. She came willingly enough, since she knew Antony was there, though I could see that she was afraid. And Kate made things harder by appearing with a tear-blotched face and throwing her arms around Patience in farewell, which set them both off crying again. I got Patience away before Kate could tell her the truth, and to try and cheer her I said, "Patience, these people are Friends, I believe; settlers with a new home a few miles downriver. Thou needn't fear field work. Thou'll be a maidservant, same as before…"

I was glad it took only a few moments to walk to the counting house. By the time she asked me about Antony we were there, and my master came forward with John Outram and his manservant.

John Outram was a powerfully-built man with a ruddy, all-weather tan. He greeted Patience with brusque kindness and told her, "Come now, wench. We have a boat waiting at the quay."

Instantly, Patience understood. She looked around, wild-eyed. "Antony?" she said. Then louder, with panic in her voice, "Antony!"

A banging began in the locked room upstairs.

"Now, Patience," my master said. "John Outram will take thee—"

"Antony!" Patience screamed. She made to break away from us, but John Outram and his servant seized and held her. Upstairs, Antony yelled to be let out. He beat on the door. "Miata!"

"Tokpa!" Patience wailed, and the two of them cried out to each other in their own language; a great stream of it poured from them, frantic, despairing. I don't know what promises and endearments they made, but the sound tore at my heart.

"Oh, let them at least see each other once more!" I exclaimed.

But the two men had already forced Patience to the main entrance. She clung to the door with both hands, screaming, and had to be prised off; I heard her struggling and crying all the way along the street. Meanwhile, upstairs, Antony hurled himself against the door of his prison with a persistent, hopeless banging.

I was left trembling with shock.

My master let out a long sigh. "Oh, that was a bad business! I'm sorry thou had to be involved in it, Jos." Overhead, the thumps and shouts continued. "But they'll get over it; they'll settle down in no time. And Patience is a good girl. She'll do well with the Outrams."

I nodded – too full of emotion to reply. Antony and Patience loved each other. They were both alone now, in a strange land, each of them separated from the only person who spoke their language and knew their ways and held a similar store of memories from childhood. They would not soon settle down – and I had helped to separate them.

For the rest of that day I asked myself, over and over: Could I have prevented this? Should I have acted differently, refused to co-operate? I did not think I could have stopped the sale. But by taking part I had betrayed Antony and Patience and proved myself one of the slavers.

Twenty

As usual my master left me to sweep the floors and lock up. Antony was still locked in the storeroom. He had stopped banging his shoulders against the door, but he was not silent. I could hear a low, faint, monotonous singing that carried a weight of sorrow in it.

My master had told me not to speak to Antony, to let him be; but as soon as he was gone I put down my broom and hurried upstairs to the storeroom door.

The singing continued, low and insistent.

"Tokpa," I said.

The sound stopped.

"Tokpa, I'm sorry—"

"I am Antony to thee."

His words cut me to the heart. He had entrusted me with his name because he thought I was his friend. Now he withdrew it.

My voice broke as I said, "Antony, I'm sorry. I could not prevent this. Patience has gone—"

"I'll follow her!" he shouted. "They take her from me but I'll find her! I'll escape. I won't let them catch me. I'll die first!"

"Antony, listen. Don't despair. I'll help thee. I don't know how, but—"

"Let me out!" The door shook as he hurled himself against it. "Let me out! Let me out! Let me out!"

His fury shocked and terrified me. I could not think what to do or say – and it was with a deep sense of my own wrongdoing that I left him banging and shouting and went back to the house.

Our evening meal began with silence, as always; but this silence was loud with unspoken thoughts. My master appeared exhausted and out of temper. Kate's eyes were red. She looked resentful, and I guessed she had been pleading with her father again, to no avail. He was a fond parent and she was not accustomed to being thwarted. We exchanged quick, sympathetic glances, and I longed to be alone with her so that we could talk.

The meal that followed was difficult. I could scarcely eat; I felt it would choke me. I watched Kate push a piece of meat around on her plate. When her father urged her to eat she said she was not hungry;

and then her lips trembled and she asked to be excused, saying she felt unwell, and went, I supposed, to her bedchamber. Hob, aware that something was wrong, whined and turned anxious eyes on us.

When, mercifully, supper was at last over, I asked my master if I should take food and drink to Antony as I had done the night before.

"No," he said. "He can wait till morning – it won't hurt him. Best not to open that door. He might even attack thee and escape."

To my shame I felt almost relieved. I dreaded encountering Antony again in his distraught condition. Even so, I argued on his behalf. "His wrists are bound."

"He's a strong man, and desperate."

"So we'll leave him bound all night?"

He lost patience then. "Yes! We'll leave him."

I went to my room on the top floor and paced about, wrestling with my sense of guilt and powerlessness. I wanted to help Antony. I *had* to help him. But what could I do? My master had made it clear that he would not discuss the matter further. No doubt he felt some guilt too, and that accounted for his distaste for the trade in what the merchants called "live cargo". But he would not go back on his word; I could expect no change of heart from him.

I walked to the window, which faced west. Golden

light was flooding into the room, laying a bright chequered pattern of small panes on the boards. We were close to midsummer; it would not be dark for hours yet. I looked out and tried to draw comfort from the freshness of the trees, the light, the songs of birds, but all I could think of was Patience, arriving by boat at the plot near Darby Creek, far from Antony and any other of her race; and of Antony, locked in that storeroom with no sight of this golden evening, forced to lap water like a dog because his wrists were bound, and no doubt feeling less than a man because he had not been able to prevent his girl from being taken away.

A light tap at my door broke into these thoughts. Mary, I guessed, sent by Isobel on some domestic task.

I opened the door – and Kate stepped into the room. "Kate!"

"Ssh!" She closed the door softly behind her. "No one must know I'm here."

Alarm at our situation – what if her father found out? – mingled with joy and relief as I gathered her into my arms. Her fair hair hung loose on her shoulders, and as she leaned against me I realized that she wore no stays. She must have been ready for bed, in her shift, and had simply flung her gown over it and run upstairs to me, barefoot and without a cap.

We clung together and kissed each other and I tasted tears on her face.

"Don't cry," I said. "Don't cry, love" – though I was crying too.

I could scarcely believe I had Kate like this in my bedchamber. It was what I'd often imagined and desired but...

"Kate," I whispered, kissing her face, her neck, "thou should not be here. Thy father – I don't know what he'd do if he caught us."

"How else could I meet thee?" she asked, drawing me away from the door, so that our whispering was not overheard. She sniffed and wiped her eyes. "Dad or Izzie is always around, and I had to talk to thee. Jos, this awful thing... Antony and Patience... Dad won't listen..."

"I did wrong. I should have refused —"

"Thou couldn't!"

"But Antony believes I'm his enemy now – and who can blame him? I've been thinking of him, trapped there. And Patience – oh, if thou had seen how she screamed and struggled!"

"Patience is with child," she said.

I drew back, and stared at her. "She told thee?"

"Yes. And I told my father" – her voice broke – "and it still did not move him. I said they should be together, that if I was with child I'd rather die

than be separated from – from my sweetheart..."
She looked down, blushing. "But he said I should
not even be thinking about such matters, that it was
unseemly in a young girl; and I said it was unseemly
for a man and a father to tear a young girl away from
her sweetheart and sell her into slavery... Oh, Jos,
we had such a big argument, and he was so angry,
and no good has come of it. He has forbidden me to
interfere in his business affairs. Jos, what can we do
to help them?"

My heart began to pound. I knew what I must do.

I realized that I had known all along, but had
pushed the thought to the back of my mind. But
Antony himself had told me. "Let me out!" he had
cried. "I'll follow her!"

"I must release him," I said. "Unlock the door. Set
him free."

She stared at me, wide-eyed, frightened. "Oh, Jos,
thou can't! My father will be furious with thee."

"Dost thou have a better idea?"

She shook her head. "Only ... to plead with my
father ... beg him to buy her back... But I've already
tried that, and he won't do it. I thought of asking the
meeting for help, but –"

"The meeting would not come between him and his
legitimate trade. And there is no *time*!" I said.

I felt fired up now, eager to act, and as I spoke

I saw the light leap in her eyes and knew she had caught my urgency.

"When wilt thou do it?" she asked.

"When it gets dark – when the household are all a-bed. I'll take him up beyond the Kites' place, towards the Schuylkill. If he wants to find Patience he'll need to cross that river and travel overland. But it's only eight or nine miles. That'll be safer than going to the waterfront here. He'd never get a boat. They'd know he was a slave."

I was thinking as I talked. Antony would need to stay hidden. He was black – recognizable. The hue and cry would begin early tomorrow morning. He'd do best to lie low for a while...

Kate tightened her arms around me. "I'll come with thee," she said.

"What? No! That won't help."

"I want to come. I want to be part of this. Then my father must blame both of us, not just thee."

"The more people, the slower we'll be, the more dangerous for Antony," I said.

She saw the sense of that, yet she still resisted me a while. I loved this recklessness in her. It surprised me, for I'd thought her strong-willed but sensible. But it seemed I must be the one to use common sense, and I would not risk putting her in danger, or being accused of inciting her to run around with me in the woods at night.

"Thou can speak in my defence when I get back,"
I said. "I'll need an advocate."

I hugged her close, aware of the enormity of what I
proposed to do. I was George Bainbrigg's apprentice,
entrusted with the keys to his counting house and the
protection of his property. I would be breaking that
trust, and yet I felt sure I was justified.

"Kate," I said, "I love thee."

"I love thee too, Jos – and will do, whatever comes
of this."

"Will thou marry me, when we're of age?"

"Oh, yes! Yes, I will."

We kissed, and clung together, and kissed some
more. I held her hard against me, felt the beating of
her heart.

A door opened and closed near by – Isobel's. We
both tensed.

"I must go." Kate was trembling.

We kissed again, this time in farewell. I felt myself
burning up with love and desire and fear of what was
to come.

"I'll watch for thee coming back," she said.

I opened the door a crack; we listened; no sound
came from the landing below. Kate slipped out, and
ran on silent feet downstairs.

The sun had set and my room was now in partial

shadow. I sat on the bed and tried to suppress thoughts of Kate and our declarations of love and the feel of her unbound hair and her soft curves. I needed to think clearly about what I must do.

The keys were in their box on the parlour wall, where I had replaced them after locking up the offices and the outer door of the counting house. All the keys were there, including the one that would open Antony's prison. I knew the name of Patience's buyer. I knew approximately where he lived. It seemed to me that I should go with Antony, help him find Outram's place. But I saw at once that I could not. I had to be back by morning to confess to my master. I could not leave Kate to take the blame. Would Antony understand a map, I wondered, if I drew one? I was unsure. But he would know what I meant by "west"; I could set him on his way.

I didn't think about how he would stay hidden or evade capture, or what he would do when he found Patience. I only knew I must give him that chance.

I took out my Bible and read from it awhile. Then I sat and waited on the inward light as the light in my room faded and the house slowly fell quiet.

Twenty-one

He heard the key rattle in the lock and was waiting for me. The first blow from his head caught me off guard and I staggered against the door. The next hit the side of my face. It was dark. I could see only the vague shape of him.

"Antony – Tokpa – wait… I've come to help thee."

I grabbed him by the upper arms, tried to push him off. His wrists were tied; surely I could overpower him? My head was ringing. He kicked me, then slammed forward again with his shoulder.

"I'll let thee out!" I shouted. "I'll untie thee!"

He drew back, breathing heavily. He would do anything to break free. But now he was uncertain whether to trust me.

"I have my master's keys," I said. I could taste blood; my lip was split and swelling. "Thou can escape now – if thou wish it."

"Escape?"

"There will be punishment if thou'rt caught. I can't protect thee from that. But if thou'll risk it – if thou want to find Patience…"

"I will find her."

"Then I'll show thee the way. Let me untie thy wrists."

I heard him turn around. The darkness hindered me and I fumbled with the knots, but at last the rope fell to the floor. I kicked it away.

He turned to face me, rubbing his wrists. "I hurt thee. I am sorry."

"It's nothing," I said, though I wondered how I would look to my master in the morning.

But morning and its retribution were a long way off.

"Come," I said. "Let's go, while we have the dark."

Jokpa

This forest is strange to me; it's not like the forest near my home, where the ancestors live. There are spirits here. I hear them and smell them. I don't know if they are friendly.

Jos says we must trust in the Light. But the forest is dark; the moon is wasting and the stars have hidden their faces.

At first I was afraid and fought Jos when he came to fetch me. With my hands still tied I kicked and butted him and almost knocked him down. I thought I was about to be sold. Jos said no, he was my friend; he had always been my friend; he had come to help me escape. I knew he too was afraid: I could smell his sweat and hear his quick breathing. He untied me. He gave me bread and meat. Then he led me out of that bad place where I'd heard Miata cry to me for help — cry that she carried my child in her belly — out into the cold night and along the silent streets, past the dark huts of his people, into this forest.

To Jos, all forests are strange. He stumbles, snaps twigs,

and is scratched by thorns. Night birds utter cries of alarm as we pass.

I put a hand on his arm. "Wait." When we wait, the darkness lightens, and we begin to see. "Now step," I say. "Feel first with thy foot. Step lightly."

We reach a sheltered place near a stream. I hear its voice as it runs over stones.

Jos says, "There are fish here; I've seen them in the daytime."

He tells me I should hide in these woods until they stop searching for me, then find a way to cross the river. He gives me a piece of paper with marks and pictures on it. He says it is a map he has drawn for me. In the faint light his finger makes a journey across the map. He tells me what the marks mean. He says with this map I can find Miata.

I say to him, "Jos, thou'rt my brother." We embrace each other, and he asks God to take care of me. Then he leaves. For a while I hear him, noisy, breaking branches; then I am alone.

There is thick undergrowth here. I crawl beneath it and shelter till sunrise wakes me. The morning forest fills with the voices of birds. I walk to the stream, strip naked and bathe. I wash away the smell of the ship, the prison room, my own fear.

I look at the thing called a map. I make a little bag of bark pinned with thorns. I fold the map small, small, and put it inside. Then I make a plaited cord of grass and hang the bag around my neck. This bag will protect me and take me to Miata.

I shall wait here, as Jos told me. I'll lie low, make a hide of leaves and branches, catch fish, find grubs and leaves to eat. But first, I will make an offering to the spirits of this place.

Twenty-two

At first, as I walked back through the dark woods along a dimly discernible track, with the wind in the trees and the rustlings and squeakings and strange animal cries of the forest all around me, I felt elated, full of a sense of mission and success, of joy that my friendship with Antony was restored, that I had set him free as far as I was able.

Of course I knew he was not safe; and I realized his pursuers would know where he was likely to be going. It had been a mad thing to do, looked at from the point of view of common sense, and likely to lead him into danger. But he knew that. He would dare anything to be free.

It was only as I came onto the road that led towards the inhabited streets near the waterfront, into the world of counting houses and commerce, that I began to think how I would explain myself to George

Bainbrigg and what might come of my actions.

I would tell him straight out, I decided. He must not be the one to find Antony gone, leaving me to confess and apologize afterwards.

The thought of telling him was daunting. And yet he knew my feelings and must surely be able to see what was so clear to me. I remembered untying the rope that bound Antony's wrists and touching, as I did so, the calloused skin and hard ridges caused by the shackles he had worn on the slave ship. It could not be right, I thought, for any man to be confined in that way – and surely my master must acknowledge that? I believed he knew it already in his heart.

When I returned to the house it was still night. I unlocked the kitchen door and went in. Hob rose from his bed in the lobby with a small pleased woof of recognition. He padded towards me, and his wagging tail thumped my leg.

"Good dog, Hob," I whispered. "Quiet, now."

I took off my shoes and crept into the parlour and replaced the keys, then made my way to the stairs. These were lit by moonlight from the landing window. I climbed up, past the first-floor landing, around the next bend – and there was Kate, curled up where the turning stairs widened against the wall, wrapped in a blanket, asleep. She must have been determined to be here when I returned but had fallen asleep on the watch. I felt great tenderness for her as I looked at her small bare feet and the way she slept with her head propped awkwardly against the wall.

I knelt beside her. "Kate…"

She woke with a gasp, and I put my arms around her and hushed her. "It's done. He is safe – for now."

"Oh!" She sat up, pulling the blanket close. Her hair hung in loose curls over her shoulders and I felt it brushing my hands. "Jos – thy face! What happened?"

"Nothing. Don't fear."

"But—"

"Go back to bed," I whispered. "We mustn't be caught here."

We stood up and kissed – cautiously, because my lip was painful. Then she slipped away while I hastened upstairs.

In the safety of my room I looked out of the window and tried to gauge what time of night it was. I thought dawn could not be far off. I wanted nothing more than to lie down on the bed and close my eyes, but I had a fear of falling into a deep sleep and not hearing the sounds of morning in the household. I knew I must be at the counting house as usual when my master arrived, ready to face him.

I opened my Bible, but the small print danced before my tired eyes. And when I closed them and tried to wait on the light my head drooped, and several times I slept and jerked awake. It was a relief, at last, to hear the first fragments of birdsong and to see the furniture in my room become slowly visible in the grey early morning light.

I waited till I heard Isobel stirring in the next room, then stood up and poured water from the jug into my washbowl. My face in the mirror showed a blackening bruise and my swollen lip was going to make it difficult to speak clearly. I washed myself, brushed dirt and bits of leaf from my hair and outer clothing, and put on clean linen. At first I yawned hugely, over and over again, and struggled to suppress it. But once I was ready to go downstairs I grew tense in anticipation of the trouble I would soon be in, and all tiredness vanished, leaving me sharp and alert.

Isobel and Mary were in the kitchen.

"Thou'rt early," Isobel said. Then she saw my face. "What…?"

I invented an accident in the yard, going out to the privy in the dark. I could see she did not know whether to believe me, but she merely asked, "Will thou have some pottage?"

"Yes, please." I tried to smile and appear normal.

"Thou'll be hungry. Scarce had owt to eat last night, thou and Kate."

I ignored this remark, with its implicit invitation

to reveal more, and merely said, "Excellent pottage, Isobel," and made sure to eat it all.

I swept the counting house thoroughly that morning, and made sure my master's desk was ready – the inkwell filled, paper, sand and quills to hand. I tidied and dusted the sales area and put everything in good order. Upstairs I cleared away the evidence of Antony's occupation, folded the blankets and stood the pallet back against the wall. Down below I heard someone come in; but it was only Zachary. I went down and greeted him, repeated my story about the privy, then sat at my desk and made up the double entries in the books for yesterday's sales, including that of Patience to John Outram. But as I wrote, my hand trembled and I felt a fluttering in my stomach.

George Bainbrigg soon came in. I heard him go into his office, calling out good morning to me through the connecting door. He sounded in good humour, as if he had put behind him the unease that had hung over us all at supper last night.

"The buyer – Isaac Shore – could be here soon," he said, as he came into my office. "Hast thou brought food and beer for Antony? We should give him something to eat, before—"

He stopped short at the sight of my face.

A wave of fear flooded me. "Antony is not here," I said.

"Not here…?" His eyes opened wide in alarm. "He's escaped? He attacked thee? Where was Zach? Why didn't thou run and tell me at once?"

"I let him out last night. I helped him to get away." My heart was pounding.

"Thou let him *out*?"

He stared at me, then strode to the door and ran upstairs as if unable to believe what I was telling him. He flung the door open, saw the empty room and came down in a fury. "Where is he?"

"I don't know."

"Thou unlocked the doors?" He sounded incredulous. "When?"

"Late last night. About midnight."

His face turned dark. He stepped towards me and I thought that for all his godly principles he would strike me. I flinched.

"Jos," he said, breathing heavily, struggling to control himself, "I'll have the buyer here at any moment. *Where is Antony?*"

"Truly," I said, "I don't know. He went out, into the night."

I would not tell him that I had guided Antony, or where I had taken him. Instead, I began to talk quickly, to steer away from that subject. "I'm sorry.

I did not mean to harm thy business. But – I had to do it. Antony was heartbroken when they took Patience. I betrayed him yesterday – "

"Heartbroken! Betrayed! Thou sound like a broadside balladeer!" He turned to the door. "I'll alert the sheriff and raise a hue and cry. He can't have got far yet. We'll catch him. I'll go there now. Thou must wait here; I forbid thee to leave – is that clear? And if Isaac Shore arrives, tell him nothing until I return."

He was gone only a few minutes, for the sheriff's office was near by. I paced around, afraid for Antony, afraid of George Bainbrigg's anger, and with a mounting need to justify myself to him.

When he returned he said grimly, "The hunt is on. As for thee, Josiah, I entrusted thee with my keys" – and now I felt his anger building – "with my keys, and my books, and the conduct of my business. It was thy duty to obey me and protect that business."

"I had a higher duty to protect Antony," I said – and felt at once that this sounded pompous and self-righteous.

"But thou hast *not* protected him!" He was shouting now, and I trembled before his anger. "Thou hast turned him out into a countryside he's never seen before, where his black face will make him stand out and lead to his capture in no time. And how dost thou think the buyer will feel when he finally gets his hands on him? The lad will likely be punished – and all to satisfy thee and thy tender conscience!"

I tried to speak, but he interrupted. "I've no time for thee now. We've that order for sugar for the Boston run. Go and help Zachary bring the hogsheads out." And then he humiliated me by calling out, "Zach! Make sure Jos is kept busy! Find him work!"

Zachary, who must have heard most of our conversation, disregarded my surly manner and involved me in manoeuvring barrels with him.

"Big trouble, eh?" he said.

I nodded. I had no idea whether he understood my actions, or approved, but his friendliness comforted me.

Soon after, the buyer arrived, and I hovered near the top of the stairs and listened to the two of them talking as they went into the office. I heard the sharp rise in Isaac Shore's voice and knew my master had broken the news. I felt guilt then – more than I had felt at depriving him of his property – for I knew how difficult it must be for him to explain. When they emerged the other man still sounded aggrieved, while my master was trying to smooth things over, reassuring him that the matter would soon be resolved.

"He cannot have got far," he said, as they parted. "I will send news to thee immediately when I have him back."

Zachary had also stopped work to listen.

"I set Antony free," I told him.

Zachary nodded. "Every man should have a chance of freedom. Took it myself, once."

"But – thou weren't a slave?"

"Bondsman – indentured servant. Not much different. I ran away from a bad master. Hid out in the Maryland swamps for two weeks before they caught me."

"And…?"

"I was beaten, five years added to my term. Then he sold me. I've been sold on twice."

Light dawned on me. "Thou'rt still indentured? To George Bainbrigg?"

"No." He smiled, showing gappy teeth. "I was, but my bond ended almost a year ago. I work here for a wage now."

I had become aware that many people in Pennsylvania kept indentured servants, but had not thought that George Bainbrigg was one of them. I must have looked shocked, for Zachary said, "He's a good man, our master. He treated me fairly. Paid me what I was due at the end. That's why I've stayed on a while. But come the fall, I plan to leave and set up on my own. Rent a plot of land. Get married."

"Married?"

He laughed. He knew what I was thinking. "I'm

not so old! I lodge with a widow, Ulla. Swedish woman. She's got two little lads. We'll be wed; have our own farm; children, too, God willing."

I was astonished. I had known nothing of this, nor thought much about Zachary's life outside the counting house.

"Antony has a girl," I said, "the one they took away. That's why he was so desperate. I wish *they* might have some hope of freedom."

"It's harder for them. They're black – folk will see them as slaves, whether they're freed or not—"

"Josiah!"

My master's summons broke into our talk. I braced myself for trouble and went reluctantly downstairs.

He was in the office, turning over the ledgers on my desk. His expression was grim.

"Was my daughter involved in this escapade of thine?" he asked.

I hesitated, unsure what would be safest to say.

He banged his fist on the table. "Answer me, boy!"

I chose the truth. "She knew of it. I would not let her come with me, but I told her what I was going to do."

He let out a breath. "I thought so. She was all of a twitch this morning – I wondered what was up with her. So she knew – but she didn't tell *me*. She kept thy secret."

I stood silent, waiting, afraid to say anything in case I made matters worse.

"I have allowed thee too much licence with Kate," he said. "I thought to be tolerant. I saw there was a liking between the two of you, and it seemed natural and right to let it flourish. But thou hast encouraged her in deceit and rebellion—"

"Kate has a mind of her own!" I retorted, for his words hurt me. I had wronged him, it was true, but not in this.

"Aye, she has, I know that. But she has never been underhand with me before."

"I love Kate," I began, "and—"

"Josiah" – he set down the account books on the table with a small thump of finality – "I want thee out of here. I'll take charge of these books. Thy work with them is finished."

For a moment I did not understand. I thought he was referring to the entries I had completed that morning. But when he spoke again there was no mistaking his meaning.

"I will settle matters with thy father later. The bond ... the money ... I'll deal with that. But thou must go today."

I began to tremble. There was a hollow feeling in my stomach. I could not believe this was happening. I had expected punishment, but never dismissal.

"Please," I said. "Please. Kate will tell thee I never sought to involve her—"

"But thou did involve her! And thou broke the terms of thy bond, and in the worst possible way. If thou had gone drinking or been slipshod or forgetful I'd have forgiven thee. But this – it was planned, deceitful; it has undermined my business and my standing as a merchant, angered my customer, caused inconvenience to him and much trouble and expense to the sheriff and officers – all of which I will be liable for."

"I know I did wrong," I said, "but I did not mean to harm thee, only to help Antony."

"Antony is my property! Thou stole him. Thou crept about my house at night while I was asleep and stole my keys." He slapped down a document on the desk. "See here, in the bond: *'He shall do no damage to his said Master… He shall not waste the goods of his said Master… He shall faithfully serve his Master … his lawful commandments gladly do.'* In all this thou hast failed, Josiah. I cannot trust thee again. Thou will come home with me now, pack thy belongings and leave."

Kate appeared the moment we arrived at the house. Her expression was wary. "Dad…?"

"Josiah is leaving us," her father said.

I had asked her to be my advocate, and now she flew to my defence.

"Oh, Dad, don't do this! Please don't blame Jos! I would have done the same. I wanted to go with him, but he wouldn't let me. We both wanted Antony to be free, to find Patience."

He grew angry with her then. "I've heard enough about those two! Thou had no business making friends with them – becoming that wench's confidante. Antony will soon be caught and sold, and that will be the end of the matter."

"But not for Jos!"

I shook my head at her, but she continued to plead. I wanted only to be gone now. I knew he would not relent.

"I'll go and pack," I said, and moved towards the stairs.

"Jos!" Kate made to follow me, but her father forcibly restrained her. "Come, Kate, no more of this," he said, and steered her into the parlour with him and closed the door. The sounds of their raised voices faded as I reached the second landing.

Alone in my room, I sat down on the bed, and at last my feelings overwhelmed me. I had lost my work, I had lost Kate, I had lost the good opinion of my master – and probably all for nothing, since the news of Antony's escape had been cried around the town and he was sure to be recaptured. And now I must go home to my family, whom I had not seen for many weeks, and instead of enjoying our reunion I must tell them of my humiliating dismissal; tell my father that once again I had failed in an apprenticeship.

Tears stung my eyes, and I sniffed and brushed them away. I had only myself to blame for what I had done, but I felt the unfairness of my master's accusations concerning Kate. Perhaps it was true that I had influenced her, but I had refused to let her be involved in my plan. I did not feel I had ever behaved improperly towards her.

I stood up and began to pack. There was little enough to remove. I took my empty bag from the chest and in a swift, angry clearance I threw into it my few clothes, my Bible, journal and writing case. Now there was nothing left of me in the room, and Isobel could change the sheets and make it ready for whatever paragon George Bainbrigg had in mind to replace me with. The thought of that person living here, in the same house as Kate, filled me with a furious jealousy.

I slung my bag over my shoulder and tramped downstairs. As I reached the hall I heard a clatter of claws on the wooden floor and Hob appeared, wagging his tail. I knelt to pat him, and then I did briefly let a few tears fall as he licked my face and hands.

"At least thou still love me," I said. And I called out, towards the parlour door, "I am going now!"

I stood up as George Bainbrigg came out. Kate hurried to the doorway, and he allowed the two of us to say a brief, formal goodbye to each other in which our eyes did all the real talking; then he sent her back in and shooed the dog in after her.

I looked at George Bainbrigg, and thought how well I'd liked this man, how glad I'd been to work for him. He must have caught some of my feelings, for he gave me a fierce, regretful look and said, "I had such high hopes of thee. We worked well together; thou pleased me greatly. But I cannot tolerate this breach of trust." His hand hovered above my shoulder and he said, "Go well, Josiah."

Tokpa

The forest was cold last night and the earth is still damp. The sun warms me as the day grows full but the ground never dries out. Always there is water in the earth and the air; the green shrubs and leaves are fat with it. I think there could never be drought in this country, nor the baked earth and dusty air that I remember from the dry season at home.

All day I stay hidden. Once, a young man passes near me. His hair is curly and shines red, like fire, in the sun. I hear him splashing in the stream. He comes back later, and I see that he carries two fish, glinting silver, swinging from a length of string.

A long way off I hear bells ringing: bells, and shouting that grows louder. Men come crashing along the path with loud voices and sticks to beat the bushes. Dogs run barking beside them. I hide well away from these enemies, in the stream, where the overhanging branches cover me and the dogs can't pick up my scent.

I eat the remainder of the bread and meat Jos gave me. When I am sure the men and dogs have gone, I move. Further on, among the trees, I see a hut. A familiar sound comes from it: the ring of metal striking metal. This is a blacksmith's forge! Now I am afraid. The blacksmith in my village was a powerful sorceror. Sometimes he helped people; sometimes he did harm. People bought charms from him to protect themselves from enemies. Maybe this blacksmith will protect me? But I am afraid and I move further away. I turn towards the west, as Jos told me, and walk on through the forest until I reach the river, and then I take shelter again as night falls.

I wake at dawn to the sound of voices: two men, who speak low and use few words. I hear a crackle of fire, and smell fish cooking. My stomach yearns for food, but I stay out of sight and listen.

The voices come again. These men are not speaking English. They are not the men I heard yesterday, shouting, breaking branches as they searched for me. These two talk like hunters, with no words wasted. I part the leaves of my hiding place and look out.

The men are squatting on the riverbank, wrapped in mantles and sheltered by a windbreak made of branches stuck in the ground. They must have been here all night, close to where I lay.

And now I see something else: drawn up on the riverbank is a canoe.

I creep closer.

Twenty-three

$\mathcal{I}$ was in heavy mood as I walked home, but when I turned the corner into Sassafras Street I saw something that momentarily drove my problems from my mind: our house was finished. In the weeks I had been away in Barbados the builders had moved on apace, and now the structure stood proud: a fine clapboard house of three storeys, with balconies on the upper floors, a shopfront on the street and a workshop extending behind.

"Jos!"

Sarah had seen me and came running. She wore a dirty apron and as usual her hair was escaping its cap. She stared at my face. "Did someone hit thee?"

"Bumped into the privy in the dark," I said, and she giggled. She walked with me, chattering: "We have moved in, and Betty and I are together, and Mam is very happy now we can wash and cook properly –

and we have two cats to keep down the mice…"

My mother came out of the house, saw me, and called to Sarah to fetch my father from the bookshop. I put down my bag inside the gate. My mother hugged me. I lied again about my injury, and fended off her questions about Barbados. "Show me the house," I said, as my father appeared. I dreaded telling them my news. The new house could come first.

My parents and I went in, with Sarah tagging along behind us, through the side entrance into the kitchen and pantry, then upstairs into a spacious room. I saw how pleased my mother was with this new home. She made an expansive movement of her arms as if to display it: "This is the parlour. The balconies face south-west so we catch the afternoon sun. The chairs and settle were made by the woodturner on Fourth Street; he is skilled and reasonable—"

At that moment we heard footsteps on the stairs and Betty burst into the room and asked, "Jos! Why hast thou brought such a big bag? Hast thou come to stay?"

They all looked at me—and I realized that my mother had sensed all along that something was wrong.

"Yes," I said. "I've come home."

I could not meet my father's eye.

My mother turned to Betty. "Go and mind the shop. Thy father is busy."

"Oh, Mam!"

"*Now*, Betty! And take Sarah with thee."

Betty scowled and turned away, and I heard her stomping down the stairs.

"Sit down, Jos," my father said. "Tell us what has happened."

He and my mother sat side by side on the settle, while I sat opposite them on a bench. It reminded me uncomfortably of our confrontation last year, in London, when I had come home drunk and bloody. But this was worse – much worse.

I told them the story at length, beginning with our voyage to Barbados and ending with what I had done and how I had been dismissed from George Bainbrigg's service. They listened in silence. Occasionally, especially when I spoke of Patience and how she had been dragged screaming from the counting house, I saw the shock and distress that I had felt at the time reflected in their eyes. But when I described how I had taken my master's keys and gone to free Antony, my father shook his head and screwed up his face as if – too late – to try and prevent me.

I looked directly at him. "So I have lost another apprenticeship," I said.

I knew I had failed him utterly. And I thought I could bear his anger, but I dreaded his contempt.

He said nothing at first. The two of them sat in

silence, heads bowed, as Friends should do when strong feelings tempt them to speak angrily.

When he looked up he surprised me by asking, "What has happened to the young man – the Negro?"

"I left him in the woods, not far from the forge. I told him to lie low awhile. George Bainbrigg doesn't know I took him into the forest. He thinks I just set him free."

"We heard the bells, husband, remember?" my mother said. "There was a hue and cry, but I was busy and didn't pay much attention. Oh, I fear they'll catch him!"

"They will, and he will suffer for it." My father's expression was grim. "But that is what happens when people are made slaves. How can they *not* try to escape?" He turned to me. "I would probably have done the same as thee."

For a moment I thought I had misheard him. Then my mother took his hand in hers and said, "Yes, thou would, husband. I know thou would."

I looked from one to the other of them. "You don't think I did wrong?"

"Oh, certainly thou did wrong," my father said. "Thou hast probably done the young man no favour, for he will be caught and punished. And thou betrayed thy master's trust and injured his business. That is unforgivable and I am not surprised George Bainbrigg has dismissed thee. I wish thou had not acted in that way. If thou had given it more thought—"

"There was no time to think!"

He sighed. "No. I understand that. And thou'rt young, and rash. I would have done the same at thy age. Thou acted out of fellow-feeling and out of thy understanding that to enslave a man is a greater wrong."

"Yes," I said. I felt a cloud lifting. He understood, after all. We were not far apart, as I'd feared; we were father and son, and thought alike.

"I will talk to George Bainbrigg," my father said. "And no doubt the meeting – the elders – will consider this matter. It may be resolved, and thou back in work again."

"He will not relent. He blames me for turning Kate against him."

"Was she involved in this?" His voice was sharp.

"She knew what I was going to do."

My parents exchanged a glance.

"No wonder he was angry," my father said.

"But I had to tell her – we were together, and … Dad, I need to *see* Kate! She must come here. We must talk—"

"Not yet," my mother said. "Let things settle awhile."

"I can't! I need to see her! And Antony. I don't

know what's happened to him. I must find out."

"We'll hear if he's caught," my mother said. "The news will be all around. Thou should sleep, Jos—"

"Sleep!" I was outraged. And yet my head and eyes, my whole body, ached for want of it.

"Let me show thee thy room. It's not quite ready yet. We didn't expect thee home to stay…"

I let her lead me up to the room, which I scarcely noticed, except that it was new and smelt of pine and had a bed that she quickly made up for me with clean sheets. She left me, and I lay down on the bed, thinking to close my eyes for a moment. I did not open them again until I woke in the early evening.

Sunlight was streaming in, for there were as yet no curtains and the window faced south-west. Someone had come in while I slept and put my bag down just inside the door. I rose and examined my new surroundings. The room was not unlike the one I'd had at George Bainbrigg's house: fresh, clean, painted in pale colours. I thought of that room; imagined the bed stripped, all trace of my presence removed.

There was a knock at the door, and Betty came in.

We looked at each other.

"So thou'rt in trouble again?" she said. Then she came and put her arms around me and hugged me. "But thou did the right thing, Jos."

I grunted. "I've slept all day! What news is there?"

"None. They haven't caught him yet."

I could see she was brimming with excitement about all that had happened.

I thought of the map I'd given Antony; tried to think where he might be. Had he somehow managed to cross the river? Would he find Patience? And if he did, what then? If he approached the house he would almost certainly be caught. My father was right: I had done him no real favour.

"Thou slept right through dinner," Betty said. "It'll be suppertime soon. Mam's getting it ready."

"I'm not hungry."

But when my mother had set supper on the table I realized I needed to eat, and my appetite returned.

Later, as the evening darkened, I walked down to Front Street with my father to find out if there was any news of Antony. But to my relief there was none.

"He may have been recaptured already and returned to George Bainbrigg," my father said.

This possibility filled me with anxiety. "We could walk back past their house."

"No." He spoke firmly. I knew he was right, and let him steer me in the opposite direction.

But it's first-day tomorrow, I thought. They can't stop me speaking to Kate after Meeting.

✿　　✿　　✿

We were late for Meeting. I had overslept, and Sarah was found to have no clean kerchief to tie over her bodice. I heard my mother scolding, Sarah snivelling, and then an exchange with Betty, who exclaimed, "Am I my sister's keeper?" and was rebuked for it.

So we arrived when almost everyone else was seated and found our usual places, a few rows back and facing the Bainbrigg household.

Kate and her father looked up as we came in and he gave a brief nod of acknowledgement. Kate looked at me with longing eyes, then turned her attention to her clasped hands in her lap. I did the same. For a long time the room was silent except for the sounds of breathing and coughing and the occasional whimper of a child. I looked up again at Kate and found her looking at me. We filled our eyes with each other. I became aware that my mother, beside me, was restless. Suddenly she stood up, and I realized she had been moved to speak.

"It is hard to be young," she said. Her voice was abrupt, nervous. She rarely speaks in Meeting. "You are full of desires you cannot act on and ideas that sweep you away and beliefs that no one else seems to share. We need to rein in our young people, to keep them from too much contact with the world. And yet we must encourage that spirit, that challenge... We need to encourage them in their adventurousness, to see the light in them, to allow the spirit to fill them like the wind in a ship's sail; for sometimes God speaks through children…"

She spoke a little longer, faltering somewhat, then sat down. Her face was flushed.

This was about me, I thought; I had stirred her to this. I felt she was on my side, perhaps defending me to George Bainbrigg. Others spoke – among them some visiting Friends from Maryland – but my attention strayed; I did not attend to what they said.

When the meeting ended George Bainbrigg got up and began talking to the Maryland Friends. He kept Kate firmly at his side, and she gave me a little shake of her head. But then my father began moving towards him, and he placed Kate with Isobel and Mary before turning aside to talk to my father. I was deeply anxious to know what the two of them were saying about me; but even stronger was the urge to speak to Kate – and now I had an opportunity. I took Betty's arm and said, "Come!" and we moved quickly across the room.

I held out my hand, and Kate took it – a brief clasp: "Oh, Jos…" Then she said, "Betty!" and embraced my sister.

Isobel turned to me. "We are very sorry, Jos – Mary and I. Sorry to lose thee." She spoke stiffly. I felt her kindness towards me, and yet I knew she must be shocked and unable to sympathize with what I had done. To her the slaves were savages, and her loyalty to her employer was absolute.

"I thank thee, Isobel," I said. "And I wish…"

I struggled to know what to say next – but before I could speak further George Bainbrigg came towards us, clearly eager to gather up his womenfolk and be gone. He nodded to me and said a polite "good morning", but then he turned away, and they left. I caught only a last quick glance from Kate over her shoulder.

Nevertheless, I had hope. Isobel would surely allow me to talk to Kate, even if she would not leave us alone together.

Next morning I was at the front early. A news bulletin was posted there every day, but today it still showed the "missing – runaway servant" message I'd seen before. The *Frances* lay at anchor in the river, and George Bainbrigg's counting house was open and busy, but I did not venture near.

"No news?" my father asked, when I returned.

I shook my head. Perhaps, I thought, Antony had found Patience. Perhaps they were together now, somewhere hidden.

My father showed me around the bookshop and printing works. The new shop was to be at the front of the house, with a drop-down shutter to form a counter on the street, while the print works was in a separate building behind the house, with its own entrance as well as a covered passage from the kitchen.

Betty joined us as we went into the print shop.

"I'm to work here," she said. "I'll be the apprentice – the printer's devil." She wore a look of happy anticipation.

It was hard to imagine that clean, empty space filled with the sound of a press and all the bustle of a print shop. But some tables had already been moved in, and my father had brought wooden font cases with him from England and set them up. Everything else was waiting to be unpacked, except the press, which had yet to be built.

So we'd have my father, my mother who had worked as a printer in London, Betty as apprentice; and all three of them could take turns to mind the bookshop. And then there was the skilled typesetter who was coming from London. All we needed now was a man to operate the press.

"You'll have me until I find a new employer," I said.

The thought came to me that perhaps no other merchant would want me. Merchants talk to one another. And merchants who are Friends, who go to Meeting, are closer still; and Philadelphia was a small place. Perhaps I had lost my reputation within less than a year of my arrival in the colony. For me, it might come down to manning the press after all.

But none of these thoughts was uppermost in my mind. That was focused on Kate. As soon as we had eaten our midday dinner I went upstairs, changed into clean linen and polished my shoes. There was nothing I could do about my bruised face, but I combed my hair, brushed my beaver hat and put it on, tilting it slightly to shade my face – though not too much, for Friends are warned against the vanity of wearing brims tilted at rakish angles. When I was happy with my appearance I set off for Walnut Street.

George Bainbrigg would be out now, at his counting house or at the Society's hall.

Isobel answered my knock. "Jos," she said, resignedly.

From the open kitchen door came Hob, wagging his tail. He bounded towards me, pushing his head against my legs. Mary hovered in the doorway. At the sight of me she flushed red and looked anxious. I vaguely wondered why; but it was not Mary I had come for.

I glanced about. The parlour door was closed. Hadn't Kate heard the commotion?

I straightened up and looked Isobel in the eye. "I've come to see Kate."

"I'm sorry. They've gone. Sailed before noon."

"Sailed?" All the bounce went out of me. "Who?"

"Those Friends from Maryland. She's gone back with them. Her father's orders."

"*Maryland!* But – she never said! She talked to my sister yesterday. Why didn't she tell Betty?" I was knocked hollow with shock and disbelief.

"He sprang it on us this morning." Isobel sighed. "We scarce had time to pack her things. Her linen wasn't ironed and ready, and I'd clothes waiting to wash for her. Men – they don't realize…"

"When will she be back?" Why hadn't I come this morning? What a fool I was! I'd waited, and missed her.

"I don't know." Isobel looked at me with a mixture of sympathy and reproach. "His friends offered. And he says the change of company will do her good."

"The change from *my* company?"

"Aye."

A silence fell.

Her face softened. "Thou'd best go, Jos. The master might call back at any time."

So I was not welcome, even on the doorstep.

I turned to leave. The dog was still there and thought I was about to take him for a walk. He gave a little bark of anticipation.

"No, Hob."

"I'm sorry," said Isobel. "Mary! Hold the dog. Let Jos escape."

I patted Hob goodbye. Mary reached to hold him; our hands brushed together, and I felt her put something – a folded piece of paper – into mine. I looked up, startled, but she had averted her face and was already taking the dog away – "C'mon, then, old dog" – and I quickly pushed the paper under the edge of my sleeve, nodded to Isobel and went out.

It was an address, scribbled in haste: *"Jerome Richmond's house at Herring Creek, Anne Arundel County, Maryland. Write to me there. I'll write when I can. I love thee. K."*

Tokpa

*N*ow I see the two men clearly. They squat on the ground like my people, and eat with their fingers. They are brown-skinned, and their black hair hangs below their shoulders; one of them has feathers tied into his hair. Under their mantles they are bare-chested and hung about with strings of beads and small pouches. Their faces are strong and fierce, and if I were not hungry, if I did not need to cross the river, I would hide from them. But they have a canoe.

I stand, and step forward, opening my hands to show I mean no harm.

They look up, startled, and seize spears. I let them see that I am alone and unarmed. I speak in English: "Please, I need help. I must cross the river." I point to the canoe and then to the far bank.

The older man signals to the other to put down his spear. They talk rapidly to each other in their own language. Then they beckon me forward, motion to me to squat. They put fish on a platter of leaves and offer it to me.

The food warms my stomach. In a mixture of speech and gestures I explain to the men that I want to cross the river, to find Darby Creek, John Outram's plot. I remember those names that Jos told me. When I say "Darby Creek", I see that they know it. But they question me. Where am I from? Why am I a fugitive? I tell them about Miata. "We are slaves. Slaves of the white men."

They talk some more. The younger one looks at me: at my hair, which is so different to theirs, my dark skin. He touches the little drum that I have kept slung from my belt ever since I left Barbados. I can see that he likes it. I untie the drum, and give it to him. He examines it, to see how it is made. I know he wants to tap out a rhythm, but the forest is listening. He fastens the drum to his belt.

The older man begins speaking to me. His English is hard to follow, but I listen carefully and watch his gestures and find I can understand. He tells me, "Our people are the Lenni Lenape. We have lived long in this land. We are at peace with William Penn's people. We want no trouble. But we will take you across the river. We will guide you to Darby Creek. No more. We will not help you steal back your woman."

I thank them. When we have cleared away all trace of their camp they take me in their canoe across the river. On the far side they hide the canoe and we walk on through the forest.

They are hunters and trappers, these men; young, strong

men – two brothers. Their faces are watchful; they miss nothing. They belong in the forest, like me. I know that when I am gone they will hunt.

We come to a creek that runs sparkling over rocks and stones. They tell me the name of this creek is Karakung.

"But the white men call it Cobb's Creek," the older one says.

We cross at a shallow place. Now the two men become more cautious. I see that some of the land ahead of us has been cleared for farming and staked out in plots. There are large tracts of woodland between the plots and we move through these until they show me, ahead, the line of another creek, bordered by willows.

"Darby Creek," says the younger brother.

Distant figures are moving about. There are carts and horses. I hear the sound of an axe chopping wood.

"We will leave you here," says the older one. "We do not know this man John Outram, but many white men settle around this creek."

They turn back, promising to watch for me if I return, and vanish silently into the woodland.

Now I am alone, and ahead of me lies the white men's land. How will I ever find Miata? I am afraid to ask any of the white men. They will know I am a runaway and send word to the city, to George Bainbrigg. I move closer, cautiously, from tree to tree, until I am within breathing distance of a man working his plot. He does not see me.

He has servants – I see them come and go – but no black people. I move on through the woodland to another plot, then another, always watching and listening. I know how to stay hidden in the forest, making no sound; but I need help, and I see no one I dare ask. Perhaps Outram's plot is on the other side of the creek? The shadows grow long.

I come to a place where I see a servant girl close by in a yard, gathering up clothes that had been spread on the bushes to dry. Her basket is almost full; in a moment she will take it indoors. She is a white girl, but this may be my last chance. If I speak to her, will she help me – or will she scream and bring people running?

I take a chance, creep close to the fence, call softly, "Sister!"

She turns, and sees me. Her eyes widen. She glances back at the house, then walks towards me. She looks scared.

"Sister!" I say again. "Help me? Please?"

"What do you want? You a runaway? You want food?"

"I look for my woman, Miata."

She begins to shake her head.

"John Outram bought her."

"Outram? Two, three days ago?"

"Yes!" My heart leaps. She knows.

"Go that way." She points. "Four plots, all new, all along this creek. The fourth is Outrams'. I heard they got a black woman."

I thank her, and go before she is caught. I travel along the line of the creek, keeping to the woodland, count four plots, *stop near the last. There is a yard with hens scratching in the dirt, a dog tied up. The house smells of new-cut timber. I wait till the light goes. The dog hears or scents me, and barks; I move further away. A light appears and glows within; people's shadows move. I think: I will stay here, under this tree, till morning. But then I see the door open, a bar of light in the yard; someone steps out.*

Miata! Even in the half-dark I recognize her from the way she moves. She has come to round up the hens and shut them away. I hear her calling them.

I don't go close because of the dog; but when she has shut the hen house and turned to go back indoors, I give a low whistling call. It's the call of a bird of our homeland and we used it at the Crosbies' as a signal.

Miata's head goes up; so does the dog's. She quiets him and creeps towards the fence. I meet her there. We reach out, touch each other, clasp hands.

"Miata."

"Tokpa."

Tears run down her face.

"They hurt you, Miata?"

"No! I cry because I'm happy to see you. So happy. How...?"

"Jos helped me escape. But they are searching for me – I must stay hidden. Miata, this land, this forest – we can hide here, we can hunt; we can live. Come with me!"

She puts a hand on her flat belly. "Soon I'll begin to grow big. When the time comes I'll need women to help me."

I tell her about the forest people, the Lenni Lenape. "They will help."

She says, with a nod towards the house, "She doesn't know yet about the baby."

"Outram woman?"

"Mmm." She grips my hand. "Tokpa, I'm afraid to run. But I'm afraid to stay here. They could sell my baby – take it away from me."

"You think they will?" The thought fills me with horror: my child, my first-born, sold away.

"I don't know," she says. "They own me. They can do anything."

She looks at me. I know she is fearful. But she says, "I'll go with you."

We make a plan. She'll come out at night, when the Outrams are all asleep. I settle under a tree and wait.

The moon is high when she appears. The dog stirs, but he knows her; she quiets him.

I help her climb over the picket fence and we move quickly away, into the woodland. When we are out of sight of the settlements, deep in the forest, we stop and embrace.

Twenty-four

"Jerome Richmond's house at Herring Creek..."

I wrote at once to Kate. Ships left frequently for the southern provinces – but how long would it be before she received it? I remembered seeing Maryland on the map in George Bainbrigg's office: it was far away; you'd have to sail down the length of the Delaware to the sea, then into Chesapeake Bay... I could only write; I could not go after her. She was lost to me until he chose to bring her back. They'd lived in Maryland, Kate had told me, before coming to Pennsylvania, and had friends there – among them, no doubt, the people we'd seen at Meeting yesterday. Kate probably knew them well – must have done, if her father had sent her away in their care. I imagined him telling them of his troubles with the runaways and how his apprentice had turned Kate against him.

There had been a woman in the group; no doubt she'd offered to take charge of Kate. I felt a great resentment of this woman.

But Kate had gone unwillingly; that was clear. And she'd somehow cajoled timid little Mary into slipping me a message without Isobel seeing. Her father would not be able to keep us apart. We'd write. We'd wait. And if he thought this separation would weaken our love for each other he was mistaken.

I thought of those other two. Had Antony found Patience? Were they safely away? I longed to feel I had done the right thing in freeing Antony.

Tokpa

We find shelter under some trees; stay there till daylight. Miata has brought food and blankets, and we make a shelter of bent branches and lie wrapped together all night. I put my hand on her belly but I can't feel the baby – "Too young! Too soon!" says Miata, laughing – but I believe he is there with us, an unborn spirit, all three of us Kpelle, far from home. Miata and I kiss and talk and ask the spirits of this land to watch over us. We hear animals snuffling and grunting, but they don't come near. In the morning we make a small offering of food to the spirits before we leave.

The day is fair and warm. We hear no pursuers. We feel happy. We wash in a stream and gather cherries to eat. We follow a trail. I think it is a trail of the Lenni Lenape people. It leads west, along the creek. We will go far from the new city, I decide. We will live in the forest, and the Lenni Lenape will be our neighbours.

Miata grows tired, and we stop to rest beside the trail.

I remember how I lay low for a day on the other side of the river and my pursuers passed me by. We would be wise to do that again, I tell Miata. We leave the trail and find a sheltered place by the creek. Miata brings out the last of the food: cornmeal cakes and berries. She lays this food carefully on fresh leaves, and offers it to me. We eat, and talk quietly together. But all the time I keep watch and listen. I know men will be out searching for us now. Once, in the distance, I hear voices, and dogs barking, and my heart beats fast; but they are far off, and the sound grows no louder.

As night falls we feel safer. We huddle under the shelter of a fallen tree and wrap ourselves close in the blankets, trusting the spirits to protect us again.

Next morning we rise early and brush away all trace of our camp. Miata rolls up the blankets and ties them for carrying. We walk on. The trail leads deep into the forest, and we hear all around us sounds of birds and running water. Squirrels leap from tree to tree above us. Once, coming into an open glade, we startle several deer that run with a crash of branches into the cover of the trees. I know these sounds might alert our enemies. We pause, and listen, but hear only birds and rustling leaves. I think: Once we are far away from the white men's settlements, once we are among the Lenni Lenape, we will be free. We will hunt. We can survive in this forest. And I stride out. I feel like a free man already.

A new sound startles me: a clink of metal?

I whirl round. "Miata —"

Voices, breaking branches – danger! We clasp hands and run, but they are all around us: men armed with ropes and shackles. They seize me, tear Miata's hand from mine, bind my arms behind my back. Miata screams. She too is caught and tied.

These men are not like those others who blundered along with dogs so that I heard them coming. These are hunters, men who know how to move silently in the woods. I see now that they have been following our tracks, all the time we thought we were free. I turn to Miata, cry out that I'm sorry, and she sobs and struggles to reach me. But they force us apart. They march us back along the trail.

Twenty-five

*O*n fourth-day morning I offered to call in at the grocer's on Front Street to fetch household supplies. Along the waterfront I noticed a group of surveyors at work, and realized they must be measuring out the area where the merchant Samuel Carpenter's wharf was to be built – the first wharf in Philadelphia. This would allow ships like the *Frances* and the *Chepstow* to dock at the harbour wall and bring goods and people ashore without the need to transfer them to boats. I thought of how the merchants and their apprentices must be full of enthusiasm for the new wharf and keen to see the work go ahead. I had lost my chance to be part of all that now.

As I entered the grocer's store I heard a buzz of conversation and knew at once that something had happened. With so many Friends among Philadelphians, there was usually little needless talk in shops or other meeting places. Today was different.

"…those runaway Negroes…"

"Taken together, the boy and girl. They hadn't got far."

Antony and Patience. Caught. It hit me like a blow.

"Poor creatures!" a woman said.

They were mostly women in the store; mild-faced women in grey homespun and plain aprons, wicker baskets on their arms: Friends, or Baptists, or others who must know what it was like to be hounded by the authorities.

I stood there, crushed by the news. So it had all been for nothing. And then I rallied, and thought: I'm glad we tried, even though it brought so much trouble. Antony had found Patience; he'd escaped with her. It had been a brief triumph for him. Their actions might lead to punishment, but they'd had time together, however short.

"George Bainbrigg will be glad to have his Negro back," the grocer said to the woman he was serving. "I heard the buyer was not well pleased."

"Will he still buy?"

"Sure to – Negroes being so hard to come by here."

I thought of George Bainbrigg's counting house, of the storeroom upstairs. That was where Antony would be now, awaiting sale to Isaac Shore. Unless he had already gone to Shore's plot. And Patience?

Returned to her owners, I supposed. I hoped, fervently, that they would not beat her. If only the two of them could have stayed hidden! I remembered those vast tracts on George Bainbrigg's map marked only as "wilderness". Antony and Patience were forest people. They could hunt, fish and farm. They could have survived out there.

But now they were caught, and it would be made harder for them to escape a second time. Kate had been snatched away from me, yet our troubles seemed as nothing compared to the plight of Antony and Patience.

Tokpa

As we approach John Outram's place, Miata begins to wail. Outram's people come out to fetch her, and she screams and falls to her knees and begs our captors not to send her back. Everyone is shouting. The dog barks and strains at its tether. Miata struggles as they untie her, drag her into the yard and shut the gate. She looks back at me in despair and we cry out each other's names; then a woman appears and pushes Miata inside the house, out of my sight. I can do nothing to help Miata.

Our captors take me away, back to George Bainbrigg's counting house.

Friend George does not beat me. But he locks me in the storeroom and sends word to my buyer.

This man comes and takes me in a cart to his plot on the edge of the city, in the woods. There he leaves me bound, pushes me into the yard and ties me to a fence post. He takes out a whip and beats me till I sag at the knees and cry for mercy. Then he unties me and says, "You run away – you get a beating. Run away again – I beat you again, harder. Understand?"

He sets me to work on his plot, clearing scrub. This is work I have done before, in the fields near our village, when we cleared the land for rice-planting. But there it was happy work. We sang and laughed together, and the women would bring us food and drink when we stopped to rest, and the fields and crops were for all of us to share. Here I have no reward but cuffs and curses, and the land is my master's.

He is a harsh, hard-working, busy man, this Isaac Shore. He lives with his wife and son and a servant woman, and all four of them beat and curse me. I will not stay in this place. I will escape again and fetch Miata, and next time we will find a better place to hide.

Twenty-six

$\mathcal{I}$ stayed at home and helped my parents for the next two weeks. We moved the bookshop from the log cabin into its new home at the front of the house; dealt with orders; put up shelves. A letter came from Nat Lacon telling us that Florian Marshall, the typesetter, was now on his way to the New World and might be expected in July. This news spurred my father on to get the printing workshop ready. He found a carpenter to build the press, and we busied ourselves arranging the layout of the workshop and unpacking the crates we'd brought with us from London.

All this took my mind off Antony and Patience and what might be happening to them. And Kate: although I thought of her often, I'd still had no reply to my letter. My mother believed our separation was perhaps for the best while her father was so angry with me.

"Let the dust settle," she said. "Kate won't forget thee."

But the dust was unable to settle, for the next thing we heard was that Antony had escaped from his new master, Isaac Shore. It seemed he had been caught almost immediately, but that very night he had broken out again, and this time had not been found, despite a hue and cry and enquiries at the Outrams' holding.

He's lying low, I thought, as he did before. And I wondered if he'd have made for the same part of the forest.

The next day, when I went to Front Street, there was still no news of him. But when I called in at the post office, as I'd been doing for the past week, I was at last rewarded with a letter from Kate. My spirits soared. I stepped out, breaking the seal as I went, and unfolded it eagerly.

"Jos," she wrote, *"forgive my hasty note to thee when I left. I hope Mary gave it thee?"* So our letters had crossed, as I'd expected. *"I did not dare ask Isobel – she is so loyal to my father. Poor Mary was frightened to death that Dad or Isobel would catch her with the note! She begged me not to make her do it, but I insisted.*

"Jos, I am so angry *with my father, and also a little angry with our Friends the Richmonds for offering to take me away, though I know they meant kindly by it. I love Margaret*

Richmond well. She says I may stay as long as I wish – but she must know I don't wish! She is so good to me. She gives me motherly advice and is very interested in hearing all about thee. *Well, I think nothing I say could make her disapprove of thee, but she warns against too much haste, impulsiveness, airiness of spirits – thou know how elders go on! She does not understand how much I long to be with thee.*

"Of course we hear nothing here in Herring Creek of Antony and Patience. Are they safely away? I told Margaret all about them, and that Patience is carrying Antony's child, and she was shocked – though I am not sure whether that was because Antony and Patience have been separated or because they are young and not married. I think she would be shocked also that I speak of such things to thee. I hope thou don't think me immodest? I believe in plain speaking.

"I also have no news of thee. Was thy father angry? Did he blame thee? Will thou work for him now? I wish Dad would have thee back. Oh, I wish all was as before!

"Write to me, please, Jos. I know it is not thought seemly for a girl to beg a young man to write to her, but I do.
Thy Friend,
Katherine Bainbrigg."

I replied the same day:

"Kate, I care not if it is unseemly – but thou need not beg me to write. There is nothing I would rather do – except be with thee, of course. It is harsh that thou hast been sent away, and neither of us deserves it."

I told her that Antony had gone on the run once more – and added, furiously, *"I hate this whole business of slavery and would never consent to be involved in it again. And yet I was happy working for thy father. It seemed right for me – not only because of thee (though that was a big part of it) but because I felt capable and confident. Maybe I can find employment with another merchant, but I fear they may all be involved in the slave trade, some perhaps much more so. Oh, Kate, I wish we were not separated like this and could at least talk! Any news I send will be out of date by the time thou receive it. I love thee and long to see thee…"*

The next morning, as usual, I joined my father and Betty in the print shop. But no sooner had we started work than my mother appeared with Judith Kite. Judith was dusty from the road and out of breath, and both women looked worried.

My father stopped work at once. "Judith! Is something wrong?"

"It's the escaped slave – Antony," said Judith. "He is with us at home; we took him in. Will, he is hurt. He has been brutally beaten."

I started forward with a cry.

"I'm going back with Judith to care for him," said my mother. She bit her lip, and the two women exchanged a glance. "Judith and I feel minded to say nothing to the authorities – at least, not yet."

My father nodded, slowly. "For now, yes, I agree.

It seems Antony is determined to escape, and if beating doesn't deter him..." He frowned. "This new owner" – he turned to me – "is he a Friend?"

"I don't know."

"If he is, he may listen to Friends' advice, otherwise the law may be the only recourse. Yes, go there, Su, and take Jos" – for he saw that I was anxious to go with them. "Antony will be glad to see a familiar face."

As we walked to the forge, Judith said, "We found him near our house last night, exhausted and bleeding from his wounds." She shuddered. "It reminded me of the old days in England, Su, when Friends were so cruelly treated and we tended to one another's injuries."

When we arrived we found Daniel at work, the fire glowing red-hot.

"I'm glad to see thee, Su," he said. "And thee, Jos. He spoke of thee – the lad – he said thy name. Esther's with him. But he seems afraid of me and Ben – maybe he can smell the fire on us; maybe some superstition his people have – who knows?"

We went upstairs, into the spacious house, then up the ladder to the loft.

"He's well hidden here, for a while," said Judith.

I was shocked when I saw Antony. He lay on his front, stripped to the waist, and his back was a mass of oozing wounds. This had been a vicious whipping. It had cut open his flesh so cruelly that it was impossible for Esther to tend the wounds without causing more pain. She was simply offering sips of water and murmuring sympathy. She looked enormously relieved when her mother appeared and took over, allowing her to escape downstairs.

"Those cuts have opened up half-healed wounds," Judith told me. "He has been beaten more than once."

I crouched beside him, touched his shoulder gently. "Tokpa..."

"Jos."

When he turned to look at me I saw that he had also been punched in the face. His mouth was swollen and bloody, and blood had run from his nose and dried.

But he was determined to speak.

"I will not stay with that man," he said. "I will die first. He is a demon. They are a house of demons." His eyes burned with anger. "When I am free I shall come back and kill them all."

I felt that I should say some word of restraint, or of forgiveness of one's enemies, but I did not. The truth was, I rather relished the thought of Antony returning and killing whoever had done this to him. And I thanked God that George Bainbrigg had not sold the two of them, Antony and Patience, to Isaac Shore.

"He should be brought before the law," I said – and I wondered how the law stood on this issue.

I sat with Antony while my mother and Judith cleaned his wounds and treated them with a salve that Judith applied with a feather so as not to hurt him too much. He bore this stoically. When they were finished they went downstairs, leaving us to talk.

Antony turned troubled eyes on me. "They won't fetch men to take me away?"

"No." I hoped I was right; the women had urged secrecy.

"The woman's husband is a blacksmith. In my village the blacksmith is powerful. He makes spells. He talks to the spirits, to the ancestors."

"Thou don't need to be afraid of Daniel, or of Ben. They will protect you."

"Good magic?"

"Yes," I said. I was unwilling to argue about the choice of words, for I felt the meaning was the same, even though Friends denied magic.

Twenty-seven

*T*he next day my mother and I went to the Kites' again.

"He's asleep," said Judith. "It's good. Sleep is healing."

She and Esther and my mother busied themselves with household matters and Judith poured beer into three tankards, set them on a tray and sent me out to the forge. There I found Ben working the bellows while his father heated a lump of iron to glowing redgold. They looked like the sorcerors Antony believed them to be, both of them black with smuts, their red curls of hair like fire. I put the tray down, turned towards the road, and saw a group of horsemen approaching.

"The sheriff," I said. My stomach tightened.

The iron was glowing incandescent now, but Daniel motioned to Ben to stop work. Then he came forward and confronted the officers as they rode into the yard.

They dismounted. The sheriff said, "We're searching for an escaped Negro. No doubt you heard the hue and cry?" He looked from one to another of us. "Have you seen anything? Any suspicious sign?"

Daniel stood four-square, hands on hips. "The man is here," he said.

"Here?" The sheriff looked taken aback. "In thy house?"

"Yes."

"Thou did not report it."

"We knew you would come before long. The young man has been cruelly beaten. He collapsed near our home. My wife is caring for him."

The sheriff turned towards the house. Daniel relaxed his stance and led the way. Ben and I followed. My breath came fast and I felt a fluttering in my stomach; I was afraid for Antony.

The group of us reached the house door as Judith opened it. My mother appeared and stood beside her.

"Thy husband tells me the Negro servant is here?" the sheriff said.

"He is," said Judith.

"We ask thee to surrender him. He must be returned to his owner."

"His back is criss-crossed with bloody stripes,"

said Judith. "He is in no condition to be removed."

"Nevertheless—"

"I cannot release him to you." If Judith was afraid, she hid it.

"Then we must take him."

Daniel stepped forward, but before he could speak my mother said, "If thou arrest Antony, thou must arrest all of us. We will not allow him to be taken."

"Friends, don't make trouble," the sheriff advised. I could see that he did not know what to do. He was a Friend confronting Friends. My mother and Judith stood together in his way and he was unwilling to arrest them. He conferred a moment with his deputy, then said, "I insist on seeing the Negro."

"Thou may see him," said Judith, "but I ask thee not to bring thy officers with thee."

She and my mother stepped aside, and the sheriff entered the house. Daniel and Ben followed, and I went after them, knowing that Antony must have heard the voices and would be terrified.

"Ben," said Judith, "stay down here with Esther and the young ones. They're frightened."

She led the way up to the loft.

When she reached the doorway she spoke softly, "Antony?"

He was not on the bed, though a few bloodstained bandages littered it. He was standing backed up against the far wall, where there was a tiny window – too small to climb out of. His eyes were wide, but he showed no other sign of fear.

"Antony, the sheriff wishes to see thy injuries," Judith said. She turned to the sheriff. "Note his face, Friend, how he has been punched. Turn around, Antony." He moved reluctantly, his eyes on me for reassurance. "We have tended his wounds, but thou can see how severe the whipping was. We will not send him back to be beaten like this again."

"But he is the property of Isaac Shore," the sheriff said. "If the man has been ill-treated, that is a matter for the law to raise with the owner. I advise you people to let us take him."

Antony remained silent, standing instinctively as far away as possible from the door and close to the window. I wanted to show myself part of this resistance, and I moved to stand beside him. From there I watched the calmness and inner certainty with which my mother and Judith and Daniel, schooled in years of confrontation with the authorities, gently refused to co-operate.

"Give us another day," Judith said. "Susanna Heywood and I will go and speak to Isaac Shore and see if we can reach an understanding with him — "

"The Negro must be taken into custody," the sheriff interrupted. "If we leave him here he may escape again."

"He is in no condition to escape," my mother protested, and Daniel said, "I will ensure that he does not. I'll answer for him. Only give the women a day."

The sheriff sighed. And yet I thought he looked relieved. "A day you have, then. I see that the man is badly hurt. But I hold thee responsible for him, Daniel Kite."

"Thou hast my word," said Daniel.

The officers left, and my mother and Judith embraced each other and wept. I knew we had avoided a violent and frightening arrest and prevented Antony from being handed straight back to his cruel master. It showed me the power that had sustained my parents and their friends through much harsher times in England, and I felt ashamed of the way I had once mocked their courage and thought it weakness.

The next day my mother and Judith went to Isaac Shore's holding and remonstrated with him about his treatment of Antony. The sheriff went with them – for protection, he insisted; but he stayed at a discreet distance and let them do the talking.

My mother told us about it when she returned.

"We struggled to reach the light in Isaac Shore," she said, easing off her dusty shoes as she sat down with my father and me in the parlour. There was a weariness in her manner, and I guessed it had as much to do with a sense of failure as with feet tired from walking. "He's an angry, ill-tempered fellow – said Antony was lazy, no good and a persistent runaway, and that he'd been misled about the Negro's character by George Bainbrigg. His wife is a hard-faced woman; you should have seen the look she gave us when we dared to reproach them! A young man, their son, lives there – and no love lost between any of them, by the look of it. There used to be a maid, too – an indentured servant – but she ran away." She sighed.

I was shocked – and surprised, for I'd never known my mother so unable to see the light in anyone. It sounded worse, in some ways, than working on a plantation – the fate John Crosbie had hoped to avoid for Antony. At least plantation slaves had one another and a network of communication through their markets. Antony was alone and at the mercy of these people.

"How *could* George Bainbrigg have sold him to such a man?" I exclaimed. All my anger against my former master was reignited.

"He cannot have known," my father said.

My mother agreed. "George Bainbrigg would have seen nothing amiss. Isaac Shore presents himself as a plain, hard-working farmer, and no doubt George approved of that."

"But thou and Judith made no headway with him?" my father asked.

"He didn't like being rebuked by us, though we told him we came in friendship."

"Well, no one likes being rebuked."

"But what can we *do*?" I demanded. "Must Antony go back to this man?"

"He must. He belongs to him," my mother said.

I remembered Antony's back with its furrows of torn flesh. "He's not fit to work yet!"

"I know. But the sheriff will warn Isaac Shore. He'll acknowledge that Antony was in the wrong to have run away, but he'll make it clear that no servant should be punished unmercifully. And Judith and I have shown the Shores that Antony has friends who care about him. We should have hope," she added. "People are often aggressive when told of their wrongdoing, but come round to the right course soon after. And it wouldn't be in Isaac Shore's interest to injure him too badly."

"When will he be taken back there?"

"This afternoon. He may be on his way already."

"I'll go and see!" I sprang up.

"No, Jos." My mother put out a hand. "Don't cause trouble for Antony."

"But—"

"The authorities have their eye on Isaac Shore.

He knows that. It's better not to harass him any more for now."

So Antony returned to the man who had beaten him. Isaac Shore's holding was in the woods to the north of the city, along rough tracks; only a few miles out, but not a direction I could find any excuse to be walking in. If I went out there I'd be noticed, possibly challenged, and might make things worse. Instead, I wrote to Kate about my fears for him. We were all anxious, too, about Patience. My mother made enquiries through the women's meeting, but heard only that there was nothing bad known of the Outrams.

My father kept me busy; and before long, to great excitement, the press arrived, and Daniel Kite came over to help set it up. The machine – the frame, the screw, the lever – was in working order, and Daniel had undertaken to create the flat plate needed for a printing press. The days were long, for it was early July, with light evenings, and by the middle of the month the print shop was up and running. Although in London I had never wanted to be part of my father's work, now I became caught up in the enthusiasm of the new venture. The day we printed our notice advertising the opening of Philadelphia's first print works I was as excited as any of us.

A week later the typesetter Florian Marshall

arrived from London. Florian came recommended by Nat Lacon. He was young, not yet twenty-two, and until last winter had been apprenticed to one of the Quaker printers in the City. We had a day of talk and reminiscence when he arrived, for he brought news of London Friends and reminders of life in England that stirred us up and cheered us and sometimes moved my parents to sadness. He brought letters, too, from Nat and Rachel Lacon, and other London Friends, and some for Betty from her former schoolfriends. We learned that Tabitha Lacon had married in the spring, and that Stepney and Ratcliff Friends continued to be harassed and fined by the authorities.

The work increased steadily. We started off printing notices of sales, and of Friends' matters. Florian set these up ready to print, and my mother began training Betty. She taught her how to daub the type with ink, lay the paper on the tympan and fix the frisket in place. My father and I took turns at the press, for it was tiring work and neither of us was used to it. Soon my parents began to talk of hiring more people: they needed a strong man to work the press, and a maidservant to help in the house so that my mother could take charge of the print shop while my father spent more time selling books.

Kate stayed on in Maryland, and we wrote long letters to each other. Her father had little contact with me and my family, though he was polite when we met on first-days. However, I ran into Zachary on the waterfront and heard that George Bainbrigg had engaged a new man – a clerk, not an apprentice.

This news gave me a pang. Zachary and I were watching a great ship being laden, the boats plying to and fro with goods; and I thought of the voyages I might have made in a year or so, to New England or Maryland or the Caribbean, as what the merchants called supercargo: in charge of all goods on the ship and empowered to buy and sell on my master's account.

But to Zachary I said, "I don't care. They're looking for men here, on the waterfront, building the new wharf. I might try for that – earn some money."

He grinned. "Well, they say the pay is good." And then he asked, "The Negro – Antony – any word of him?"

"No." He had touched on the unease I felt about Antony.

"Maybe he's settled down?"

"Maybe."

But in that isolated holding, out in the forest, who knew what brutality might be hidden?

Tokpa

*I*saac Shore glares at me. "You think the Friends are your *friends*? Think they can protect you? You cross me again, boy, and I'll beat you till you can't stand up. Then you won't go running to the Friends for help. You won't go anywhere."

I believe him. He is a man who has terrible rages. I have seen him punching and beating his son, and sometimes his wife goes about with dark bruises on her face and arms. He could kill me if he loses his temper, so I work hard and keep out of his way.

I feel crushed, even though I know I have friends. I fear I will never escape this place, never see Miata again.

Isaac Shore does not trust me. At night he locks me in a shed. He puts a shackle on my right ankle and chains it to the wall. When the door is locked I sit in darkness, and evil spirits gather around me. I sleep at last, and wake to see light shining through the cracks in the walls. I remember how we sat and waited on the Light in Barbados. Sometimes I close my eyes and let my spirit go where it will. I see my village, whole, unburnt; I see my brothers and sisters and hear our squeals as we run and play; I hear my mother laughing; I see my friend Manhtee; I see a bright-winged bird I once caught and tried to keep. And then I weep because I understand now that I can never go home again.

Each week there is a market day in Philadelphia and people come to town from farms all around. My master's wife takes me with her to the market to carry goods for her. I don't try to escape when we go to town; I know I would be caught. The mistress chooses meat, fish, plums, apples, vegetables. I carry everything in a pannier on my back. One day, as I wait for her to choose, I look around and see a girl – it is Miata! She walks with a sway of her hips, balancing a basket of fruit on her head. Her belly is only a little rounded, but her breasts are large and full and her face is plumper than it was; her hair is braided and gleams with oil. She is beautiful. I leave the mistress paying for plums and step into Miata's path.

"Tokpa!" Her eyes tell me she loves me still. How she outshines the pale, beak-nosed women! Now that I see her, all my hope comes rushing back.

"Miata, are they kind to you – the Outrams? They don't beat you?"

"No," she says. "They treat me well. But you...?"

I tell her quickly how much I hate my master, how the

blacksmith's wife cared for me after I was whipped and ran away. "Oh, but it gives me hope to see you—"

"Antony!" My mistress's voice is angry. "Get over here!"

I touch hands with Miata and leave her.

My mistress stares after Miata and frowns. "Don't you go sniffing around every black girl you set eyes on. Get back on the road. I'm finished now."

Twenty-eight

J was working as a labourer on the new wharf the day Kate returned to Philadelphia.

I had told my father, "They are calling for skilled men – carpenters, bricklayers – but also for men to load carts, lift and carry. The money is good. It will help the family."

He was resistant at first, but soon saw the sense of it. He had wages to pay to three people now: Florian; Abel Lawton, the burly ex-seaman he'd hired to operate the press; and Phoebe, my mother's maidservant.

"It will do for now – for a short while," he said. "But I intend before long to get thee settled somewhere more suitable."

So, in August, in the heat of summer, I began a very different kind of work: lifting, loading, laying paving stones, shovelling gravel. At first the work nearly broke me: every muscle in my body ached and it was hard to get started each day. But after a week or two I realized I was much stronger.

"Thou hast muscles, Jos!" said Betty, squeezing my arm.

"What's more," I said, jingling a handful of coins, "I've got money!"

We laughed. I felt glad to be earning again. Perhaps, I thought, I could go on like this, never bothering with an apprenticeship.

George Bainbrigg came by the new wharf one day and, seeing me, was obliged, out of courtesy, to stop and speak. He expressed some surprise at my choice of work.

"It's honest toil," I said. "Good for my strength and health, and no shame in doing it."

If he felt the barbs in this speech he did not respond to them. "Well said," he agreed, "and certainly there is no shame in it. But thou hast other abilities, Josiah, that not everyone possesses. I hope thou will use them again."

He nodded to me and left.

Afterwards I thought: When is Kate coming home? When may I visit her? How long is this separation to go on? I should have asked when I could see Kate, instead of getting on my high horse and prating about honest work.

As it was, I was obliged to wait.

I knew from Kate's letters that she'd hoped to return soon, but I'd had no news for nearly two weeks. In late August, on one of the hottest days of the year, I was working in a team laying paving stones on the new wharf as it grew steadily closer to the riverbank. I wore a straw hat, my shirt was untied at the neck, and I was sunburnt, slick with sweat and covered in a film of dust.

I saw a ship anchor in the river and, as always, I watched the boats lowered and passengers being helped down into them and rowed to shore.

Perhaps Kate would not have recognized me, but I knew her at once, and before I could stop myself I hollered across the water, "Kate!"

My workmates whistled and laughed, and the two dark-clad Friends who accompanied Kate looked startled, especially when she waved back.

I left my work on the instant and ran along the wharf, leapt the last yard to the bank, and was waiting for her when the boat was tied up.

She came towards me with the Friends, her face alight with happiness. "Josiah, here are Jerome and Margaret Richmond. I have been staying with them in Herring Creek."

"I have heard much of thee, Josiah," said Margaret Richmond, and I knew her eyes – and probably her nose, too – were taking in my dirt and sweat and dishevelled clothing. It was not the introduction I would have chosen.

Kate, however, was looking at me with undisguised admiration, a faint blush rising on her cheeks.

I knew I had begun blushing, too. I pulled the neck of my shirt together and tied it, and said, looking at the two of them, "I am sorry to greet you like this."

"Thou look appropriate to the work in hand," said Jerome.

"Indeed." I seized my advantage. "And we are building a wharf. You will not have to come ashore in a boat in the future."

"Well, thou had best return to it," said Margaret, glancing back at the place I had come from, where the foreman stood frowning.

And Kate added, "I hope to see thee again soon."

I wished them all good-day and ran back to the wharf. I had a lot of chaffing from my workmates, and the foreman docked my pay for leaving the team, but I didn't care.

My work on the wharf began at sun-up and finished early, before our printer's and bookshop closed. The day after Kate returned, I came home and went up to my room to wash and change my shirt. I was drying myself when Betty tapped on the door.

"Jos! Kate is here."

"Where?" I flung down the towel and seized my shirt.

"In the bookshop. May I come in?"

"No! Yes!" She entered. "Is my hair dusty?"

"A little." She brushed at it with her hand. "Give me thy comb."

"Here. Ouch! That's enough."

I peered at myself in the mirror. I did not look too dirty now, but my face and neck were brown from the sun.

"Come on!" said Betty. "She'll think thee fine, however thou look."

"And what about thee? Still ogling Lars Andersson?" I teased, as we went downstairs.

"Oh, *him*!" Betty rolled her eyes dismissively, and I laughed.

To my disappointment, Kate was not alone in the bookshop. She was browsing among the history books while my father was in animated discussion with a group of Germans – pulling out one book after another and answering their questions. These men all spoke good English, though I heard them talking in their own language among themselves. They seemed to me rather old-fashioned and formal in their manners. They nodded to Betty and me as we came in, but did not doff their hats, so I knew they were either Friends or members of some similar group.

Kate turned, and we looked at each other. Betty moved discreetly away.

"Kate," I said. I stepped forward and briefly took her hands. In a low voice I asked, "Does thy father...?"

"No. But" – I heard the impatience in her voice – "he must *guess* that I will not stay away from thee, otherwise why did he send me to Maryland?"

"Have the Richmonds had enough of thee?" I asked, and we both smiled.

"Probably. And my father agreed it was time I returned home. Margaret was much taken with thee."

"She *was*? I thought—"

"Oh, she is not as stiff as she looks. She is on our side, and will try to persuade my father to relent towards thee."

"He can't *forbid* us to meet – can he?"

"He can make it difficult. We are not yet of age, after all. Jos, what news of Antony and Patience?"

At once our mood sobered.

"My mother says the Outrams are Friends and are known to some members of the women's meeting. They have seen Patience and know she is well. But Antony... There has been no more trouble reported since my mother and Judith visited him, but I wish I could *talk* to him! I wish I knew how he is faring."

"We can't go there?"

"I walked out there once – don't say anything to

my father; he doesn't know. Someone pointed out Isaac Shore's holding to me. I saw it from a distance and caught a glimpse of Antony in the yard with another man. So I know he's still there. But I didn't dare approach the place for fear of causing trouble for Antony."

We had been talking softly, and now we became aware that the Germans had gone. Kate turned to my father: "Friend William, I hope thou don't mind us meeting here?"

He said diplomatically, "I assumed on this occasion that it was by chance. But I cannot go against thy father's wishes, Kate." His look included me. "Perhaps Jos and Betty might accompany thee when thou walk home? There can be no harm in that."

"Those Germans..." said Kate, as we walked along Third Street. "I have been studying the German language all this year, and yet I could not understand *anything* they were saying. It's very disappointing."

"They come from near the Dutch border, that's why," said Betty. "Dad told me. They speak a dialect called Hollandisch. It's quite different."

"Oh! So I am not so stupid?"

"Not at all!"

"That's good." She gave a little skip. "Because I've been thinking about my future, what I should do – for

I want to do something useful. Margaret Richmond used to teach in a girls' school in Herring Creek – a Friends' school – and I thought I should like to do the same here. There must be a need for more teachers, with new colonists arriving all the time. What do you think?"

"Thou would be an excellent teacher," Betty said. "Don't thou think so, Jos?"

"Yes, indeed."

It would get her away from the house, I thought, and from her father's domination. And she'd be good at it. I could see that.

"Thou put me to shame," I joked. "I'd better find another employer – someone who needs a clerk. A labourer can't go courting a schoolmistress."

"*Thou* could," said Kate. "But yes, thou should be a clerk. Or a merchant's apprentice..." She turned to Betty. "It seems I should be studying Hollandisch?"

"I reckon they have their own schools, up there in Germantown," said Betty. "Still, it could do no harm. Perhaps we could learn it together? Dad likes these Germans well. They read, and study, and discuss ideas; and he says they are true Christians and that their lives speak the truth."

What clever women I am surrounded by, I thought. Kate a schoolteacher, Betty a printer, my mother in charge of the print shop. And I felt again that I had lost my way, that I needed to find my place, my purpose in life.

As if she guessed these thoughts, Kate said, "I think Dad would like to have thee back, Jos, only he's too proud to say so."

"I'm not sure I'd want to go back," I said. I had my pride, too. "Hasn't he found a new man?"

"A clerk, yes. But he's slapdash, and Dad hates that. He won't last."

When the wharf was finished, in late summer, we began to feel that a real modern city was emerging. The wharf was Samuel Carpenter's, but other merchants and ships paid to use it, and it was a great convenience to all. Soon plans for more wharves were being put forward, along with a design for a meeting house where the growing number of Friends would have more space than in one another's homes. William Penn himself was gone to England on business, but had plans afoot for an estate of his own some distance upriver from Philadelphia.

In September I found work as a grocer's assistant, keeping accounts, serving in the shop and making deliveries. It was responsible work, though it held none of the challenge of the merchant's life.

Meanwhile, George Bainbrigg's insistence that I keep away from Kate remained. It infuriated Kate, who argued with him and took every chance she could to slip out and meet me. There was some delight and excitement to be had in these secret meetings, and in the notes and messages that passed between us, usually via Betty; and they carried us through the late summer and autumn. But before long we began to tire of the enforced secrecy – and we knew that come winter our meetings would not be so easy to contrive. Early in November we decided to make a stand. I'd go to the house, and together we would confront her father.

We made our plans, but before we could act on them, an English ship, the *Isabella* of Bristol, sailed into Philadelphia's harbour; and during the events that followed, all thought of such a meeting was put to one side.

Twenty-nine

We were aware of the *Isabella*'s approach some time before she docked at the new wharf. Any ship attracted attention, and I joined my employer and several customers at the door of the grocer's shop on Front Street and watched as this one drew nearer. She was a large, two-masted vessel with square sails.

The grocer and his customers discussed her appearance.

"Not one of our merchants' ships. Not seen her before."

"English, I'd say."

"Looks like she's been through some rough weather. See the state of those sails?"

As the ship drew nearer I saw on her side the name *Isabella*, and her home port, *Bristol.* She was, indeed, battered and in need of repair, and I wondered what route she had followed. It seemed unlikely that she had come straight from England.

We returned to our work, and by the time we left, the *Isabella* was tied up at Samuel Carpenter's wharf and sailors were beginning to come ashore, bandy and still rolling with the ship's motion.

It was then that I knew – even before we heard the news. An odour had reached us – faint, and overlaid with cleansing herbs; but no amount of scrubbing could ever remove that smell. I had encountered it once before and would never forget it. By morning the news was all over town: the Bristol ship *Isabella* had sailed direct from the west coast of Africa and was carrying a cargo of a hundred and fifty slaves. They were to be sold by auction on the waterfront in four days' time.

I went home at noon for dinner and found an auctioneer at the print shop with a draft of a notice he wanted printed:

"James Furlong, master of the Isabella *of Bristol, offers for sale PRIME NEGROES – men, women and children – newly arrived from the coast of Guinea. To be sold by Public Vendue on Thursday the ninth day of November 1684 at 10 of the forenoon, at Front Street, Philadelphia."*

My father read the notice, frowned, and gave a slow shake of the head. He handed it back. "I am sorry. We cannot undertake this work."

"You are too busy?" The auctioneer seemed surprised.

I waited, tension growing in me. I knew my father must feel torn. The print shop was newly set up; he was beginning to attract customers but was in no way settled in business. To turn down work was risky. But his face was set firm; and I knew my mother would support him.

"I cannot print a notice for the sale of slaves," he said. "It is against my conscience."

A cheer rose inside me.

The auctioneer said, "You won't change your mind? We must draw it up by hand otherwise. It will make no difference."

I knew this was true, but still I was glad my father said no.

Within hours notices had appeared outside the Blue Anchor, the post office and the Society of Traders' hall. A standard form had been used – including a woodcut of a black man, naked except for a loincloth – and the details filled in by hand. As the auctioneer had said, it made no difference.

The news struck Philadelphia and its surrounding farms like a hurricane. There were almost no black slaves in the colony, but the desire for them was huge. Over the next few days, as the word spread, settlers began pouring into town by boat, in carts and on foot.

The Blue Anchor's rooms were full and people were sleeping in their carts. New customers thronged the grocer's shop, and I heard their talk – heard how badly they needed strong men to clear and plant their holdings; of the high cost of Negroes ("but they are better than bondsmen because once you've bought them you have them for life"); of their cooking and household skills, and their cleanliness, thought to be superior to that of many indentured servants. Foremost was the issue of cost: unlike bonded labourers, who must eventually be provided for, slaves were your property, and if they bred you owned their children. I felt an inward shiver as I listened to their talk, which seemed to me without compassion. I awaited the event with both fascination and dread, remembering the unease I had felt at the auction of the *Chepstow*'s cargo. And that was household goods. These were men and women.

My parents appeared subdued by the arrival of the slave ship. I saw that it burdened their spirits, as it did mine. After supper, on the night before the public vendue, my mother lit candles and we sat and listened while my father read to us from the Bible, as was his custom of an evening. When he closed the book we remained silent for some time. I felt that we were preparing ourselves for the events to come.

My father spoke once. "There is something unholy

in this rush to auction," he said. "I thought Friends would not wish to own slaves." And I knew he was as shocked and disappointed as I was.

Many more buyers gathered in town the next morning. "Almost the entire colony must be here," my employer said. He looked forward to extra sales. From his shop on the front we were able to watch the preparations being made. A large area of Front Street was cordoned off, and a wooden stand set within it. This stand would accommodate, I guessed, seven or eight slaves at a time, so the vendue would be a prolonged affair if the Negroes were to be displayed in such small lots. Larger groups had been brought up in batches onto the ship's deck earlier in the day for some of the merchants to go on board, look them over and have first choice – and a fair number were sold in this way. I did not see George Bainbrigg among these merchants.

I thought of Antony. Was he here, with his master, in the crowds? It was a day when almost everyone had come to the waterfront. Even if Antony was not here, he would know what was happening. How must he feel, I wondered, seeing others about to be sold as he had been?

The auction began with a boy ringing a bell. In the shop we all rushed to the door, and saw the auctioneer mount a block and shout, in his strong, carrying voice, that the proceedings were open. The first captives were brought off the ship, and my heart almost stopped as I saw their terror: the uncontrollable shaking, the rolling eyes, the way they wept and tried to cling to one another. Some were so afraid that their knees gave way and they fell down in a swoon and had to be splashed with water by the sailors and hauled to their feet. I remembered my conversations with Antony in Barbados, how he'd said that when he arrived there, and was put up for auction, he'd thought the beak-nosed people surrounding him were demons who would kill and eat him. These men must be feeling that same dread. As soon as they were in place on the stand, shackled, almost naked, exposed to all, and in the grip of fear, prospective buyers rushed forward and fell upon them, pushing, prodding, turning them around. The settlers' hands were in the men's mouths; they forced their jaws open, made them bare their teeth, stick out their tongues. They examined eyes, skin, hair, private parts.

Some of the Negroes were clearly worth having, for the settlers pushed and argued with one another over who was first. I saw a fight on the brink of breaking out before the auctioneer's man calmed it.

The first batch was sold, and next from the ship came a group of women, forced up onto the stand. They wore strips of cloth like little skirts around their hips, but their breasts were bare, and I found I was staring at their nakedness despite myself. Some of these women had young children with them – one a toddler no higher than its mother's knee. And there was a girl, perhaps thirteen, still slim-hipped and with breasts just beginning to show. She stood with head down and tears falling. Nearly all the women cried, and some were so afraid they could not stand and had to be dragged upright. But a few, I noticed, remained still and quiet. These were mothers, and I believe they controlled their fear in order not to frighten the young ones.

I returned briefly to my work, but female shrieks drew us all to the door again. Two of the women were being separated from their children. Their despair was harrowing. I could not bear it, and turned away.

"They settle down," the grocer said. "Screech and wail, but get over it fast enough. Like cows, when the calf's taken."

They are not like cows, I thought. They are like my mother. Like Judith. Like Miata.

Another group was brought up, and I felt the ripple of excitement that ran through the crowd. Each time a new group was brought forward onto the stand a roar erupted and people pushed forward. As the auctioneer began the bidding I saw the eager, greedy faces, the hands shooting up, and I imagined again, as I had at the time of the *Chepstow* sale, the auctioneer as an agent of the Devil, whipping up souls to evil. Perhaps Antony was right, and demons did indeed stalk the world.

The auction continued until well into the afternoon. We heard that all the captives had been sold – and for cash.

"Which means there will be scarcely any ready money left in the colony and everyone will be asking for credit," the grocer said gloomily.

I thought of the captives who, over the next day or so, would be taken out to farms and smallholdings in the countryside, far from others of their kind, lonely and afraid, unable to speak the language or understand the customs of their owners. No wonder slaves often kill themselves, I thought; or run away and endure cruel punishments, only to run away again. I had tried to help Antony by letting him escape. But it was not in my power truly to set him free. It seemed we were all caught in this evil trade and could not escape from it.

When I returned home I found the ordinariness of our family life a refuge from the scenes of avarice and despair I had been witnessing all day. The hens ran clucking to Sarah as she tossed them handfuls of grain; my mother set the table; Betty scrubbed ink from her hands in the yard. We sat down to eat, and waited in silence on the light.

We ate mostly in silence, too, in the manner of

Friends, but afterwards we moved to the parlour, where Betty and my mother took up their sewing and Sarah struggled with her letters on a slate.

"This has been a dark day," my father said. I saw that he was shaken. An auction like this was something we had never thought to see in Philadelphia.

"We must hope that since most of the buyers are Friends they will treat their slaves well and endeavour to bring them to the Truth," my mother said.

"Is that all?" I burst out – angering my father, who said, "Do not shout at thy mother."

I apologized, but with an ill grace, for I was full of pent-up rage at what I had witnessed on the waterfront.

"We cannot alter the fact that they are slaves," my mother said. "All we can do now is to urge Friends to care for them, body and soul, and eventually to set them free."

"Mam, if thou had seen the greed, the cruelty in the faces of those buyers, thou would not believe them capable of caring."

"All are capable," my mother said. "And the buyers are all Christians."

"Would *thou* have bought a slave, Mam, if we needed one?" I demanded.

"Thou know I would not."

My father intervened: "Thy mother understands that we now live among people who keep slaves and must appeal to the consciences of those people to behave rightly towards them. George Fox said as much; and William Penn has said they should be freed after fourteen years."

"It is not enough!" I said.

"It is not. But once a sale is made it is all we can do. And people *do* change, Jos, over time."

"But what use is that to those who are suffering now?"

Nothing they said could satisfy me.

I was still brooding on the scenes I had witnessed when, two days later, we heard news that shocked us all.

Tokpa

*O*nce again I glimpse Miata on a market day. Several moons have passed since we last met, and I see that she is now big with child. She doesn't see me. There are several stalls between us – one heaped with gourds, another with corn; and although I fix my eyes on her and try to will her to look at me, she doesn't turn. Her mistress leads her away, and they disappear into the crowd. I feel more bitter than ever at the loss of Miata. It cuts my heart to see my own woman heavy with my child and have no power to reach or touch her.

We go back to the farm and I work with Isaac Shore and Enoch, his son, clearing the fields ready for next spring's planting. Both men use any chance to cuff or punch me. The scars on my back are healed but I have many hidden cuts and bruises. Isaac Shore has made a switch of some flexible twig with sharp thorns, and he uses it all day long on me, pricking and stinging my face, neck, ears and arms. It maddens me and my hatred of him grows. Father and son grunt and snarl at each other, and Isaac hits out at Enoch as often as he does at me. That night, as always, he shackles me in the shed and locks the door. The nights are long now and the bad spirits crowd around me.

If I had power I would avenge myself on this man.

Next day Enoch goes to town, and when he comes back I hear the three of them talking about a ship from Africa full of slaves in Philadelphia's harbour.

At once I am full of hope, and fear. Who are the captives on this ship? Could my people be among them – my family who were left behind? All my love and longing for my people returns and torments me. I want them to be at home, in our village, and yet I want them here with me. I both want and dread to see the captives come off this ship.

There will be an auction, Enoch says; and the woman, Isaac Shore's wife, begins to chatter like a monkey with excitement, and says she will have a wench – a little wench to help her in the house.

So we go to town: the four of us, me with an iron collar around my neck to mark me out as Shore's if I should run.

I smell the slaves and the slave ship as soon as we approach the harbour. Everything has been cleaned, and the Shores don't seem to notice the lingering odour – but they are white people, used to living in filth; they don't mind the stink of it.

The smell reaches me and fills me with remembered terror.

My knees feel weak and my mouth is dry. As we approach the harbour the noise surrounds us: the auctioneer shouting, the yells of the crowd, raised hands, eager pointing fingers. We enter the harbour front and the scene bursts upon me. I see a row of black men on a long stand, naked except for loin-cloths, staring-eyed and shaking with fear. My heart pounds. I know they expect to be killed and eaten by demons. I see the auctioneer in his cocked hat and his blue coat trimmed with grimy lace. A man leaps up from the crowd and grabs one of the captives, forces open his mouth, prods and pushes him. Words begin to fly back and forth between the crowd and the man in the blue coat. Hands shoot up, faces redden, calls come faster. The auctioneer bangs a stick on the block and the cap-tive is unfastened and led away. I see these captives and hear their voices and I know they are not of my people. They speak a different language, but their terror takes root in me and I am back in the harbour in Barbados with the whiskery man and the cart full of people stinking of fear.

"They are bringing the women up now," says Enoch. And he runs his tongue over his lips. His mother looks up with an eager face.

The women are weeping, trying to cover themselves with their hands. A young girl appears. None of these people is Kpelle; I know now that I will not find my family here. But this girl is about the age my sister Musu would be now; and I wonder, as I have so often, where Musu is, whether she is still alive, whether someone is hurting her. The girl stands with tears running down her face. I feel such pity for her that my own eyes flood.

Shore's wife is excited; the monkey-chatter bursts from her again. She goes up on the stand and examines the girl and calls down to her menfolk that she's pleased. The bidding begins. This girl is cheaper than the grown women, I suppose, and therefore many people want her. Voices rise. Isaac Shore continues to shout and raises his hand; his wife squawks.

But they lose. The girl goes to someone else, and I'm glad. I hope she will be with a kind woman.

My master and mistress try for another girl later, but again they are outbid. We go home without having bought a slave. Husband and wife quarrel all the way about whose fault it was.

We carry on working next day. Some of this plot was not cleared last year, so we are cutting down trees, chopping firewood, building a bonfire to burn the scrub and bushes. Isaac Shore lights the bonfire and smoke billows up. The woman comes out and shouts and bad words fly between the two of them. I know she is still angry about the girl.

Isaac Shore turns on me and flicks at me with the switch and tells me to work faster. The bonfire burns all afternoon as we feed it with small branches and tangles of knotted roots and weed. As evening falls it crackles and throws up showers of sparks into the darkening sky.

I think of Miata and our child. I think of the captives I saw yesterday, of their fear and humiliation. I think of the young girl who looked like Musu. I look at the fire, feel the heat of the flames, and remember my mother and Musu and the little ones running screaming from their burning hut.

"Get on! Move!"

Stinging pain strikes my neck: Isaac Shore with the switch.

A red bloom of anger rises in me.

He raises the switch again. I whirl round, snatch it and throw it into the fire. I seize a burning branch from the flames and thrust it towards him, forcing him to leap back. I rejoice to see the fear in his eyes.

"Enoch!" he shouts – and his son comes running. "Quick! Grab him! Shackle him!"

I brandish the branch at both of them. I shout curses. The woman comes out and shrieks.

The brand is burning down towards my hand. They see that and run to tackle me.

"Get him into the shed!"

I will never be shackled there again.

I hurl the branch onto the roof of the shed. The thatch ignites with a roar like a beast's. Flames leap up. Soon the whole building is alight. Before they can move I pull out another brand from the fire and run with it to the house and toss it up onto the roof, which explodes in flame. The woman runs screaming across the yard.

"Fetch neighbours!" her husband shouts. "Fetch the sheriff!"

The two men overpower me, knock me to my knees, tie my hands behind my back. They pull me upright and force me into the burning shed; but it's too hot, they can't fasten the door, and I stumble out, sparks of fire burning in my hair and on my clothes. I roll on the ground to smother the flames, and see father and son scurrying with pails of water, trying to save their house. But it is already lost; the hungry fire will devour it.

Sparks burn my face and hands and smoke scorches my throat. Neighbours come, and – later – the sheriff and his men. Still with my hands tied behind my back I am taken away, in a cart lit with a lantern, along dark woodland tracks. When we reach the town they take me into a big house and put me in a cell and untie me. There is water to drink and a pallet on the floor. My jailer goes out, and a key turns in the lock.

What will they do with me? Surely they will kill me now.

Thirty

"*In jail*? Why? What has he done?"

"Burned down his master's house and outbuildings, it seems." The grocer enjoyed being the bearer of early morning news on the waterfront. The shop was already filling with customers, and I was busy weighing out dried peas for a servant girl.

"He'll hang for that, won't he?" she said, her eyes widening.

My breathing slowed. I felt cold. Surely not? This was not England, where you could be hanged for stealing a loaf of bread. And yet – what rights did slaves have?

At noon, before I went home for dinner, I hurried along the waterfront to the lock-up where unruly troublemakers were kept overnight, and where I guessed Antony was being held.

The guard led me downstairs. He was a young fellow, not much older than I. I asked, "They won't hang him, will they?"

He shook his head. "I don't know. I know he thinks they will. Sits there all turned in on himself. Won't eat or drink."

"When will he be tried?"

He shrugged. "No one tells *me* anything."

He opened the door of the cell.

Antony was squatting on a pallet, hunched and miserable, as the guard had said. He looked up, dull-eyed – but at sight of me a spark returned and he rose to his feet.

"Jos!"

"Oh, Tokpa! How did'st thou come to be here?"

We hugged each other. I noticed that hanging around his neck was a little bag made of bark pinned with thorns. Some good-luck charm, I supposed.

He told me briefly what had happened. It seemed it was the slave auction that had finally driven him to fury. That, and the switch; I saw its small scars all over his neck and arms, some of them festering.

"They will kill me," he said.

"No!" Please God I was right. "Thou'll be tried, and probably found guilty, but thou must not fear Pennsylvanian justice."

I looked around. The cell was clean, with fresh

rushes on the floor, blankets, and a necessary bucket with a lid.

In my childhood, in London, I had visited my parents in prison – at Newgate, New Prison, and other places – and had seen people lying on stinking straw, plagued by lice and rats, and with the smell of excrement and a raucous clamour of voices all around. This place was bare, but decent. More than anything, its decency gave me hope.

"This country – this colony – is a refuge," I said. "People have come here from all over Europe, fleeing persecution…" I saw that I had lost him; he knew nothing of our history. "Thou'll have a fair trial. Thou may be found guilty – but the jury will know Isaac Shore provoked thee. And thou hast friends, Tokpa. We'll speak up for thee, and hold thee in the light."

There was no time to say more, except to urge him to eat and not to despair. I left him, and hurried home, feeling far less certain about the justice he would receive than I'd tried to sound.

I saw from their faces that my family had already heard the news.

"Dad," I said – and my voice cracked – "they won't hang Antony for this, will they?"

The girls looked up, startled, and my mother put her arms around me and said, "Oh, Jos – no! Be sure they won't. This is what we came across the sea for.

We have true justice here in Pennsylvania."

"William Penn's Great Law for the colony allows the death penalty only for murder and treason," my father said.

"Even for a slave?"

"The law must be the same for everyone."

"Then what punishment *will* he suffer?"

"That's for the judge to decide." He frowned. "The usual punishment would be a fine – in goods, if necessary. But Antony can't pay a fine. I don't know what they could take away from him that he has not lost already."

"Isaac Shore is a brute!" I said. "*He* should be the one to suffer."

"Well … he is now without shelter – and winter is coming on," my mother remarked – to which Betty retorted, "Good!"

"And George Bainbrigg, who sold him to Isaac Shore," I said. "He is to blame, too."

"George Bainbrigg didn't know what Isaac Shore was like," my mother said.

"He didn't care!" I retorted. "He sold him for profit – reckless of what harm might come of it."

And I shared that blame, I knew. I had helped separate and sell Antony and Patience.

"Sit down and eat," my mother urged us. "Jos, eat thy dinner or thou'll be late getting back to work."

We sat in silence for a moment before turning to the food.

After we had eaten – and I could manage little, thinking of Antony, isolated and afraid – my father said, "It's first-day tomorrow. This should be a time for reflection, not blame."

"I won't go to Meeting," I said. I was so angry about the auction, the great influx of slaves into the colony and the thought of Antony's suffering that I felt I would never go again, never have anything more to do with Friends.

"Come, Jos, and bring thine anger with thee," my mother urged. "Bring it into the light."

"I don't want to listen to a lot of old men speaking platitudes."

But in the end I did go – not from any noble ideal, but because I had not been able to see Kate for several days. I was desperate to talk to her about all this, and to take up again our plan to confront her father; and I knew she would be at Meeting.

As Friends came into the meeting room there was, as usual, almost no conversation; people were already in a quiet frame of mind, their thoughts turned inwards towards God. No doubt most of them had been reading their Bibles. I too had done so, seeking vindication for my feelings about the slave auction. I found little there about slavery, but much about compassion, and about our duty of care to one another. With these words of Christ in my mind I went to Meeting.

Kate was there, but her father kept her close to him and we could not speak before they went to their seats. I looked around, and saw many people I knew: the Kites, Tom Appleyard, David, Zachary, Florian Marshall, our neighbours the Parkes.

The meeting began to centre down. I withdrew my attention from others, let my thoughts go and felt myself drawn into the silence. Usually I would daydream and find it hard to become one with the meeting, but that day all my being was absorbed by its power. I thought of what I had read in the Bible that morning, of the significance of every soul, of forgiveness, of love. I thought of Tokpa, torn from his home and family, separated from Miata, and now in prison awaiting trial. And I relived the scenes I had witnessed at the slave auction and the horror they had aroused in me.

These thoughts and feelings filled my mind, and I became aware at the same time of the deep stillness and silence around me. I sank into it; became part of the gathered meeting. After a while I began to feel light-headed. My hands shook. An intense agitation overwhelmed me. I thought, I am about to speak. And then, I *cannot* speak; I have never spoken before. I looked at my mother, who sat next to me, but she seemed unaware of the force that moved me. The shaking spread to my whole body. I could not resist it. The spirit took hold of me and I rose to my feet.

People noticed then; their slight movements stirred the room.

My voice broke from me in a rush. "We think ourselves Christians," I said. "We have been persecuted and cruelly treated. We come here to Pennsylvania because others who call themselves Christians oppress us. Here we have liberty of conscience, a better life, a new society. Freedom. Yet we deny freedom to others. Here, in this colony, are people who have been stolen from their farms and villages and sold as slaves – brought across the sea in a manner so cruel that when I heard of it I could not imagine how they survived – and then sold again and again; everything taken from them: their friends, their families, their dignity, their clothes, their very *names* taken from them, their lives of no account. I know because I have taken part in it myself, to my shame as a Christian. I have locked up a man and helped to sell his woman and unborn child away from him…" I kept my gaze on the back of the room; I could not look at George Bainbrigg. "And I'll regret that to the end of my days."

I paused; then, in the hush I felt around me, plunged on: "Imagine what it must be like, to have your village burnt, to be taken captive and forced to march, day after day, until you reach the sea; and then to be sold into a strange country – your wife, your children, your friends gone. Who would do this to any of their own people? We may say, 'These people are here through no fault of ours, so why not buy them, and have the use of them, and bring them into the light of Christianity?' But if we do this we are no better than those who capture and buy them in Africa. I cannot do it. I cannot be part of it. I will stand against this traffic, here, in Pennsylvania. We came here seeking Eden. But this – this is not Eden, where men have liberty of conscience but use their freedom to keep others in slavery."

I sat down, my heart hammering. The silence was profound. And yet I knew silence was to be expected; Friends do not engage in argument or direct response at Meeting. They would be meditating on what I had said. Even so, I trembled. I had been moved by the spirit, but they might not like what I had said. They might think me too young, and my ministry presumptuous, argumentative, not sufficiently reflective.

My mother took my hand and held it.

Later, Friends began to speak: some on other matters, some on the moral dangers of the marketplace, some on the necessity to attend to the souls of people bought as slaves and to ensure that families were not parted and Christian marriage was encouraged between them. George Bainbrigg remained silent. I glanced at my former master, wondering how he would respond now to my request to court his daughter. And yet, whatever the outcome, it was a relief to have spoken.

When Meeting was over and people stood up and began to mingle, I caught Kate's eye. Her look told me that she was in complete accord with what I had said, but we had no chance to talk.

The next time I saw her was at Antony's trial.

Thirty-one

The trial took place two days later, before the deputy Governor (since William Penn was in England) and a jury of Council members, all Friends. There was limited space in the room, but a large number of concerned Friends crowded in. My parents and the Kites were there, and George Bainbrigg and Kate, several members of the women's meeting, and some people I guessed were neighbours of Isaac Shore. I had persuaded the grocer to give me time off work so that I could go; I think he hoped that in return he would receive prompt news of what took place.

Even though I knew it would happen, it still distressed me to see Antony led into the dock. I could sense his fear. And because he was afraid, he looked wild-eyed and dangerous, gripping the rail and staring out at all the faces. I worried that his appearance might count against him. When his gaze alighted on a man who sat to one side of the dock I knew at once from the look of hatred that crossed his face that this was Isaac Shore – and was surprised to see that this cruel master was a small, nondescript man with nothing about him to show his true nature.

Isaac Shore gave his testimony first, describing how Antony had seemed to go insane. "He was like a wild animal – threatened me with a firebrand, and then, when we tried to restrain him, he burned down my house and farm buildings."

His tone was that of an aggrieved but reasonable man. Antony, under questioning, admitted to deliberately setting light to the thatch. He glowered at Isaac Shore and his answers sounded aggressive. I began to think it would not go well for him and was seized with anxiety.

But almost at once the mood began to change. The court was told that Antony had attempted to run away several times. The sheriff was called, and he described the injuries he had seen on Antony after his whippings by Isaac Shore.

"They'll leave him scarred for life," he said.

Then came a neighbouring farmer who told how his family had taken in and protected the Shores' bondservant when she too ran away complaining of harsh treatment.

Next, to my surprise, George Bainbrigg spoke. He told the court of Antony's previous good character throughout his time in Barbados, and admitted his own feelings of guilt at having separated Antony from the girl he regarded as his wife. He said he was willing to buy back Antony from Isaac Shore and find him a new master, if Isaac Shore would agree. And he added that if Antony could be joined in Christian marriage with Patience and a way found for them to live together as husband and wife he believed there might be no more trouble from him.

The judge then summed up, and the jury retired to consider a charge of arson. They quickly came back with a guilty verdict. I clenched my hands. What now? Everything in my life so far had made me afraid of courts and prisons. Would today be different?

"Antony has committed a crime and must be punished," the judge said, "but the plaintiff, Isaac Shore, must take much of the blame for his harsh treatment of this young man who, until now, has shown good behaviour. I also bear in mind that although Isaac Shore has suffered considerable loss and expense it is not possible for a slave to repay him for the damage done. There is only one way Antony can make recompense, and that is to work on the speedy rebuilding of the plaintiff's house and outbuildings. I therefore sentence Antony to work under the supervision of those neighbouring colonists who have offered to help with the rebuilding – and, to this end, he is to be released immediately."

I let out a breath of relief.

"I hope," the judge continued, "that the remedies others have spoken of – that Antony and Patience should be married, and that George Bainbrigg should buy back Antony and find him a new master – may be brought about. But these matters must be left to the discretion of those involved."

And so the trial was over. I felt enormous satisfaction at this outcome. It restored my faith in Friends' justice. And I knew I had misjudged George Bainbrigg; clearly he wanted to make amends for his hasty sale of Antony and Patience.

Antony was taken away, and I saw George Bainbrigg already in discussion with Isaac Shore. Kate and I found each other in the throng as people were leaving.

"This is good," she said, "good for Antony."

"I think well of thy father for what he said – and what he's trying to do."

"He *does* care, Jos. I always knew it."

"We must speak to him soon – about that other matter. There will never be a better time."

She agreed. "Tomorrow," she said. "Come after work. I'll let thee in."

I appeared, I hoped, respectable enough. It was now winter; my labourer's tan had faded, and I looked more clerkly; and I had taken care to dress in a clean and sober manner. Even so, my heart was beating fast as I knocked at the front door of the house in Walnut Street.

It was opened at once by Kate. Our arms went round each other. I felt her body pressed against mine, breathed her breath and smelt the scent of her skin. I love her, I thought. I can't give her up.

"Come!" she said, releasing herself. She opened the parlour door.

George Bainbrigg had heard my knock and was already on his feet. We entered and stood facing him, side by side and holding hands.

"Josiah? What's this?"

We had caught him off guard, as we'd intended.

"George Bainbrigg," I said, "I come to ask permission to court thy daughter – with the intention to marry her when I am of age and able to set up home and provide for her and any children God may grant us."

Having delivered this speech I turned hot and looked down at my feet.

"We want to be free to meet in plain view," said Kate. "We are sweethearts, and want folk to know that."

I glanced up and saw that her father was not angry; indeed, he looked, I thought, almost relieved.

"Well, Kate," he said, "thou'll have thy way, as usual. Watch out for her, Jos, or she'll rule thee." I permitted myself a smile. "I'd not be one to stand between sweethearts, and I doubt the meeting would approve if I did. Jos, I was moved by thy ministry on first-day. It spoke to my heart, to my unease about the trade in Negroes. I've felt guilty for a long time about my lack of care towards Antony and Patience. I was too eager to be rid of them. But Antony belongs to me now. I bought him from Isaac Shore today."

And Kate added, "Antony is up at the Shores' now, but they know my father owns him, and the neighbours won't let any harm come to him. We needn't fear."

"I'll visit John Outram in a day or two," her father said. "He may be willing to buy Antony – or to sell Patience. I will find a way to keep them together – and to see them married."

"I'm glad of that," I said. "We all are, and thank thee for it."

He gave a wry smile, and shook his head. "I've been angry with thee, Jos. I believed thou had involved Kate in thy wrongdoing and turned her against me. But that's all in the past. We'll say no more about it."

"I *did* wrong thee," I said, "and I'm sorry." I was determined to be as conciliatory as possible. Kate squeezed my hand.

"Kate tells me she wants to be a schoolteacher," he said.

"Yes." Kate and I exchanged a smile.

"And thou, Jos? What are thy prospects with the grocer?"

He'd been keeping an eye on me and my doings, then, I noted.

"It's steady work," I said, "and useful. Not what I'd hoped for earlier in the year, before – before..." I stumbled, despite my wish to be in control.

"Before our falling-out, yes," said George Bainbrigg. "But thou hast no plan to change?"

"I might consider change," I said guardedly.

George Bainbrigg let out a breath. "The fact is – I'll be blunt – the man I took on to replace thee is no good. He's older than thee; he's not an apprentice; he's a clerk, a man with some experience. But he makes mistakes. He's not careful. I'd like thee back, Jos. What dost thou say?"

I was startled. I hadn't expected this, even though Kate had hinted at it a while back. It seemed I had changed in an instant from outcast to apprentice and future son.

"I ... I can't," I said. "Thou heard what I said in

Meeting. I cannot bear to deal in slaves. It is against my conscience. I won't do it, no matter how much…"

"I've no wish to deal in slaves again myself," he said. "I feel much chastened by recent events. But the fact is, Jos, we live in a world where these folk are bought and sold, and we cannot avoid all contact. But I can promise I would not ask of thee again what I asked on our Caribbean venture."

And as I stood, uncertain, he said, "I've missed thee, lad, and I'd like thee back. That's the truth. And as for my daughter, I know you are sweethearts and I won't come between you. Thou may marry Kate whether thou work for me or not. I don't make it a condition. Think on it, lad. Talk to thy father and mother. Talk to Kate. Take her back now, to see thy parents. Hast thou had thy supper yet?"

"No."

"Take her back with thee, then. Thy mother'll find a sup for her, I reckon?"

"She will, gladly."

I did not hold out for long. I had my pride; but excessive pride, I knew, was a sin. Of more concern was my conscience. I'd seen how my father had refused to print notices for the slave auction and had admired him for his stand. As a merchant's apprentice, I might at any time be confronted with a similar situation.

"A merchant is always looking for profit," I said.

We were sitting around the table at home: my parents, Kate and I. Looking around the room – comfortable enough now, though with unpainted walls, plain-weave curtains and wooden boards underfoot – I thought how much was needed in the way of earnings and labour to make a living and create a home for a family.

My father laughed. "We all hope to make a profit, else how will we live – and pay for our children's apprenticeships? Thou must deal with each challenge as it comes, Jos. If thou know, in thy heart, what is right, thou'll have no difficulty."

"But I'll be an apprentice – not free to choose."

"We are always free to choose. And thou won't be an apprentice for ever. Four years is not long."

It seemed long to me.

"He'll send thee out to trade on thy own," said Kate. "He did that with Matt Peel. Matt was often away."

Voyages. Independence. A chance to see more of the New World. Better that than being a grocer's assistant. I saw that I must seize this opportunity and use it.

"Don't rush to give him an answer," my mother advised. "Sit in silence and wait on the spirit."

"I will," I said.

But already my mind was made up.

Thirty-two

"She's a bonny sight, the *Frances*," George Bainbrigg said.

The schooner was no longer anchored in the river but tied up at Samuel Carpenter's wharf, not far from the counting house on Second Street. We stood in the doorway, looking out at her through a gap between the buildings. It was an evening in early autumn, almost a year since I had taken up my apprenticeship again with George Bainbrigg. I had been working hard all day with Richard Grey and the crew, gauging the ship, overseeing the lading and writing up the necessary papers. We were making ready for a voyage first to Maryland and then north to Boston – a voyage on which I would be in charge of the sale and disposal of the cargo and the purchase of goods in exchange. We would go out laden with woollen cloth, grain and tools, and would buy tobacco and indigo in

Maryland, dried cod in Boston. The sails were furled, the hatches battened down. We were to sail in the morning, early. This was my first trading venture on my master's behalf, and I was sick with anxiety and yet more exhilarated than I had ever felt in my life.

"Excited?" my master asked.

"Yes, indeed!"

"And terrified thou'll do something wrong or plain foolish?"

"Yes."

He patted my shoulder. "Don't worry. Richard Grey will look after thee. And I have confidence in thy good sense – I wouldn't trust thee with my goods, else. The traders will deal kindly with thee; they're mostly Friends. And thou'll see new places and different ways of living. It'll set thee up, give thee confidence. Thou hast thy letters of introduction?"

"I have." I patted my side, where I had a pocket hidden inside my coat.

"And the mail for Friends in Anne Arundel and Boston?"

"Everything is safe."

"Well, I'll close up here tonight. Go back to the house now. Thou'll be wanting to say thy farewells there…"

He meant Kate.

I said, "I thought Kate and I might go out and

take the air, since it's a fine evening."

"Aye, do that! It'll be a while till thou see her again."

I had already said goodbye to my parents the evening before – though I knew my mother would be on the quay to see me leave. I would only be gone a month or two, but she'd be watching the weather and ships for my return.

"Be pleased for me!" I'd said, hugging her.

"I am, son. And glad thou'rt back with George Bainbrigg, and all mended between you."

My father had returned the money for my apprenticeship, which had continued as if it had never been interrupted. By February next I would be nineteen and almost halfway through my term.

I went back to the house and found Kate in the parlour, seated at the table with pen and paper, and making notes from several books. She jumped up, put down her quill and came into my arms.

"What's that you're doing?" I asked, nodding towards her work.

"Oh, it's for the school. I shall be teaching them English history and thought I should remind myself of dates and kings."

"Mam says thou hast brought Sarah on greatly. She can read and reckon quite well now."

"Oh, Sarah was a challenge!" She smiled; it was good to see her enthusiasm for the work she had chosen. "Her health is better, and that helps. But mostly she needed to come out from under Betty's shadow. Betty is so quick."

"She is." I turned Kate around and gave her a little push towards the table. "Put thy work away now and come out with me. We can take Hob as an excuse – though I don't think we need one tonight."

"No." She put the lid on the inkwell and replaced the quill in its case. "Dad understands."

We called the dog, and went out with him, turning away from the waterfront towards the unfinished centre of the city, where the roads soon turned to tracks through woodland. Hob trotted beside us. Once we were past most of the houses we held hands.

Kate turned to me. "I wish Patience could be as happy as I am! Those two have so little, compared to us."

My master had been unable to persuade John Outram either to buy Antony or to sell Patience. They liked the girl, he said, and would not part with her; but although they had need of another man they could not afford to buy Antony. Instead, George Bainbrigg had agreed to hire him out to them three days a week. Patience had her own cabin, and on those days Antony stayed there with her and the baby, Kpana. So they were together some of the time, and Friends had seen to it that they were married and attended Meeting. And in time John Outram would perhaps buy Antony. But they were still slaves, property – to be disposed of if necessary. They could be sold to pay a debt, given away as gifts, separated, their daughter taken away.

"The only right way forward," I said, "is for Friends to refuse to take part in the slave trade."

Nothing engaged me so strongly as this concern. There was a group of us who prayed and talked about it regularly: Kate, my family, the Kites, Florian, and some of the Germans my father had met in the bookshop. Change would happen; it must. We all felt sure it was God's will, and were working towards it.

Kate and I had come to a part of the forest where the road was no more than a track and only a few plots were occupied. A series of clearings marked where settlers had moved in. We turned onto a woodland path that led alongside a stream. I put my arm around her waist and we walked along closely entwined.

As soon as we were out of sight of the main track we let the dog run free and stopped under an oak and moved closer into each other's arms. We lay down on the grass and leaf mould beneath the tree and kissed and embraced each other, and came as close as we dared to the act of love – closer than ever before. Our passion was the stronger for knowing that tomorrow I would be gone and it would be many weeks

– perhaps months – before we could expect to meet again. I knew Kate was fearful for me – of the dangers at sea, of pirates, hostile Indians, illness. She clung to me and cried, and as I kissed away her tears I longed to be free to make love to her, to marry her now, not to have to wait. And I thought that perhaps it was for the best that I should make these voyages from time to time; the pain of separation might be easier to bear than this enforced chastity.

"Thou won't forget me?" She pressed closer, and we lay with our hearts beating together, kissing and murmuring promises. Yet all the time, underlying my sadness at leaving her, there ran a current of excitement and a longing to be on my way, off on my own adventure. These mingled feelings fought in me.

Hob thrust a wet nose under my hand and licked us both. Kate giggled and sat up.

"It'll soon be dark." She looked flushed, her lips red and her eyes bright with love.

"Thou'rt beautiful," I said. I would remember her like this when I was away.

We stood up and brushed leaves and grass from our clothes. Kate's kerchief was crumpled and lay askew over the neckline of her dress. I untied it, laid it carefully in place around her neck, and retied it with a kiss. "Let's go home," I said.

❋ ❋ ❋

Next morning I was on the wharf in good time, rechecking the cargo, receiving last-minute instructions from my master, and stowing on board my personal goods, few as they were. I was to have my master's cabin, which pleased me greatly. It had a desk and writing materials, and a shelf of books: works by Robert Barclay, George Fox, William Penn and others. I had brought my journal to write up and also, secretly, paper and inks for drawing. Hidden in my pocket was a sketch of Kate, done when she was sewing, that pleased me, for it caught her likeness a little. I carried it with me as worldly folk would carry a painted miniature.

I spent time disposing my belongings around the cabin, reluctant to go out and say goodbye to everyone until the last moment. I wanted all the partings to be over with quickly.

Richard Grey knocked on the cabin door. "Josiah?"

When I came out I saw that the crew were hoisting the sails. The canvas snapped and cracked as the wind caught it, and I felt the ship move like a live creature straining to be gone.

Outside on the wharf stood George Bainbrigg, Kate, and my parents and sisters, as well as the usual gathering of passers-by who are drawn into watching a ship depart. I stepped ashore; hugged all my family in turn; held Kate close for a long moment.

And then, in the crowd, I saw Antony. Eagerly, I called him over.

"Tokpa…" I felt tears pricking my eyes. I'd wanted so much to be a true friend to him, not only to help him, but to be at ease with him, as I was with Ben or Florian. Perhaps that would come in time, as Africa faded to a memory and he grew more like us. But it would be hard to achieve, for our lives and our destinies were so different. Now, as always, the two of us had little to say, but we put our arms around each other in a wordless gesture of affection.

Then he slipped away, back towards the counting house.

George Bainbrigg took my hand and wished me farewell.

"God send thee fair winds and a prosperous voyage," he said. "Go well, Jos."

I sprang aboard. The rope was cast off; and the ship, her sails filling, moved slowly away from the wharf and out into the river, to begin her long passage towards the sea.

Afterword

When I began work on *Seeking Eden* I didn't expect to be writing about slavery. I knew of course, that there were slaves in America at that time, but I never thought Quakers would have owned them or traded in them. My research soon showed that I was wrong, but even so I was shocked when I read of the 1684 sale of 150 slaves from the English ship *Isabella* to eager settlers in Philadelphia.

The Quakers are well-known for their opposition to slavery, but this opposition came into being later in the eighteenth century. In 1684 there was no anti-slavery movement – though even from the earliest times there were individuals who spoke against slavery.

Some of these individuals were Quakers from the German-Dutch community at Germantown, near Philadelphia. As early as 1688 they sent a protest to Pennsylvania Friends, and their sense of outrage can be felt across the centuries that separate us:

"There is a saying that we shall do to all men like as we will be done ourselves; making no difference of what generation, descent or colour they are. And those who steal or

rob men, and those who buy or purchase them, are they not alike?... In Europe there are many oppressed for conscience sake; and here there are those opposed who are of a black colour... Pray, what in the world can be done worse towards us, than if men should rob or steal us away, and sell us for slaves to strange countries; separating husbands from their wives and children. ...therefore we contradict and are against this traffic of men's bodies. And we who profess that it is not lawful to steal, must, likewise, avoid to purchase such things as are stolen, but rather help to stop this robbing and stealing if possible. ... (For) if this is done well, what shall we say is done evil?..." (This letter has been abbreviated and the spelling modernized. You can read the original at http://www.yale.edu/glc/aces/germantown.htm).

I imagined that Josiah, young and idealistic, would have felt a kinship with these German-Dutch people who spoke so powerfully to their fellow colonists. But it was to be nearly a century before Friends declared themselves against slavery, and not until the mid-1800s was the slave trade finally outlawed.

Ann Turnbull

Ann Turnbull grew up in south-east London but now lives in Shropshire. She has always loved reading and knew from the age of ten that she wanted to be a writer. Her numerous books for young people include *Pigeon Summer*, *A Long Way Home*, *House of Ghosts* and *Alice in Love and War*.

Seeking Eden is the final story in Ann's Quaker trilogy, and follows *No Shame, No Fear* (which was shortlisted for both the Whitbread Book Award and the Guardian Fiction Prize) and *Forged in the Fire*. Ann says, "When I left Will and Susanna together in 1667 with their newborn son, Josiah, I knew that as Quakers they would suffer increasing persecution. But I also discovered that in 1683 William Penn would at last realize his dream of founding a Quaker colony in America – and from that grew the idea for *Seeking Eden*."

Find out more about Ann Turnbull and her books by visiting her website at www.annturnbull.com

no Shame, no Fear

"Don't cry. We won't be parted, I promise."

1662 – England is reeling from the after-effects of civil war, with its clashes of faith and culture.

Seventeen-year-old Will returns home after completing his studies, to begin an apprenticeship arranged by his wealthy father. Susanna, a young Quaker girl, leaves her family to become a servant in the same town.

Theirs is a story that speaks across the centuries, telling of love and the struggle to stay true to what is most important – in spite of parents, society and even the law.

But is the love between Will and Susanna strong enough to survive – no matter what?

Shortlisted for the Whitbread Book Award
and the Guardian Fiction Prize

Forged in the Fire

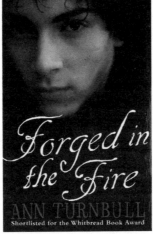

"The plague. Please, God, I thought, not Will."

England 1665 – 1666

Will, now a Quaker, travels to London to find work.

Waiting for him in Shropshire, Susanna becomes increasingly worried: Will's letters grow fewer as the plague spreads and the city gates are closing.

Susanna sets off in search of him, but hopes of marriage fade as an even greater threat looms.

The riveting sequel to *No Shame, No Fear*, shortlisted for the Whitbread Book Award and the Guardian Fiction Prize